FIRES OF SATAN

FIRES OF SATAN

E.C. TUBB

WILDSIDE PRESS

CHAPTER I

After the third drink he felt ready to face the night and, muffled in his thick coat, gloves and boots, paused before the big window that gave a view of the observatory. Snow had fallen earlier leaving the area covered with a thin, white blanket. A pity, had it continued to fall the dome would have had to remain closed and he could get on with checking the pile of accumulated records in comparative comfort. There was still a chance of more bad weather, but if there was a possibility of clear skies he must be ready, which meant long hours of tedium.

Experience dictated that he was warmly dressed and carried a flask despite regulations. Rules easy enough for Hammond to make but the Director didn't have spend a freezing winter's night in the opened dome. To hell with him.

Ice crunched beneath his boots as Spragg left the house, slamming the door then pushing against it to make sure it was locked. Up here there was little risk of vandals but old habits died hard. Ice crunched as he strode down the path and on the road, which led up the hill. Above him, touched by the snow with an air of enchanted mystery, the great dome loomed. Time and custom had changed that but, for some, it still remained.

"Professor? Is that you Professor Spragg?"

She stepped towards him from the shadows, tall, lithe, her body shapeless beneath a fringed garment. Despite the cold her head was bare, dark hair hanging in an untidy mane. In the softly luminous light cast by the reflective snow he could see wide, deep-set eyes, a generous mouth, dimpled cheeks.

"Yes," he snapped. "Who are you?"

"Myrna Parkin. I'm doing post graduate work and—"

"You're here to assist me." He closed the space between them. "Why didn't you wait inside?

"I couldn't. The door is locked."

As he should have known. McGregor was on vacation, Reilly was sick, and Dowton would have locked up at dusk. A habit permitted by Hammond for the sake of the saving in overtime—unlike astronomers the janitor worked by the hour.

"Sorry," said Spragg. "I should have remembered. Were you coming to meet me?"

"To visit you, actually." Shivering the girl added, "It was better than just standing around to freeze. Please, Professor, couldn't we go inside?"

A decade earlier Spragg would have joked, insisted she called him 'Mal', trying to warm their relationship in optimistic anticipation of potential reward. Now he busied himself with the keys, throwing open the door and passing through before her in order to switch on the lights. The place was as cold as an iceberg and he hurried into the small compartment used for recreation; a place where those who smoked could and hot drinks and snacks could be made. Radiators glowed to life as he hit the switches.

"Tea?" He gestured towards the electric kettle. "Make some and I'll join you."

"I'd prefer coffee if there is any."

McGregor drank the stuff and there was a jar of instant tucked away at the back of the cabinet. Sipping his tea Spragg stared at the girl.

"Postgraduate, you say?"

"Yes."

"Studying?"

"Quarks, quasars and black holes," she smiled. "Physics and astronomy fascinate me. The universe—the secrets waiting to be solved out there—" She dropped her hand, a little self-conscious, he guessed, of the displayed enthusiasm and not sophisticated enough to be careless of his reaction. "The majesty of it all. The splendour. The tremendous implications of the discoveries we are making."

He said, dryly, "Is this your first stint in an observatory?"

"I've been in others."

"But this is your first time as an acting assistant?" She nodded. "I thought so, but don't be ashamed of it. We all have to learn."

"You think I'm foolish?"

"No."

She put down her cup. "Sometimes I get carried away but how can anyone not respond to the mystery of the universe? It's so enigmatic and yet, all the time, I've the feeling that if we only had one more scrap of knowledge, one more piece to fit the jigsaw, the whole puzzle would become clear and we would have the answer to everything. Is that being childish?"

"No," he said quickly. "It's just that it's been a long time since I've met anyone honest enough to admit to such enthusiasm. I find it a refreshing change."

"Which means that you had it once yourself," she said.

"A long time ago, perhaps."

"You talk like an old man."

"I am an old man."

"Not that old. When I first heard about you I thought you'd be stooped and grizzled and—"

"Absent-minded and senile and on the make?" He shrugged. "Why not? We are like other men."

"No." Her hair flew as she shook her head her eyes serious. "Not as other men. You belong to a dedicated breed."

A monk, he thought bitterly, they too were dedicated to something larger than themselves, restricted by onerous duties; hours governed by a bell which was governed by a clock which, in turn, was governed by the stars. And they too could be tempted by someone coming to them in the night. Damn the girl, why had she displayed such enthusiasm? It gave them something in common, a shared emotion, a shared motivation.

"Professor?"

His tea was cold. Irritably he flung it into the sink.

"Impatient, Miss Parkin? We have the entire night before us." He smiled, remembering the impetuosity of youth. "You saw the sky out there and must know it won't clear for a couple of hours at least. Which means there is no point in opening the dome just yet. But, I'll admit, we can check the instruments and you need to be taught the basic routines and the system we use here. And, of course, you'd like to inspect the installation, right?"

"That's why I'm here, Professor."

He looked at her appraisingly. The fringed outer garment she wore was a poncho of some kind. Below her legs were covered with the inevitable jeans, her feet with the inevitable boots. "You'll have to get rid of the poncho. "It swirls too much and could hit things or catch in things and the equipment costs too much to be risked. Now get it off while I find you something better."

Beneath it she wore a uniform-like shirt and he paused as he turned from the cabinet, McGregor's parka in his hands, staring at the taut fabric.

"Here." He handed her the parka. "Belt it tight and if you get too cold don't be afraid to let me know. You'll find gloves in the pocket but you won't be able to wear them all the time. Those other observatories you've been to," he said shrewdly. "All down south?"

"Yes."

"Well, up here things are a little more primitive." He smiled. "The Director would say we operate in a more old-fashioned way which is another way of saying we're so far behind the times it's a laugh. In fact you're standing in the middle of a scientific fossil. I'm sorry."

"Why? You have a telescope haven't you?"

"Yes," he admitted. "We have a telescope. In fact we've had one for a long time now. Too damn long." He resisted the impulse to take a drink. "That's half the trouble."

When the eccentric Lord Althene had been smitten with the urge to dabble in Natural Philosophy his interest in astrology had directed his attention towards the stars. If the course of the planets could be plotted with greater precision then it was obvious horoscopes could be cast with a higher degree of accuracy and more definitive predictions made. Fired with enthusiasm and brooking no opposition he had been checked by only one consideration—where would the proposed observatory be sited? Ivegill had seemed ideal. A few miles to the south of Carlisle, served by roads and water an area rich in stone and timber and with plenty of cheap labour to construct the essential buildings. Lord Althene owned the land for miles around and had large holdings close to the city itself. In the early spring of 1857 the first sod was cut and the first dirt removed for the foundations.

Seven years later the observatory was complete.

But, in the late nineteenth century the internal combustion engine was yet to come and, while the smoke from open fires was a nuisance, there weren't enough of them to create a problem. At the turn of the century the old 6-inch refractor was replaced by a 32-inch reflector and later photographic equipment was added. The Althene Observatory gained a modest reputation for efficiency and strengthened that reputation when, in 1927, several small discoveries were made as to the disposition of some of the larger asteroids.

Then came the second world war, the massive increase in the use of cars, the population explosion, the motorways, pollution, death-duties and near-chaos. Things Spragg explained as he guided the girl around the installation.

"So now we're a trust," he said. "Enough was saved from the estate to provide an income from a scientific foundation. It suited the government to give its seal of approval and so we get certain tax advantages. But as far as real use is concerned we're in the same class as the dodo."

"Why? It seems a nice place to me. Better than others I've seen."

"Better, maybe, but in the wrong place. You've visited Greenwich? You know the Royal Observatory had to be moved to Herstmonceux?" He didn't wait for an answer. "Pollution, that's why. And the traffic—the vibration was hell. The same here." He gestured beyond the walls. "The M6 runs past barely a half mile distant. Big lorries carrying loads to Carlisle, not to speak of the endless stream of cars. And we mustn't forget the airport, planes with lights and turbulence and heat-distortions from their jets. A mess. If we get a couple of prime hours seeing a week we're lucky."

"Then Althene—"

"Is a mess." Spragg was blunt. "We do our best but the odds are against us. This is a backwater, girl, a dead end. You should be in a place where you can meet the right people, make contacts, sow the seeds for later advancement. A few years and you'd be climbing and, if you're lucky enough, then—"

"I know," she said bleakly. "A discovery, my name in the papers, my report published in the journals and all those who want to jump on the wagon will be offering me posts and position. But if I don't make a discovery? If I don't get the publicity? What then?"

"You'd make out."

"Yes," she said and, subconsciously, inflated her chest. "I guess I would but maybe I'd rather not do it that way. I want to be known for my achievements not because I was born with a good body. I want what you have, Professor Spragg."

"Me?"

"You've made your mark and it hasn't been forgotten. You're respected and admired and none can argue with your reputation. That's why I wanted to come here. To learn what you can teach."

She was putting him on, she had to be, and yet it was impossible to resist the glow of satisfaction from the knowledge that he hadn't been forgotten. Someone had remembered, had thought him worth seeking out to share his labours. Then he shook his head, remembering, the small discovery he had made years ago now quickly swallowed in the doors it had opened. Had Hammond used it to obtain a willing girl to act as cheap labour?

"I need the experience," she said when, bluntly, he asked. "Theory isn't enough, you know that."

You had to sit and freeze or roast according to the season, to fight cramps and thirst and impatience and learn not to cavil against circumstance when, after days of patient waiting, some trifle ruined everything. Like the time when a complete batch of recordings had been wiped because an assistant had misread an instruction. Like the time when some fool had set the woods aflame at the time of a critical observation, the distortion making all measurements useless.

And the time when Jashir had slipped and fallen to his death when climbing up to the eyepiece to make an adjustment.

A bad time and he had seen it all. Heard it all too, the gasp, the strangled cry, the scream and then, after too long a time, the sickening, squashy thud as a head had hit metal and burst like an overripe melon. A bad time and he had been fortunate not to have been alone for the police, oddly, had seemed suspicious and were probing with their questions. Yes, he had ordered the adjustment. No, he had no reason to suspect Jashir had been drinking. The reverse in fact, the man was a Moslem—had been a Moslem and no believer in Islam drank. No, he had not tried to help. Yes, it had been an accident.

Cold and heat and boredom and disappointment and even death—the girl was right, theory wasn't enough.

He said, "Are you living in the village?"

"Yes. I've got a room with Mrs Turney. The Director recommended her to me." She looked at him. "And you? I suppose you've got a house."

"Yes."

"Married, of course?"

"Of course." He wondered at her directness then realised it could be the product of shyness. In his own time such shyness would have found refuge in silence and a reserve which had too often been mistaken for sullenness but times changed and so did customs. "But not any longer," he added. "Astronomers shouldn't marry."

"The hours?"

"She grew tired of sleeping alone and decided to do something about it. I discovered what was going on. There were no children so—" he made a gesture "—end of marriage."

And the end of a friendship, which could have meant so much. Later, thinking about it, he realised that his anger had been directed more at his loss than at Irene's infidelity. Bob could have grown so close but had turned from him to accept the forbidden fruit so freely offered. A stupid metaphor—since when had sex been forbidden to any thinking and intelligent person.

"So you're free," said Myrna, "Don't you ever get lonely though?"

"At times. I've a woman who comes in to clean up."

"And?"

"You haven't met Mrs Elphick." He looked into her eyes, searching for mockery but finding none. "And you? I guess you have a man."

"I had. He didn't want me to come. In fact he threatened not to see me again if I did. So, naturally, I had to take the position. I'm selfish."

"If wanting to do what we want to do is selfish then yes, we are," he said. "As I'm going to be now. I want to open the dome and get to work. Let's move!"

Once it had meant sweat but now electric motors did the job and Spragg watched as the segment moved to one side exposing a narrow section of sky. It was clearing, stars winking through a faint scud of cloud, the cold increasing as the trapped heat escaped from the building. A moment and he completed the cycle, the segment wide open now, held fast, the lattice of the telescope etched against the heavens.

There was a moon for which he was thankful but from the city a suffused glow rose to paint the thin wisp of cloud a rosy pink while lower-lying mist held a deeper hue. High above the winking signal lights of a jet made traces towards the west while, from the motorway, the sound of traffic made a loud thunder.

"I don't believe it." Myrna tensed. "It sounds so close."

"It is close but this makes it worse." Spragg gestured at the interior of the dome. "Open it acts like an ear catching and concentrating the noise. You'll get used to it."

If she stayed which was doubtful but, would he ever get used to her? Already she had won him so that, even when not looking at her, he was conscious of her presence. An old man, old enough at least to be her father—he should have more sense! And yet, why not?

"Ready, Professor?" She was standing at the foot of the lattice waiting for instructions.

"Did Hammond explain the programme?"

"Only roughly. He said you'd fill in."

He would, his golf would be waiting, but maybe he shouldn't judge the man too harshly. It couldn't be easy to act the professional beggar, which, basically, was what the Director really was.

"We're running a correlation check on the Jovian Moons," said Spragg abruptly. "Just an excuse for staying in business, to let others know we're alive. Others being the government and various benefactors who are willing to make a donation that they can set against taxes. With me?"

"You're bitter," she said quietly. "You shouldn't be. There are those who would—"

"Give their right arms to be able to play with an installation like this. I know. I get letters from idiots who want to send messages. Nuts who are convinced there are secret symbols on the moon. Fools who know just where to look to find the aliens who are manipulating us."

And the others, she thought, the dedicated amateurs who were often more skilled than the professionals. A professional was merely someone who got paid and a person who worked for love was surely more worthy than one who laboured simply for gain.

Spragg?

She had been warned about his temper, his irascible nature and gratuitous sarcasm. Warned too about his penchant for women, a trait he had betrayed with his eyes when handing her the parka. But there was more and she had caught a hint of it when talking about his circumstances. A yearning, an empty longing quickly masked with a brash facade which she knew too well. And the taint of alcohol on his breath when they had met, normal enough at such a time on a man who worked during the day, but for him it was tantamount to drinking at breakfast.

A man under strain, she decided, and perhaps one who was slipping and knew it. The Dutch courage, the irritability, the attack when there was no cause and the defence when there was no need. The demeaning of his chosen profession. The cynicism, which he wore like armour.

"As I was saying," said Spragg. "And if I continue to hold your interest, we are checking the Jovian system of moons."

Spragg blew on his hands, his breath a cloud of vapour.

"It is barely possible that we may be able to isolate and identify the satellite in question and, if we can determine that it is hitherto unknown as a moon of Jupiter we shall have made history. But don't hope for too much. Personally I believe the mysterious object to be a wandering asteroid, which has an erratic orbit. A few more years and it will have vanished from the vicinity of the planet."

"An asteroid?"

"Why not?" He guessed her objection. "The size? All we have seen is a speck of light. A high albedo would give the impression of great dimension if the reflected light were diffused. But you know all this. What you may not know as yet is how we work here. It is a matter of making the best of a bad job. As we can never be certain of clear skies we have to rely more on records than direct observation."

"That's normal."

He shrugged. Given time she would learn but for now it was best to use her as a pair of hands. "It's time we got to work. Aim for Capella. You—"

"It's in the constellation Auriga," she said coldly. "There's no need to treat me as if I were an ignorant child."

"I was going to say that you may find it difficult to maintain alignment," he said. "The drive mechanism is a little sloppy so we've worked out a system of signals. When I give the word you make sure we're on target. When you're satisfied let me know. I snap the shutter and we wait to do it over again. With luck we'll get maybe a dozen useable exposures."

"That many?"

"We're using a special emulsion coupled with a light magnifying analogue device rigged up by McGregor. It isn't as good as the commercial installations used by the big observatories, but it'll do." Spragg glanced at his watch. "Up you go now. Watch yourself and, if you get too cold, let me know."

She climbed with the easy agility of youth and he looked away, remembering Jashir falling. An incident which, tonight, was not repeated. As the girl settled he checked the equipment, electric motors humming as the telescope moved to point at the selected region of sky—an eye peering into the universe.

And, despite his age and the coating cynicism, the magic remained. The stars, the mystery they held, the enchantment. The endless spaces illuminated with scattered suns. The whole glory of the universe spread out before him to be probed and questioned, explored and chartered, loved and feared and, even, worshipped a little.

"On target," said the girl. "Clear seeing."

"Check." Luck seemed to be with them but it would be stupid to miss the opportunity. A photograph, any photograph, was better than none and if she could maintain the alignment at least she would have proved her worth. "Hold!"

A click and the camera was working, small lamps glowing on the panels and casting tiny patches of various colours to illuminate hooded dials. Now, if the seeing lasted and she could hold the alignment a record would be made of the Jovian sector of space.

With nothing to do but wait Spragg moved restlessly beneath the opened dome. The girl shouldn't have to be watching the target-star. She shouldn't have to freeze in winter chill. They should have a better mechanism, better mounts, a better position away from towns and motorways with their attendant haze and vibrations. How the hell could they be expected to work without proper equipment?

How had Galileo?

"Professor! We're shifting!"

From the motorway came a steady roar. Heavy trucks shaking the concrete, the terrain, the very foundations of the building itself. A minute quiver accentuated by magnification so what should have been steady points became blurred haloes. Scowling Spragg ended the exposure and triggered fresh film into the holder. He'd be lucky to get a couple of usable exposures.

"We'll try again later. A few hours before dawn is the best time. Traffic is thin then and, if there is no mist, we should get decent seeing." He looked up to where she sat. "Come down and get warm. I'll make some coffee."

She was shivering as she gripped the cup. From the cabinet Spragg took a heavy sweater and a string vest.

"Put these on," he said. "The vest under your shirt." Then, as she hesitated, he snapped, "I won't stare if that's what bothers you."

"It doesn't. I've been looked at before."

A certainty, he thought sourly, and by men too young to realise their luck. Then, understanding her reluctance, he said, "Go ahead. Those things are clean. I keep them here for emergencies."

He turned away as she doffed the parka and shirt, hearing the soft rustle of fabric over skin. Small sounds that held a poignant familiarity and carried associations of warm intimacy.

She said, "Thank you, Professor. I hadn't realised it would get so cold."

"It'll get colder before dawn. Can you get a hot bath at your lodgings?"

"I doubt it. Mrs Turney needs time to heat the water. Later, maybe, but not just after dawn."

He said, slowly, not looking at her, "If you'd like to come back with me I can provide a hot bath. A hot meal too if you want."

"Thank you. That would be nice."

Spragg set down his cup, feeling suddenly cheerful, confident now the night would not be wasted.

CHAPTER 2

James Hammond walked into his office, placed his Holmberg neatly on the rack, then his topcoat, and adjusted his jacket with his usual attention to sartorial perfection. The jacket belonged to a suit that had originated in Savil Row, the shoes were of hand-made leather, the shirt natural silk. Hammond liked good clothes and, as Director, he was justified in wearing them. The observatory had at least to appear prosperous.

The office was panelled in wood mellowed with time, glistening with the patina of years of wax polishing. Framed certificates spoke of past achievements and photographs showed previous members of the staff standing stiffly, whiskered and dressed as at the turn of the century. On the wide desk stood a heap of mail but Hammond ignored it, moving to the window and standing to look at the drive beyond, the hedges flanking the narrow road. Spring was coming, the sward dotted with the stars of primroses, the fading blooms of snowdrops. Soon would come the crocuses, the daffodils and tulips. Soon, too, would come the bills and, inevitably, trouble with the staff.

Hammond sighed as he thought about it. McGregor was restless as was Reilly. Dowson would want an increase as would the gardeners and maintenance men. There would be talk of 'differentials' and interviews with union officials and the haggling and all the rest of the stupid business. They seemed unable to accept the fact that the observatory was not a government institution with unlimited access to taxpayer's money.

"Good morning, Director." Susan Keating had followed him into the office, holding a tray bearing a steaming cup of coffee, which she set carefully on the desk. She smiled as he turned. "Did you have a good trip?"

"Comfortable, anyway." He knew it wasn't the answer she wanted. "Sir Edward was most interested and saw the value of sponsoring the sciences now there is so much interest in the latest new Voyager missions. Incidentally, should enquiries be made, use our highest figures for attendance and don't forget to emphasise the foreign interest."

A gilding of the lily; their peak year for visitors had been caused by tour operators having been persuaded to include the observatory in their itineraries. The foreign interest had stemmed from the Middle East when certain oil-rich sheiks had become interested in buying the land. Visitors now were less and the interest negligible—things she knew better than to mention.

Susan lingered and Hammond could guess why. She had worked at the observatory for thirty-two years, a confirmed spinster and, while officially his secretary, was more his spy. As she had been for other Directors before him.

Casually, she said, "I think Miss Parkin has settled down. When I spoke with her last, she seemed quite happy with her duties and position."

"No complaints about Spragg?"

"None. They seem to get on well." Susan added, dryly, "I understand she is now lodging with him."

To the benefit of the observatory. With the girl as bait Spragg would be reluctant to look for other employment and with decent comforts the girl would be more likely to remain. Two birds with one stone— Hammond wished his other problems could be solved so easily.

"Anything else, Susan?"

"Nothing important, Director." She glanced at the heap of mail. "A gardener has given notice and one of the machine-room staff was caught pilfering metal. And we are low on chemicals. I've taken all necessary action." Again she glanced at the piled letters. "I've printed out the e-mails, and they're in with the letters. I didn't sort them, Director, I hadn't time, but if you would like me to do it now?"

Her confession was a signal and he shook his head, smiling as she left, sitting and reaching for his coffee as he wondered what bombshell the mail contained. She knew, of course, and could have told him, but a rigid code of ethics prevented her from admitting to any hint that she pried.

Putting down the empty cup he reached for the mail. Spragg, as usual, had the most, a motley collection of letters addressed mainly to The Chief Astronomer but some others bearing his name; typed, scribbled, scrawled, printed. One held an unusual calligraphy, the letters neatly formed with graceful flourishes. The writer knew of Spragg's academic achievements and gave not only his title, but his qualifications. Hammond added it to the rest and looked at the others. Myrna Parkin had three of little obvious importance. His own mail was as he'd expected; some official communications, some invitations a few of which he would accept, a reminder from the golf club that his subscription was due. Hammond disliked playing golf as much as he did playing bridge but was good at both and suffered them for the sake of the contacts they provided.

Two letters caught his immediate attention.

Both had arrived airmail and were obviously what Susan had wanted him to find. One, addressed to Doctor Sean Von Reilly was from the Observatiorum der Dutschen Tautenberg, the other, addressed to Ian McGregor, was from Rand Optics Inc. California, U.S.A.

The one to Reilly from Germany was thick, and Hammond recognised the typical shape and heft of application forms. Reilly must either be sounding out the prospects or seriously intending to quit the observatory. The other to McGregor from the States was more dangerous. Thinner and somehow more sinister it could well be in an invitation for him to apply for a position or official notification that he had been accepted.

He could destroy them both, of course, and perhaps nothing would come of it and he would be able to retain his staff. But for how much longer? Althene was a backwater; both were as high as they could go.

As Hammond was himself and, like him, they must know it. Sighing he gathered up the letters and, though it wasn't his job, decided to deliver them personally.

McGregor was big, thick-set, and bearded, which added to his image of a wild Highlander. He grunted when Hammond handed him his mail, holding the letters in broad hands, the spatulate fingers belying their sensitivity. Reilly, thin-faced, long-lipped, a brush of hair falling about his ears, stared at his own through rimless spectacles.

"Any luck, Sean?"

"An answer from Germany." Reilly ripped it open, glanced at the wad of forms and scowled. "I wrote asking for a job and told them everything they needed to know. Do I get the job? Like hell I do. I get a load of bumph to fill in instead. You?"

"One from the States." McGregor examined it, opened it, read it again and whistled. "My friend, someone up their must like me. Rand have offered me a job."

"Just like that?"

"Just like that—with a little help from a mutual friend. Remember Bob Arkwright?"

"Vaguely. He was before my time but I've heard talk about him. Some scandal, wasn't there?"

"He ran off with Spragg's wife, about eight years ago. Spragg went home one night and caught them red-handed. The next day Bob and Irene left and later, so I heard, went to the States. He must have got a job with Rand because now he's a big wheel in their research department. And now this." He waved the letter. "What about you? Did you ever hear from Jodrell?"

"No vacancies now or in the foreseeable future. The same from Yerkes, from Lick and, naturally, form Herstmonceux. I should have been a plumber."

"You'll get something."

"Sure. I'll get the ice-cream concession on open days or be allowed to sell programmes or find a job spieling at a planetarium or—"

"That could be a good job," said McGregor, quickly, eager to change the subject. Reilly's illness had left him lacking some of his normal bounce. "Say, have you had a chance to study Spragg's new assistant?"

"I've seen her."

McGregor sucked in his breath. "A looker! Spragg is one lucky bastard."

"That girl? You're joking."

"I'm serious. She must have a father-complex or something but she's moved in with him. He probably bribed her with hot baths and hot breakfasts and she gave him a hot bed in return."

McGregor glanced at the rest of his mail. Bills, advertisements, the usual rubbish. A list of electronic components available from a discount warehouse, a copy of a trade magazine, two requests from optimists for the circuit diagrams of his light analogue. A note from a girl he had met while on vacation in Iceland. A letter from a woman in Carlisle. A worrying communication with hints of coming trouble caused by a careless interlude and a firmly held religious conviction. Irritably he threw it down. The offer from the States had come at a good time but he hated to be pressured. Now if Carla had only looked like Myrna Parkin—damn it, a girl like that would be worth marrying!

* * * *

Spragg thought so too as he looked to where she sat facing him across the table, littered with the remains of a slowly-enjoyed breakfast. A good breakfast was essential after a night at work and the more so when he now needed the extra sources of energy. Why couldn't he have found a girl like Myrna when he'd been young?

"Mal?" Myrna was looking at him, her face freshly clean, hair round with a braided cord, her body nude beneath the robe she had donned after her bath.

"Something wrong? Thinking of the job?"

"I was thinking of the weakness of youth," he said with sudden honesty. "It's strange how quickly we forget. If we didn't the young wouldn't regard us as dinosaurs and we wouldn't think of them as an alien species. We'd remember how we were at their age and make allowances."

"Do you make them for me?"

"I wasn't thinking of you, you're—well, different."

"I'm a woman."

"Yes, very much so."

"And you are very much a man." She frowned. "So there are a few years between us, so what?"

More than a few, a score at least.

"There's a repeat of the new Voyager films tonight at eleven," said Myrna lowering the newspaper she had been reading. "I'd like to see it."

"You will."

"How? We'll be in the dome."

"I'll be in the dome," he corrected. "You can stay here and catch the programme. Better yet you can record it so we can see it again later together." He gestured towards the television set and the video and DVD player. "We might as well use the damned thing."

"It's crazy," she said. "Here we are studying the Jovian system night after night and only a short while ago actual films were taken and transmitted of the areas. You remember? Ganymede, Io, Amalthea and the rest."

"Pictures," he said. "Interesting, but they told us nothing of the overall pattern. No matter if the Voyagers had stayed out there we still wouldn't be certain about a new satellite. We have to do it the hard way."

"Too hard." She was bitter. "And it's crazy. A Schmidt would do the job without sweat."

Something the observatory couldn't afford. A Schmidt was a camera-telescope and could not be used for visual observation. It took wonderful photographs but even so few observatories owned them. Palomar, naturally, and Uccle in Belgium and Kvistaberg in Sweden and, he was sure, the Tautenberg in Germany. Althene would never possess one unless they were given away.

"We keep pegging away," said Spragg mildly, "and maybe we'll find the answer. Our main tool is patience—that's what astronomy is all about."

"It seems such a damned waste. We could spend years on a project when, with the right equipment, we could end it in weeks— I'm being stupid, aren't I?"

"You're just tired," he said.

And forgetful. It wasn't just a matter of equipment; they were dealing with space and time and things that moved did so in their own frames of reference. And movement was what they searched for, the drift of a minute particle of light against the unchanging backdrop of the heavens. A tiny mote which was drowned and swallowed by the universal brilliance; the glittering host of stars which bloomed in the lens of even a low-powered telescope and was dazzling in the eye-piece of a high-powered instrument.

"Why don't you get off to bed?"

She stood up and stretched, and he rose with her, reaching out to embrace her.

"Myrna, my love, I—"

"Don't talk!" Her voice was a strained whisper. "Don't talk, Mal! Just—"

She broke off, stiffening, as the doorbell made its discordant clangour. Hammond said, blandly. "Thank you, my dear, this is excellent coffee."

"It's instant."

"Even so it is excellent." The Director was determined not to take offence, guessing at the reason for her abruptness, Spragg's reluctant invitation to enter his house. "And let me apologise once again for having disturbed you. I know how it is when you have to work at night. All you want is a hot bath, a hot meal and a soft bed, right?"

"We want more than that," snapped Myrna. "Something to keep us warm in the dome at night for one. New gears on the drive-mechanism on the reflector. A Schmidt—"

"Why not ask for the moon while you're about it?" Hammond smiled thinly. "I'm sorry you appear to be dissatisfied with the conditions here Miss Parkin and if you choose to leave I will understand." A studied pause then he added, "As I'm sure others will when and if they may ask. I assume you intend to gain your degree?"

Spragg heard her sharp intake of breath and moved forward before she could call the Director the bastard he was. He said, quickly. "We're on our own time, James. What do you want?"

"Another cup of this excellent coffee would be welcome. Thank you, my dear." Hammond smiled as the girl took the cup; gracious once having gained his victory. As she vanished into the kitchen he said, "A fine girl, Mal, I'm pleased to see you are getting on so well. A proof of the old saying about life in old dogs, eh?"

"You've a dirty mind," said Spragg, bluntly. "And a vicious disposition. Did you have to threaten her?"

"You know me better than that, Mal, but I had to do something to keep her here. Mostly I was thinking of you." Hammond reached into his pocket. "Here, I brought you your mail. It's a nice morning and I felt like a walk and thought I'd see how you were getting on with your new assistant. How long has it been now?"

"Eight weeks. From the end of February," Spragg added, "You should do as she suggests about getting some heat in the dome. A couple of times there was ice on the lattice."

"I'll try to arrange something before next winter. Infra-red projectors could warm the working areas at least and I might be able to find someone to supply then." Hammond looked at Myrna as she returned with his coffee. She was now fully dressed. "Going out?"

"For a walk." She handed him the coffee. "Is there anything else you want? No? Then I'll get off. See you later, Mal."

The door slammed behind her leaving a sudden emptiness filled with the ghosts of what-might-have-been had Hammond not chosen to call. Spragg scowled, remembering, wondering if ever such a moment would come again.

Hammond took a chair. "Sit down, Mal. I need to talk. Have Ian or Sean mentioned they are leaving?"

"No, are they?"

"I don't know, but if they should we'll have a problem. An observatory can't run without trained staff and we haven't enough as it is. Either or both of them could be hard to replace."

"You should have thought of that when you threatened Myrna."

"Don't fight her battles, Mal, she's big enough to fight her own. And post-grades aren't hard to come by. What I'm asking is, should the need arise, do you know of anyone interested in joining us? Old friends, maybe, old associates. As Chief Astronomer, it's your problem as much as mine. And if they are thinking of leaving and you can change their minds—" He let it hang, cunningly changing the subject. "Anything interesting in your mail?"

"It's my mail."

"I know but there was one letter which caught my eye. One with unusual script. You don't see calligraphy like that nowadays and I wondered if the contents carried the same precision." Then, quietly, Hammond added, "I heard about Irene, Mal. Interested?"

"No. She chose her life and I wasn't a part of it."

"She's left Bob Arkwright—a Las Vegas Divorce. She has a position with the new Voyager promotional campaign as a designer of plastic models, plaques and pennants. Under licence from NASA, naturally."

"The souvenir business." Spragg shrugged. "Well, what of it?"

"I thought you'd like to know."

A lie, Hammond knew of his feelings towards Irene, so what was his real motive for coming to the house? To check on the domestic arrangements with Myrna? To ask his help in retaining the services of the others? Spragg doubted such obvious motives; the Director was known for his deviousness and was rarely so direct. His anxiety about the others leaving was misplaced—always there were more astronomers than telescopes and even in installation like Althene could find willing staff. And his interest in the letter.

Spragg studied it, nothing the script but not overly impressed. A screed from some raving nut, most probably, wanting him to look for fire-demons on the surface of the Sun or the drifting remnants of the Atlantean space fleet destroyed in some imaginary war with Mars.

"Mal," Hammond cleared his throat. "I had dinner with Sir Edward Thorne last night. He is most interested in the observatory and would be willing to make a sizeable donation if he considered it worthwhile. He became really enthusiastic when I mentioned your project. He even hinted, and you'll appreciate the joke I'm sure, that the new moon should be named after him if—well, you get the point."

"Money," said Spragg. "A bribe."

"A consideration," said Hammond quickly. "A small favour for a man willing to support the observatory. Damn it, Mal, it happens all the time. How else to win patrons? Now if I could tell Sir Edward that you were on the verge of announcing the discovery of a new moon of Jupiter and it would be named after him he would be more than grateful. Mal?"

"Lie if you want," said Spragg. "But don't include me in your schemes. You know damned well we have a long way to go before we can be certain we've checked out the Jovian system."

"How long?

"Too long to satisfy Sir Edward." Spragg wasn't shocked by the proposition, as Hammond said it happened all the time, but he was still proud of his reputation because, without it, he had nothing. To terminate the discussion he ripped open the envelope and grunted at the mass of papers it contained. "Someone's been busy."

"An amateur?"

"Obviously." Spragg riffled the sheets that bore the same calligraphy as the envelope and found the covering letter. "From Laggan, Inverness—up in the Highlands. Sent by—" Spragg scowled at the signature—"the Reverend Aird Gulvain. Somehow that name rings a bell."

"What does it say?"

Hammond waited as Spragg read on, looking around the room now untidy with a domestic intimacy absent before. He crossed to the window and stood looking at the bulk of the observatory pictured against the sky, A movement and he saw Myrna walking from it towards the house, her long legs scissoring in a mannish stride, hair a cascade of darkness over her shoulders.

As she passed the gate and vanished down the road he wondered just what he had interrupted.

"Well?" He turned back to Spragg. "Anything of interest?"

"For once, perhaps." Spragg leaned back thoughtfully. "Gulvain is an amateur but a damned good one—I met him about ten years ago when he presented a paper to a conference I'd attended. An old man as I remember. A retired parson—he must be in his eighties by now. Anyway he thinks he may have discovered a new asteroid."

"So, naturally, he wrote to you." Hammond nodded. Fifteen years earlier Spragg had made exactly the same discovery; isolating and plotting the orbit of a scrap of planetary debris found between Mars and Jupiter. "He wants confirmation, naturally."

"Yes."

"A pity we can't give it to him. A discovery, even of a minor asteroid, would do the observatory no harm. Sir Edward—" He broke off. "Can you suspend the programme?"

He knew the answer before Spragg shook his head. It was the old problem; not enough telescopes and not enough nights in the year for all the observations waiting to be made. A pressure compounded at Althene by the bad viewing conditions. In time the potential discovery would be checked and, if verified, another notation placed in the books. But, by then, Gulvain could be long dead and Sir Edward's bounty dispersed elsewhere. If only—

Hammond said, "Mal, we can't afford to let this slip. If Gulvain is right we can use the discovery. Sir Edward would be pleased to have even an asteroid named after him."

"It's Gulvain's find."

"True, and he won't be forgotten, but we have to take the long view. You could explain that to him, Mal. Tell him of our need for new equipment. A Schmidt, for example, with a plaque attached saying it was to gift of Sir Edward to Althene on behalf of the Reverend Aird Gulvain. As long as Thorne gets his name in the papers he won't give a damn about the scientific histories—who reads them, anyway?"

"I do."

"You and a few others but who usually has the time?" Hammond shrugged. "Did he invite you to visit him? I thought so—the true Scottish hospitality. Why not accept the invitation? You could study his equipment and make an assessment of his capabilities. After all we can't ignore him."

Spragg said, flatly, "You want me to visit Aird Gulvain and to stay with him as his guest. To check his findings and verify if he's made a discovery. And, if he had, you want me to steal it. Right?"

"Of course not!" Put like that it sounded raw. Smiling Hammond added, "All you'll be doing is visiting a colleague. You could use a break and the programme can run without you for a while. After all Gulvain could have made a mistake—you said he was old. All I'm suggesting is that you check his figures."

"And leave the rest to you?"

"Exactly."

"I'm not going to see him robbed."

"Damn it, Mal, I do have ethics. All I suggested was a mutually beneficial compromise, an arrangement. I realise that it is a little unusual for a Chief Astronomer to visit an amateur but this is a special case." Hammond's voice hardened a little. "When will you be ready to leave?"

CHAPTER 3

He travelled by train, liking the comfort, the opportunity to think. Relaxing in a window seat of an almost empty compartment Spragg studied the rugged beauty of the Grampian Mountains, the vista of the Forest of Atholl, the distant shimmer of lochs and streams running like silver thread over the wide expanses of dusky green heather. Reflected in the window his face held an odd detachment and he wondered at the passage of time which had added depth to the lines running from the corner of his eyes, those marking his cheeks. His hair was flecked with grey and the soft bulge of a second chin showed beneath the first. A battleground on which emotions had raged and left their marks.

What had attracted Myrna? His achievements? Reputation as a scholar or reputation as an admirer of the female form? Or maybe his comfortable house, the expenditure saved by giving up her lodgings?

He looked past his reflection towards the darkening scene beyond, remembering how it had happened. She had moved in as if it had been the most natural thing in the world. After the first few weeks in which her return for a hot bath and food had become a routine and then, quite simply, she had moved in.

They had eaten breakfast and it was time for her to go and he had left her while mounting the stairs to his bedroom. He had lain beneath the covers, a little tense, subconsciously aware, perhaps, that this morning would not follow the usual pattern so that when she came to join him he was ready and unsurprised.

And after, as she had lain beside him, sleeping, her lashes resting like trapped moths on the smoothness of her cheeks, he had wondered, as he had so often in the past, what it was made a woman such a splendid creation.

"Sir?" An attendant stood beside him in the aisle a tray in his hand bearing empty paper cups and packets of biscuits. "Coffee, sir? A snack?"

"Coffee."

He paid and watched as the man moved down the compartment leaving the empty paper cup standing before him. Within minutes another attendant bearing a steaming pot followed the first. Seeing the signalling cup he paused.

"Black or white, sir?"

"Black. No sugar." Spragg glanced through the window. "Where are we?"

"Yon's the Glen Carney. You for Inverness?"

"No, Newtonmore." A hired car could take him from there on to Laggan. "How long before we reach it?"

"About an hour, sir. We halt a while at Drumochter to let through the express."

An hour—he must have dozed a little thinking of Myrna.

Spragg sighed as he again studied Galvain's letter. It had been a week since it had arrived and there had been no answer to his own announcing his intended arrival. Maybe it was still in the post. Hammond had been adamant he should leave and waste no further time. Others could have been contacted, he'd pointed out, and something had delayed the original letter; it had been dated ten days earlier than the time received. Even now the discovery could be lost to the observatory.

The train slowed and came to a halt in the brooding stillness. Framed by the windows the external scene took on an added air of mystery and Spragg found it easy to imagine ghosts moving through the heather; Picts and Calendonians who had ruled in ages past, Clansmen of more recent times kilted and savage in their determination to remain free. Other ghosts too; those of men who had fought and died to protect their homes in the south and crofters who had been evicted to starve so as to clear the land for the estates of the wealthy. The highlands had a blood-drenched history.

A jerk and the train was moving again towards the looming bulk of the Cairngorms. At Newtonmore taxis stood before the station. Spragg headed towards the first in line, jerked open the door of the rear compartment and threw in his single bag.

"Can you take me to Laggan?"

"Aye." The old driver squinted at his fare. "Where to in Laggan?" He blinked at the answer. "The ald minister's hoose?"

"You know him?"

"Aye, that ah did. Mon, dinna ye ken he's deed?"

* * * *

"Dead?" Hammond's voice came strongly over the phone. "How?"

"Pneumonia and I'm not surprised. The place is as damp as a marsh. He must have been ill when he wrote the letter and that accounts for the delay. Someone must have found and posted it. My own was unopened. No phone, of course, I'm speaking from the hotel."

"And?"

"He had something, James. I've checked his figures and diagrams as best as I can and he knew what he was doing. He managed—"

"The discovery?"

"Tentative as yet but highly probable. We'll have to check it out. I want you to tell Reilly to get all the plates taken on that area over the past few years. As many as he can find. Ask Ian to run an elimination check. Then contact all observatories owning a Schmidt and request copies of any plates they may have taken of that particular area. Then—"

"Hold on, Mal." Hammond was sharp. "Do you realise what all this could mean? There'll be questions asked. What can I tell them?"

"Say it has to do with our work on the Jovian moons. We're searching for any aberration in asteroidal orbits, which could give us a clue leading to the new satellite. Who knows? We may even find it. And tell Myrna—" Spragg paused, what could he tell Hammond to say?

"I understand," said the voice on the phone. "You miss her and look forward to seeing her again, But, Mal, it's only been three days."

A lifetime, or so it seemed, and it wasn't yet over. Gulvain was dead and buried but his spirit lingered on and not just as a skilled amateur astronomer. The man had belonged to a fanatical Calvanistic sect and, though old, some of the fire had lingered. And his heirs, with stubborn insistence, had refused to allow him to take away any of the old man's papers or notebooks.

Which left Spragg with only one alternative to outright theft.

Back at the house, his purchases hidden beneath his coat, Spragg went to the old man's study. There he was permitted to read and make notes of Gulvain's work and, at times, be assailed by the rantings of the dead man's nephew, a gaunt and aggressive person whom he could barely understand. Fortunately, today, the man was absent and, with the door firmly closed, Spragg set to work to photograph every scrap of writing the dead man had left which he could find.

At dusk he made his last pilgrimage.

A few hundred yards from the house, housed in an old byre, Gulvain had built a small observatory, which housed the six-inch reflector he had made himself.

Gulvain had gone better than mere size. His instrument included a secondary mirror, which, by re-reflecting the image, made for a long focal length with a relatively short lattice. An aid to higher magnification as the incorporated drive mechanism was to prolonged observation; the device keeping the telescope aimed at one point in the sky so the observed stars seemed to be motionless.

But the man hadn't been interested in stars. He had searched within the Solar System for drifting masses of rock inhabiting the asteroid belt; a study that had once been Spragg's own major interest.

Now he touched the shrouded telescope, imagining Gulvain in his place, old, shivering from the cold yet firmly determined to prove something. Fighting age and stiffness and weakening eyes. Fired by his dedication and conviction of what must be.

"Professor Spragg?" The voice came from the house and he turned towards it as a woman came towards the byre. "If you want a lift I'm leaving now."

Janet Gulvain, Oxford educated but still with the slight lilt of the Highlands in her voice, dampened now that she was speaking to a Sassenach. Spragg moved towards her.

"Here." He gestured with his head. "I was saying goodbye to a really superb amateur observatory. What is to happen to the telescope?"

"It will go as a gift to grandfather's old school together with the firm hope that they will use it."

"As they will I'm sure." Spragg slowed a little. "My bag?"

"Is in the car. I saw it and guessed you'd want to catch the next train. Did I guess right, Professor?"

"Yes. And you?"

"I have things to do as yet." As they reached the car she said, "What did you make of his papers? I'd appreciate the truth, Professor."

"They show a painstaking attention to detail. Aird Gulvain was a remarkable observer and a most precise recorder of what he saw."

"A human camera?"

"In a way, yes. In the old days there was no other method they could use. Every tiny point of light had to be marked on a chart by hand. They had to be compared and checked against other charts and other seeing. Your grandfather was one of the old school."

"Why are you so interested, Professor?" She sent the car moving down the road then, without waiting for him to answer she added, "Is it because you think he was mad?"

"Mad? Of course not!"

"Normal, then?" She turned to look at him then concentrated again on the road. "Old, yes, and a little absent minded and even perhaps a little senile, you agree?"

"I didn't know him."

"I did. When I was young. That was twenty years ago now and he terrified me. You've heard of the old Biblical prophets, well he was one. Hellfire and damnation and threats of the vengeance of the Lord. I had it as a steady diet. You've met his nephew? He's nothing to what my grandfather used to be. I think he was a little insane."

"But clever."

"Yes, very clever, the insane often are." She slowed as they came within sight of the station. "But how many long for the end of the world?"

* * * *

NASA had been more than helpful sending a heap of appropriate material and Spragg wondered if Irene had helped to select it. Had she touched the models of the two Voyagers? The slides taken from the transmitted films? The three-dimensional postcards of the Jovian moons? He looked at one, recognising Ganymede, and imagined Irene holding it as he held it now, looking at what he now saw.

"Mal?" Myrna had come into the room, her arms loaded with brightly coloured brochures. Her hair was a veil that she blew with sudden irritation to clear her eyes and Spragg wondered why the hell she didn't tie it back as Irene had. "Where shall I put these?"

Like himself she was tired and irritable and resentful of the duties attendant on open days at the observatory. And now, with the Voyager promotional campaign adding extra work, her temper was short.

He said, "I need a drink. Join me?"

"Here?"

"Why not. Get some cups and mixers and ice if you can. We need a break."

Staff had privileges and soon Spragg lifted a paper cup filled with ginger ale, ice and whisky from his flask. "Slarg!"

"Cheers!" Myrna returned the toast. "You learn that up in the Highlands?"

"From television. They—" He broke off, she hadn't been born when he'd seen the programme.

"I'll be glad when today is over." She sat, long legs covered in faded blue denim, breasts prominent beneath her uniform-like shirt. "Do we have to mess about with this stuff?" Her gesture embraced the NASA material. "The latest Voyagers have left the Jovian system, and are headed outward. Why make all the noise?"

"Money." He shrugged at her expression. "Don't kick it, my dear. It keeps us in food and drink and what comforts we enjoy. And the Voyagers aren't finished yet. There are the other major planets to be checked before they leave the Solar System for ever—perhaps in ages to come to be discovered by some alien race."

"Who will then have the ineffable pleasure of being able to listen to some typical earth-sounds such as dogs barking, horns blowing, babies crying and a pop group!"

"Have another drink."

Spragg poured as she held out her cup then replenished his own.

She said, "Sean's making progress. He's persuaded Hammond to authorise the purchase of computer-time so as to check Gulvain's figures."

Something Spragg hadn't known and he felt a quick jealousy that Reilly had taken her into his confidence. What else had they talked about?

"It isn't through yet so he didn't want to tell you," she continued. "But I overheard Susan talking on the phone and it's pretty definite. You know Ian's quitting?"

"I know he was thinking about it."

"It's definite." She held out her cup for more and he freshened her drink. "He's got a woman in trouble and wants out."

"He told you that?"

"When he called at the house one day while you were away. He wanted a shoulder to cry on. I let him use mine."

"Just your shoulder?"

"That's all." Her tone was sharp.

"You want to lend him your shoulder that's your business. You want to lend him something else that's your business too. Right?"

"Damned right." She scowled into her cup. "I'm not property, Mal, and I'm not cheap either. You I like, Ian I don't. It's as simple as that."

The new morality was something he couldn't appreciate. A woman's body was her own and she slept around as she pleased but he didn't like it and never would. In that he was as old-fashioned as old-fashioned as Gulvain had been and he felt a sudden urge to get back to the main problem at hand; the need to check out the potential discovery. But right now he was stuck with the duties always present on an open day at the observatory.

As usual there were questions.

"Sir!" A small boy raised a sticky hand after his simplified lecture. "Sir, what stops the moon from falling on Earth?"

Patiently Spragg explained.

"Sir, where did the asteroids come from?"

"We can't be certain, of course, but most probably they are the remains of a planet which once orbited the sun between Mars and Jupiter." Spragg used the pointer to touch the distorted representation of the Solar System hung against the wall behind him. "Back in 1866 a German astronomer, Johann Daniel Titus, devised a numerical system to express the distances of the planets relative to the sun. How they were first discovered makes a fascinating story, and you will find his numerical system explained in full detail in the appropriate booklet attainable at the bookshop next to the main entrance." Having dutifully plugged the shop he went on: "You must remember that only the six inner planets were known in Titus's day. Now, following his table we find a correlation with every number to a planet aside from the fifth, between Mars and Jupiter. Instead at that distance we find the asteroids. Incidentally the series is better known as Bode's Law because he wrote about it in 1772 and he was more famous than poor old Titus." He paused to allow the dutiful chuckles to die. "Any further questions?"

"Please, sir, when was the first asteroid discovered?"

"On January 2st, 1801," said Spragg promptly. "It was first seen by a German physician, Heinrich Wilhelm Mattias Olbers who was born in 1758. It is named Ceres. Later he discovered two more, Pallas and Vesta, which shows what can be accomplished by an amateur. Olbers practiced astronomy as a hobby."

"Sir—"

There were more questions and Spragg answered them mechanically, his mind on a lonely old figure at his telescope in the Highlands. An amateur as Olbers had been. Had he also left his mark on time?

Reilly thought he had.

"The man definitely found something, Mal. I've been over his figures and charts and through he was weak on math there's nothing wrong with his observations. But, to be sure, we have to run comparisons."

"Any news on the computer-time?"

"We've got it and they're running the data now." Reilly didn't ask how Spragg knew. "I sent them copies of everything we have—well, almost everything. That stuff you photographed at Gulvain's had some pretty off notations. What are they?"

"Biblical references." Spragg had worked that out on the first study of the prints. "His grand daughter told me he was a bit of a fanatic and I guess he could have seen more through a telescope than most of us. Maybe it kept him at it."

"And maybe it helped him to see what he wanted to see." Reilly shrugged. "At home we talk of the little people, what do they have in Scotland?"

"God knows." Spragg yawned, suddenly aware of his fatigue. "Let's not confuse things. Where's Ian?"

McGregor was in the laboratory working on his light-magnifying analogue. Myrna was leaning against the bench beside him and Spragg fought a momentary twinge of jealousy. She looked up as he approached.

"Hi, Mal. Got any of that whisky left?" She took the flask he handed to her. "Here, Ian, it won't cure but it may help."

"Thanks." He drank from the bottle. "Myrna, you're an angel. Why not come to the States as my wife? Just say the word and I'm yours."

Spragg had the uneasy conviction the man wasn't joking. "I'm fit, able, and potentially rich. If the beard offends you I'll shave it off."

"And the girl in Carlisle?"

"To hell with her! I'm talking about us. Well?" For a moment there was silence then Spragg relaxed as Myrna shook her head. "No?" McGregor shrugged. "It seems as if you win again, Mal, but I'm keeping the Scotch as a consolation prize." He tilted the bottle. "Fair enough?"

"Sure. Go ahead and finish it." Spragg looked at the mechanism on the bench. "What's wrong with it now?"

"Bugs."

"But you had it working."

"I had it on test," corrected McGregor. "Up to a point it works fine enough but the gain is less than that obtained by an ordinary image intensifier even though the field of view is greater. I wanted to get something comparable to a Schmidt plate but with boosted magnification. And I know I can do it given the right facilities and help."

Myrna said, "What's the problem?"

"Bugs, as I said. Above all we need fine resolution, which means accurate components and a total absence of interference. It's easy to intensify an image—any electronics technician can do that, it's basically a matter of television, but I want more. I want to be able to take an image and both enlarge and intensify it while at the same time, filtering out all error caused by local conditions. Once I manage that all you need do is to take a sight lasting for only a fraction of time and electronics will do the rest." He growled at the apparatus on the bench. "But I'll never do it here. Now get the hell out and let me get on with it. I'll need something to show Rand."

Outside darkness softened the surrounding country, turning the trees into dim shapes of mystery, the dome into an enigmatic silhouette against the sky. Somewhere an owl hooted and Myrna shivered.

"A bird of ill omen," she said. "So the Romans believed."

"And you?"

"I'm not superstitious." She stared at him, her eyes shadowed. "Why do you ask?"

"Because I'm interested in you. I'd like to feel closer to you." Spragg reached out and caught her by the shoulders. "Would it be stupidly old-fashioned for me to say I love you?"

"No, Mal." Her voice was softly gentle. "I don't think so. Not as long as you mean it."

* * * *

Hammond said, briskly, "Mal, you know better than to think I'm trying to rush you but we can't afford to delay any longer. Either Gulvain found something or he didn't. If he did and we don't make the announcement then we'll lose the discovery."

"And if he didn't?"

"Then he made a mistake. An old man with bad eyes and a softening brain. It's understandable."

"But not that easy. If we make the announcement then we're the ones responsible. We can't blame an old man for being careless."

"Why not? He's dead."

Spragg shook his head. "You've been mixing with too many tycoons. They can find and use scapegoats but we can't. What you're demanding is that I put my reputation on the line. Well, forget it."

"But when will you be sure?" Hammond paced the floor in his agitation, oblivious of the dead eyes watching him from the photographs. "Reilly's had his computer time and checked the figures. You've taken sightings. What else do you need?"

"The Schmidt plates of the area. When they get here—"

"They won't. I didn't send for them."

"Why the hell not?"

"I didn't want to take the chance. One hint would be enough to set the others on the trail and they've better equipment than we have. Damn it, Mal, don't you understand? It's our lives I'm fighting for. This discovery could put Althene on the map. We could get government backing once we gain the right influence. Sir Edward—"

"To hell with him!"

"Later he can roast all you want but for now we need him." Hammond released some of his own frustration in a blaze of unexpected rage. "You bloody academic, what do you know about it? You, locked up in your nice ivory tower with that girl, playing at being a scientist—what do you know about how the world runs? I've got to beg, beg, you understand, for money to pay your salary. To buy materials. To pay for equipment. To employ a gang of useless bastards none of whom could do a good day's work if their lives depended on it. I've got to eat food I detest, play games I abhor, be nice to people I despise and for what? So you can stand there and play Pollyanna. You and your precious reputation! Just see how much booze it'll buy once you leave here!"

"You want me to go?"

"No, I don't want you to go." Hammond paused, breathing deeply, dabbing at his face with a scented handkerchief. The outburst had relieved his tension buy he maintained the emotional level. "But I tell you frankly if you want to quit I won't argue. I can't work with those unwilling to cooperate with me. And I won't be threatened."

But he could be pushed and Spragg had a shrewd idea who was doing the pushing. Sir Edward Thorne, eager for prominence, using implied threats to accelerate results. Hammond's fault, of course, he should have kept his mouth shut but, on the other hand, he could have tried a bluff that had misfired.

Now he said, more calmly, "Mal, we've known each other too long to quarrel like this. What am I asking? Just your permission to announce that a new discovery has been made. It'll buy us time if nothing else. Even if a mistake has been made we can turn it to our advantage. An old man, dying, pleading for our help. How could we ignore him? How could we disappoint his family? A respected member of the community, a minister, a man dedicated to his hobby."

And one safely dead.

Spragg looked at the photographs on the walls and wondered if the men depicted could return what they would have thought. Probably they would have sided with Hammond—they had lived in a hard and practical age. He remembered Titus, his reputation overshadowed by Bode. Of Others who had lost credit which should have been his. Of Humason who had come so near to discovering Pluto, actually photographing it but not knowing what the object was.

"Mal?"

Spragg said, "Gulvain found something but we aren't too certain as to what it is. I want to be sure."

"But there's something there?"

"Yes. A point of light that shows no apparent movement. It isn't a star—all those in the area have been listed for years. It can't be a planet and I doubt if it is an asteroid."

"Why?" Hammond was sharp. "Couldn't it be one with an eccentric orbit?"

"If it's eccentric enough it can't be classed as an asteroid. No more can a comet. It could, of course, be a rogue."

"A wanderer from interstellar space?" Hammond smiled. "Mal, that's just what we need! Sir Edward will be delighted. Thorne," he mused. "Thorne—it should be worth a new spectroscopic laboratory at least. Why didn't you tell me this earlier?"

"Because there's something odd about it. Gulvain records apparent movement but we can't spot any." He added, pointedly, "If you'd got those plates I asked for I'd have been certain much earlier."

"We're as certain as we need to be," Hammond said. "Can you tell me anything more about this object? Size? Mass? Albedo?" He shrugged as Spragg shook his head. "Well, it doesn't matter, the important thing is to make the announcement before anyone beats us to it. No movement, though, that's odd. How do you explain it?"

"No *apparent* movement," corrected Spragg patiently. "Which means the thing could be just hanging there which is impossible unless it's a self-motivated object of some kind. Or, and so Gulvain believed, it is coming straight at us." He smiled at Hammond's expression, enjoying the moment. "That's right, James. The wrath of the Lord sent to smite the ungodly—I told you the old boy was a nut."

CHAPTER 4

Susan Keating entered her office and, closing the door behind her, surveyed the neat array of her desk and furnishings. The desk matched her nature; items set in mathematical precision, and included an ashtray for the use of visitors who were insensitive enough to smoke, in and out trays for correspondence, a plaque engraved with her name and the record of a long-past athletic achievement.

A normal office but one on which she had set the stamp of her own personality. The carpet, won after long struggle, was the shade and pattern she had wanted. The colour of the paint, the pictures on the walls, the curtains, even the lampshade spoke of her presence. And all spoke of her success.

Straightening she crossed to her desk and sat with a happy sigh. She checked that all was in the order she had left it and then she reached for the phone.

"Joan, get me the offices of the *Sun*."

There was a protocol about such things. Joan, the secretary cum typist would make the connection, transfer the call and the person at the other end of the line would be suitably impressed.

A ring and the phone was in her hand.

"City desk." The voice was bored. "What is it?"

"I want to speak with the science editor."

"Lady, this is the *Sun*. Can I take a message?"

"I am ringing to find out whether or not your science editor received the communication from the Althene Observatory which was dispatched yesterday. It is a communication of some importance. Will you please ask him to contact me at his earliest convenience."

"Who should he contact?" The voice grunted as she gave her name, telephone number, and address. "OK. I'll pass the word."

"It is a matter of the utmost importance. It concerns a new discovery by the Observatory. A hitherto unknown planetoid in the star region—"

"Stars?" The voice sighed. "Sorry, but we get our horoscopes from the regular source."

"I'm not talking about horoscopes!" Susan made an effort to remain calm. "This is a great moment in the history of astronomy. A discovery of tremendous importance. Now please make sure your science editor contacts me as soon as possible."

A boor, she thought as she broke the connection. No respect for academic attainments and none of the deference due to a person in her position. Well, she had tried and the *Sun* could not blame her for having neglected them.

"Janet, get me the *Daily Mail*." Susan added, "And make sure I am speaking to the science editor."

The *Daily Mail* was more polite. Yes, they had received the official communication. No, they did not intend making a front-page display of the news as yet. Yes, they were interested.

"Of course," said the voice, "this has been verified by the Royal Observatory at Herstmonceus?"

"Not as yet. The observatory has been notified, of course, but they have to fit the investigation into their programme."

"I see." A pause. "Well, maybe you'll let us know when it's been done."

The *Mirror* was almost as bad as the Sun. The *Guardian* was interested and promised to use the information if they had the room. The *Daily Telegraph* was cool, the *Times* was frigid, the *Star* couldn't have cared less.

The man she contacted at the *Express* took time to explain.

"Lady, we've got three strikes, the threat of two wars, racial violence in five cities and talk of a new election. We've almost three million unemployed and two Miss Worlds had a fight in public last night. You see the problem?"

"No."

"Your news isn't of much interest now, is it? A dot of light in the sky—who cares?"

"It's new."

"So was the Star of Bethlehem and you know how many were interested in that? Three. And that was a pretty big star. Important too."

"So is Thorne."

"Thorne?"

"The new discovery. We named it after Sir Edward Thorne who is a patron of the observatory. Sir Edward is a prominent figure in the textile trade." She added, cunningly, "His firms probably spend millions on advertising."

"Not in this paper, they don't." The voice softened. "Sorry, but all we can give you if we use the item is a mention later in the week. You been a PRO long?"

"I'm not a Public Relations Officer, I'm a Personal Assistant."

"I see, a shame, maybe you should get yourself a good PRO." And then, just before ending the communication, the voice said, "Say, why not try the locals? You're near Carlisle right? Get in touch with Sam Eagan at the *Argus*. 'Bye."

Eagan was a round, plump man addicted to drink and strong tobacco. His suits looked as if they had been slept in and his head, now bald was rarely seen without a bettered hat bearing a stained ribbon. A reporter of the old school his heart had never left Fleet Street even though his body, impelled by the results of certain manipulations while in pursuit of a story, had felt it diplomatic to leave the metropolis.

"*Argus*." He blew smoke into the mouthpiece. "Eagan speaking." He listened to Susan's careful enunciation. "Thorne? Edward Thorne?"

"That is correct. Sir Edward is—"

"I know who he is." Among other things the man owned the *Argus*. "How is he connected with this? I get it. Anything special about the discovery? I see. Has it been verified? When do you expect it to be? Yeah, I understand." Eagan glanced through the window. It was a nice day for a drive and Sir Edward's involvement justified further investigation. To Susan he said, "I'll like to make a spread of this. You know, personal interviews, photographs, plenty of human interest. Could you arrange that? You can? Good. Be with you in an hour."

From where she lay sprawled on a blanket spread on the grass Myrna said, "Mal, what does Rev 9:1 mean?"

"It's a biblical notation. Shorthand so you can find a place." He reared up from his deckchair. "Didn't you ever have religious instruction at school?"

"I skipped it."

"Haven't you ever read the Bible?"

"No, I was too busy with text books. What does it say, Mal?"

"I don't know."

"Find out. Haven't you a Bible?"

There was one in the house and he went to fetch it, pausing as he returned to the garden to look at the girl. She was wearing a scarlet bikini. A young and vibrant animal basking in the sun which, given time, would coat her with gold.

"Mal?"

"Coming." He walked to his chair, conscious of his growing paunch, the wasting of his thighs. Signs of age which he would have preferred to have kept hidden but she had insisted he join her in her worship of the sun. "You'll burn," he warned. "Shouldn't you be using oil?"

"Later." She turned, the movement of her breasts catching his eyes. "I want to get rid of this fish-belly whiteness first. What does the Bible say Mal?"

Seating himself he turned the pages and quoted "And the fifth angel sounded, and I saw a star fall from heaven unto the earth; and to him was given the key of the bottomless pit."

"And?"

Spragg continued, "And he opened the bottomless pit; and there rose a smoke out of the pit, as the smoke of a great furnace; and the sun and the air were darkened by reason of the smoke from the pit."

"And? Go on, Mal."

"Read it for yourself if you're interested." Spragg closed the Bible. "It comes from the Revelation of St. John the Divine and depicts what is supposed to happen at the Time of Judgement."

"The end of the world?"

"You could call it that. Fire and plague, destruction and all hell breaking loose. Starvation, flooding—you name it and it's there with all the sinners being punished and only the true and faithful saved. It used to give me nightmares when a kid, You can see why Gulvain made that notation on his papers."

"The star which fell from heaven," she said thoughtfully. "If he was really around the bend he could have imagined his discovery to be the actual fulfilment of biblical prophecy. Mal, he couldn't have been serious!"

"Why not?"

"He was an educated man. An astronomer and a mathematician. He couldn't have believed that space was inhabited by angels and all that nonsense. His eyes would have told him better."

"Would they?" Spragg looked at the clear bowl of the sky. Aside from a scud of fleecy white cloud the blueness was unmarked. "If you had never seen anything other than the sky as it is now and I told you that there were bright points of light beyond the blue—would you believe me? Or if, at night, I told you that there were objects sending out radio waves and that these waves held regular patterns—would you accept it? Of course not. For that you need to have faith in the discoveries of others. Well, Gulvain had faith in his religion. He believed in heaven and the Bible and the things it contains. As a minister he would have had no choice but to believe, to have faith. Faith that God does exist. That the end will come. That punishment will fall on the unrighteous."

"And that a star will be sent against us to destroy the world? Mal, you're having me on!"

"A little, yes," he admitted. "But it does make an odd kind of sense when you think about it. And the descriptions in Revelations are pretty graphic of what to expect if something from space should hit earth. Not a star, naturally, they had no other terms for such objects in those days. But a planetoid, perhaps, even a big meteor—maybe legends existed of what had happened way back when one had landed and John used available material."

"Now you're going too far. I think I'll—" Her fingers reached for the fastenings of her brassiere, "Hell! Visitors!"

A mistake, Sam Eagan was alone. He approached smiling, snapping with the miniature camera in his hand, talking as he snapped.

"Professor Spragg? Miss Keating said I would find you here. And Miss Parkin? Sunbathing, I see. A most attractive sight. Allow me to introduce myself—Sam Eagan of the *Argus*."

"A reporter?"

"Yes, Professor, and I won't take up much of your time. It's just that your discovery is of great interest and I'd like to get a few things straightened out. As I understand it the object could be either an asteroid, a planetoid or a new moon of Jupiter. Right?"

"We aren't sure as yet."

"But you can make a guess. Would you call it a meteor?"

"Hardly," said Spragg dryly. "A meteor only becomes that after it hits the atmosphere. Before that it's a meteoroid."

"Which is small?"

"Yes, too small to be what we've discovered."

"Something larger, then? An asteroid?"

"Doubtful. Asteroids have been observed for years and all the large ones are known." Spragg added, "At a guess, I'd say it was a planetoid."

"How far away is it?"

"We can't tell as yet. Relatively close, though. It has to be for us to be able to see it at all."

"And heading towards us?"

"Heading towards the inner planets, yes." Spragg did his best to mark his impatience. "You've been given all the facts we have at this time. The object is new. It is relatively close. It is relatively large and is heading in our general direction. I'm afraid that is all I can tell you. Is there anything else?"

"No Professor." Eagan took one last photograph. "That is enough."

* * * *

The story broke two days later. Spragg stared at the newspaper, his hands shaking, filled with the desire to kill. All night he'd been working in the dome and now to come home to this—

"What is it, Mal?" Myrna came to stand beside him. "That isn't the *Argus*."

"But the story came from the bastard who called on us." Spragg jabbed at it with a hand. "Eagan, wasn't it? I'll teach the swine a lesson."

Swine or not the man knew his trade. The headline screamed EARTH DOOMED! Beneath it was a photograph of herself artfully touched to emphasise her breasts. The article began;

"Today, when interviewed by our special correspondent, Professor Malcolm Spragg admitted the object he had sighted in the heavens was heading directly towards Earth. The strange new planet, which he named Thor—the Hammer of God—was discovered by chance and as yet little is known as to its nature and speed of approach. Even so, as Professor Spragg confessed, it has to be unusually large. The Professor, obviously a deeply religious man, was finding consolation in his bible when our special science corresponded called at his luxurious home in the landscaped grounds of Althese Observatory set in the delightfully unspoiled village of Ivegill some twenty miles to the south of Carlisle. Despite his outward composure his voice, at times, tended to break a little and he admitted his fear at having to keep facts to himself for the benefit of Mankind in general. The devastation that would visit the Earth once hit by this marauder from the depths of space is too awful to contemplate. The total abolition of all forms of life together with the actual rending of the crust is inevitable. The fact that the menace is so near, as Professor Spragg admitted, is cause for the greatest alarm. When pressed the Professor—"

Spragg groaned. "Why do they print such rubbish?"

"To sell papers." Myrna took it from him and continued reading. It was the usual mass of repetition, half-truth and biased slant of emotive words that comprised such journalistic masterpieces. The photograph of herself, designed to catch the eye and hold the attention, was an added touch. Doom and sex—the twin props of the national press displayed side by side.

"My reputation!" Spragg snatched at the paper. "Who will ever take me seriously after this?"

"Don't worry about it."

"How can you say that? What about yourself? Your picture spread all over the page? It makes you look a tart."

"So what? Men like tarts."

"It—" He broke off, conscious of their different values, the impossibility of his ever really being able to understand her indifference. Didn't it matter to her that her near-nakedness was flaunted to all? That the photograph had been taken and used without her permission? "You could sue them," he said. "They had no right to print your photograph. And they had no right to lie about what I said."

"So sue them."

She was joking but he didn't take it like that. For a moment he glared at her then snarled, "By God, I'll do just that. But first I'll see that bastard Eagan!"

"No, Mal! Don't be a fool! The more noise you make the more they'll like it. Can you think of anything more stupid than an outraged professor?"

"So I'm stupid now, am I?"

"For Christ's sake grow up, Mal," she said impatiently. "Let it die. Just don't give any more interviews. Susan will have to take care of that side of it. Forget Eagan. And forget this tripe." She kicked at the discarded paper. "In a couple of days it will all be forgotten."

She was wrong.

The silly season was at hand and the public needed titivation. The story was a change from the usual run of sex-mad vicars, salubrious escort agencies and massage parlours, death-spells cast by inspired, teenaged witches, black magic rites conducted in deserted graveyards, and the tired old spate of potential disasters presented by nuclear power stations, biological laboratories, climatic changes and population explosion.

The Hammer of God beat them all.

Pacing his office Hammond said, "For God's sake, Mal, what came over you? Sensationalism is the last thing we want. Susan's been swamped with calls from nuts of every description. Sir Edward's having second thoughts about his support and what do you think this will do to our hopes of getting a government grant?"

"Don't blame me."

"Who then? That reporter? Are you saying he lied?"

"He added two and two and came up with five. He twisted my words—all that crap about the end of the world! Invention!"

Hammond said, flatly, "Susan walked with him towards your house to show him the way. She heard you ranting on about fire and damnation and the Day of Judgement."

"For Christ's sake, man! I was reading from Revelations!"

"Eagan must have heard you."

"And jumped at the opportunity to embroider the story. The bastard! If it hadn't been for Myrna I'd have sued!"

"It's just as well you didn't," said Hammond dryly. "We don't want to aggravate the situation. But things can't be left as they are. The media are after us, Mal. The more we put them off the more certain they are we are hiding something. So I want you to come out into the open. Be blunt. Tell the facts. Lie if you have to but kill this stupid rumour for all time."

"Lie?"

"Shape the exact truth. Do you honestly believe we are in any danger? Of course you don't and it's your duty to remove any doubt from the minds of the idiots who believe all they are told. So I've arranged a television interview. I suggest you act as if you're giving a lecture but Farmer will advise you about that. He's the interviewer. Just do everything he says."

"Like hell I will!"

"Don't be difficult, Mal. I'll be frank—I've had a request from the government. You know how important it is to avoid panic and so I promised you would kill this stupid story about a planet crashing into the earth. A planet! Where did they get that from?"

A question repeated by Stan Farmer later that day before the watchful eyes of television cameras.

He was a short man with manicured nails, over-dressed hair, cosmetic teeth and a contemptuous arrogance that Spragg found hard to swallow. But he knew his job and Spragg responded with the rehearsed answer.

"I said nothing about a planet. The word I used was 'planetoid' which is a far different thing."

"How different, Professor? Smaller?"

"Very much smaller. In fact there is no real comparison. It is almost like calling a pebble a mountain. As a matter of interest there are many such small objects in the skies."

"And some of them actually hit us?"

"Often. Look up into the sky and you may see a trail of light. Children call them shooting stars and they are small pieces of stone and iron which have reached us from space." Spragg, remembering his cues, gave a broad smile. "We get hit by such meteoroids several times a day but they obviously don't do us much harm."

"But there are other masses, aren't there, Professor? Larger ones?"

"Yes, of course, our own moon is one. But I imagine you must be referring to the Apollo-objects. There is nothing mysterious about them. They are merely asteroids that follow paths, which, at times, take them closer to the sun than our own planet. Obviously, in order to do that, they must cross out orbit. However the chance of us both being in the same place at the same time is astronomically remote."

"You mean it couldn't happen?"

"Not in the foreseeable future." One of the 'lies' Hammond had suggested—no one had bothered to check. "And while we're on the subject and in case anyone gets the wrong impression these objects are also known as Earth-grazers. But a graze, in astronomical terms, is a considerable distance—far beyond the orbit of the moon, for example."

"So we are all perfectly safe." Farmer nodded. "Well, Professor Spragg, you've certainly put my mind at rest. But you stated the object you discovered was coming towards us. What makes you so certain of that?"

"I said it was heading in the general direction of the sun," Mal corrected. "Not towards our planet. I may also have mentioned the inner planets or even the Solar System—it wasn't possible to be precise as there was no way of checking the distance."

"Why not?"

"Imagine you are standing on a deserted road at night. It is perfectly dark and all you can see is a small gleam of light directly ahead of you. You have no idea what it is and so can have no conception of its size. It could be anything; a glow-worm, the window of a house, a flashlight, the headlamp of a car. But if, while watching it, it seems to grow larger you can assume that it is heading towards you. Of course it needn't be. The light could be a fire which merely is burning brighter."

"Like a star that had gone nova?"

"Exactly."

"Which is what the object you discovered could be?"

"It could be that, yes." Inwardly Spragg winced at the damage to his reputation then hastily added, "But remember we are moving through space all the time and that means our planet is moving from a straight-line path to the object."

Farmer beamed, obviously convinced by the expert he was interviewing. "Thank you, Professor, that's even better. We are moving away from the visitor—if it is a visitor—and that's an extra bonus for safety. So what would you call all the recent fuss? A storm in a teacup?"

"What else?" Spragg smiled. "There's nothing to worry about."

Not then and not until the end of the following month when Spragg received an invitation to visit the Observatorium der Dutschen Tautenderg.

CHAPTER 5

Sat at the dressing table Myrna said, "Are you taking me with you to Germany?"

"The invitation said nothing about a companion."

"And, of course, I'm not your wife." The sweep of the brush through her hair made a thin, spiteful sound. "I'm just your mistress and that makes a difference."

The brush trembled in her hand as if she fought the desire to throw it at him then lifted to attack her tresses with greater force than before. "How long will you be gone?"

"It depends on why they have asked me to come. A few days, I guess. A week at the most."

Rising he moved towards her and dropped his hands to the smooth roundness of her shoulders, feeling the fine strands of hair covering the flesh, the scent of the shampoo she had used. Hair that tickled his nose and cheeks as he kissed the top of her head. Flesh which slid beneath his questing fingers as his hands dropped lower, down over her upper arms, to her waist.

Hands that caressed a statue.

He sensed her tension, the coldness that she maintained even while being touched. He kissed her again, lightly, then returned to the bed.

She said, as if nothing had happened, "I heard from Ian yesterday."

"Oh? How is he doing in the States?"

"Fine. It's been four weeks now and he's settled in. Rand helped him to find an apartment and he has a car and everything."

He said, "As long as McGregor's able to produce he'll climb. As soon as he stops he'll fall. That's the way Rand works."

"He won't fall." Myrna set down the brush and said, casually, "He asked me to join him."

"Interested?"

"I'm thinking about it. After all he did ask me to marry him."

"No," corrected Spragg. "You've got that wrong. He didn't. He offered to make you his wife if that was the only way he could get you. Now, it seems you're willing to be bought. Will you be leaving before or after you get your degree?"

"You bastard! Don't you care?"

"Would it make any difference if I did?"

"It would help. I don't like to be taken for granted."

"And you don't like to be owned." Irritation sharpened his voice. "Damn it, Myrna, you can't have it both ways. You want to go then you'll go but I'm not going to beg you to stay. I'm not going to give you and Mc-Gregor that to laugh over like—" He broke off. "Never mind."

"Like Bob and Irene? Did you beg her to stay, Mal? Did she laugh at you? Do you think she is still laughing at you?"

"Go to hell!"

"No." She rose, tall and lovely in her newly acquired tan. "I won't do that but I will go and dress. Why not get some rest, Mal? You look all in."

And with reason. It had been a hard few weeks since the interview with Farmer and Spragg felt the tension of fatigue that threatened his ability to make correct decisions. More interviews had followed the first, many necessitating travel and delays. There had been a press conference in which he had been quietly made to appear a fool. In Carlisle a woman had spat in his face and called him a traitor. Hammond had been elusive and there was trouble with the telescope.

And now Myrna's threat.

Lying, eyes closed, Spragg thought about it. He had told her he loved her and had meant it—then. She had told him the same and had, probably, been equally as honest. But propinquity had worn off the bright newness and now the initial flush of passion had died small faults were becoming more obtrusive. The way she was careless about kitchen-hygiene, for example. The scatter of garments in the bedroom. The clutter of deodorants and cosmetics in the bathroom. And, above all, the eternal jeans.

"Mal?" She was back, dressed, breasts firm against the taut fabric of her shirt. "I'm just going into the village. Want anything?"

"No."

"You worried about Ian?"

"No."

"Can't you think of anything else to say?" She turned in a huff towards the door.

"Only to say that I want you."

"Then want on."

She looked offended but he wasn't fooled—she was woman enough to be pleased by his outright declaration.

As she left the house he leaned back, closing his eyes again, almost drifting into sleep before being jerked fully awake by the ringing of the doorbell.

"You!"

Sam Eagan smiled and lifted one hand in a gesture of peace. The other held a brown paper package. "Keep it cool, Professor."

"Go to hell!"

"Now why be like that? Here I come bearing gifts and you act hostile. Where's the harm in a little talk?"

"The last time we had a little talk you almost cost me my job and most probably have ruined my reputation," snapped Spragg. "Now crawl back into your hole before I forget I'm supposed to be civilised."

"Why blame me for the job?" Eagan took the butt of his cigarette from the corner of his mouth and flicked it to one side. "You're a man of the world, Professor. You know how it is. One hand washes the other, right? So I sold the story to the nationals but if I hadn't someone else would have done. And I touched on a few facts you didn't want mentioned but that's the job as I see it. To dig a little. To find out things. To make the news interesting. Have you any ice?"

"What?"

"Ice. I've some of the real stuff here." Eagan hefted the package. "Top-grade malt, export stock, a friend supplied me. You enjoy a good whisky? This is the best. My way of apologising. Accepted?" He beamed as Spragg, reluctantly, nodded. "Good man! Well, let's get at it."

As he'd promised the whisky was superb and Spragg felt both fatigue and animosity begin to vanish beneath its influence. Eagan was a louse but he was a decent louse and he'd had experience of the cut and thrust of the professional world. Anyway there was nothing to be gained by continuing enmity.

"Slarg!" Spragg lifted his glass.

"Prost!" Eagan killed half his drink. "Where's the girl? Out? A fine figure and a nice face. You're a lucky man, Prof."

"Is that what you came to tell me?"

"No." Eagan became serious. "Listen," he said, "I'm a reporter and a good one. Ask anyone in the street if you want confirmation. I didn't always work for a crummy rag like the *Argus*. I just happened to make a mistake and had to pay for it." Eagan refilled the glasses. "Did you never make a mistake, Prof?"

"My name is Malcolm so call me Mal. That or Professor Spragg."

"Sorry. As I was saying, Mal, didn't you ever make a mistake? Every-one does. Mine was in following a lead down the wrong alley and winding up with a story no one dared to print. Not unless they wanted to wind up in jail. Official secrets—need I say more?"

"So they censored you?"

Eagan sipped at his drink. "It happens. I moved while I still had enough reputation to get another job but I didn't leave my brains behind. Or nose for a story." He added, casually, "When did you take your last observation, Mal?"

"Some time ago now, before the initial interview with Farmer. But I've been busy and—"

"Kept on the move, right?"

"Yes, but that isn't all. There's something wrong with the drive mechanism of the telescope so I can't use it anyway."

"Convenient."

"No, damned inconvenient. I wanted to—" Spragg broke off. "Are you suggesting that the telescope has been deliberately sabotaged?"

"Could it have been?"

"Yes, but who would have wanted to do a thing like that? For what reason?"

"Orders, maybe?" Eagan took another sip of his drink. "What made you give that first interview? And why did you agree to shade the truth? You were rehearsed, right? Well, what made you agree to play along? You put your reputation on the line and you must have known it."

Spragg said, "I agreed to the interview because it seemed a good idea to avoid any panic your story could have started."

"Fair enough. Your idea?"

"No, Hammond's. He said he'd promised to see it done." Spragg looked at the reporter. "Promised someone high in authority."

"You believed him?"

"It seemed logical. We were swamped with calls and the stories had grown out of all proportion to what I originally said. So—but what does it matter?"

"That's what I'd like to know." Eagan took a hand-rolled cigarette from a tin, lit it, coughed and beat at his chest. "All right, I know these things are killing me, but who wants to live forever? Now tell me if this makes sense: you made a discovery and reported it, right?"

"The Reverend Aird Galvain made the discovery. I checked and found the object he had seen."

"Let's leave Galvain out of this, he isn't important. You, a noted astronomer, make a discovery and report it. What would normally happen next? Wouldn't other observatories check and verify?"

"Yes, but they need time. Observatories work to prearranged programmes and they don't like to have their schedules upset. If a new discovery is made they can't stop everything just to take a look. In any case there is always room for error; the discovery could be an old object found again as has happened several times with the asteroids."

"From an amateur, yes," said Eagan. "You're a professional. They must know you would have made certain it wasn't a mistake yet they still ignore you. Why?"

"Time as I told you. And you can't really say they are ignoring me."

"I checked with Herstmonceux and got nowhere. The Royal Observatory itself and yet, with the country in near-panic as your Director claimed, they couldn't be bothered to issue a statement. Palomar the same. Licks, Yerkes— Silence all the way. I'm curious as to why."

The man was incredible. Spragg looked to where he sat, the battered hat pushed back on his balding head. He had taken a serious scientific discovery and made a joke out of it and now wondered why others were reluctant to get involved.

Myrna shrugged when, later, he mentioned it.

"He wants more pap to feed his public. Scandal, gossip, anything he can turn into a story. The man's a scavenger." She sniffed at the air. "A pity he didn't take his stink with him."

Smoke and whisky—the fumes had lingered. Throwing open the windows Myrna said, "Did you tell him about the German invitation?"

"No."

"Thank God you had that much sense. Are you still going?"

"Yes. I'll make the arrangements tomorrow."

"For both of us?"

"No." He didn't look at her. "I'm going alone."

* * * *

The observatory had provided a guide. She was tall, slim, golden hair neatly framing a rounded face. Her clothing was vaguely reminiscent of a military uniform with its stark white blouse, severely cut jacket of powder blue with the pleated skirt to match falling level with her knees. Black nylon covered her legs and shoes her narrow feet. Her perfume held the scent of spring. Hilda Brandt had been an unexpected bonus. Now she paused, pointing, dull shimmers reflected from her polished nails.

"There, Herr Professor. Accommodation for the staff. It is not always convenient, you understand, for us to travel into the village."

And little room if they did. The observatory was tucked away in an isolated region and had almost doubled the natural local population. Spragg looked at it with envy—the place put Althene to shame. The buildings were bright and clean and warm, the equipment modern, the whole installation a tribute to Teutonic thoroughness.

"There is the spectroscopic laboratory," continued his guide. "And there the film processing laboratory and there the projection room. For plates from the Schmidt," she explained. "You have seen the Schmidt?"

"Not yet."

"You will see it tomorrow. It is the largest in the world. Larger even than the one at Palomar which has a mirror of—"

"Please." Spragg smiled to remove offence. "I do know these things."

"Of course, Herr Professor. You will forgive me?"

"Anything at any time, Frauline. Is that the Solar complex?"

"Yes, there we study the sun. You wish to see it?"

"Tomorrow, perhaps. Now I feel a little tired. If I could go to my quarters?"

He had been given accommodation at the observatory and someone with unexpected consideration had provided a bottle of schnapps, which rested together with glasses on a small tray on the desk set against one wall. As Hilda left he stepped toward it, opened the bottle and helped himself to a stiff drink. He hadn't lied about his fatigue; it had been a long journey by plane and train and later by car.

Relaxing, he looked at his accommodation. It was equivalent to that provided by a first-class-hotel; a large room fitted with a wide, double bed, a desk, chairs, a television with radio fed from a master control beside the couch, a telephone fitted with a panel of buttons. A window gave a view of the valley and the road winding down towards the village. In the growing dusk the place held a strange air of unreality as if he looked at a scene from another dimension, another time and for a long moment he studied it, imagining Teutonic knights climbing up the slopes to attack the castle in which he stood.

Finishing the drink, he felt the warmth of the spirit ease the tension of his stomach. A bathroom was attached to the chamber and he moved towards it, adjusting the flow of water into the tub before stripping and plunging in, the bottle set within arm's reach. Lying back he half-closed his eyes and let his thoughts drift as the hot water caressed his body.

He thought of Hilda, her tall, lithe slimness...

"Mal!" The voice accompanying the knocking at the door of his quarters was vaguely familiar. "Mal, are you asleep?"

He had been on the verge of it, dozing while his mind toyed with erotic fantasies. He rose from the water and, wrapped in a towel, opened the door.

"Carl!" He smiled with genuine pleasure. "Man, this is a surprise."

"A pleasant one, I hope." Carl Waldemar, a few years younger, a lot fitter and better dressed, stepped into the room. His grip was firm as their hands met and he smelt of an expensive cologne. "Alone?"

"Yes."

"But your Frau— Sorry, I should have remembered. A long time now. But you have no other? No friend?"

Spragg thought of Myrna. "Yes, but I didn't bring her."

"A wise man. Why carry—what is it you say?"

"Coals to Newcastle. Did you provide the bottle?"

"Could I do less? After your hospitality to me when I was in England? You remember that night in Carlisle? And the time when that little waitress wanted to learn German?" He laughed at the memory. "Well, I taught her a few words at least." He raised the glass Spragg had put into his hand. "Prost!"

"Prost!"

"I carry an apology," said Carl as he refilled the glasses. "Ernst Kassel is absent and so is unable to welcome you. A last-minute arrangement, you understand."

"Nothing important, I hope?" Kassel, the Director, had sent the invitation.

"Nein. No, not that. He had to go to Berlin. To confer with those from Potsdam and the Berlin-Babelsberg." Carl lifted his glass. "To old places and old friends!"

"Cheers!"

Spragg leaned back in his chair. It was good to have met Carl again after so long, good that the man should remember him and have made him feel welcome. He covered his glass as again Carl lifted the bottle.

"No more for me. Keep this up and I'll be as high as a kite. Carl—what's all this about?"

"Uh?"

"The invitation didn't go into detail. Kassel just asked me to come along for mutual discussions and general observations. I came because, to be frank, it suited me to get away for a few days. I guess you've read the papers?"

"Of course."

"Then you know what kind of a fool they made of me. The press crucified me!"

"No, Mal, not quite that." Carl was serious. "But you are lucky, here in Germany our press has no restraints such as yours has. So we know how to evaluate what is said and printed. Forget it. I assure you it has no bearing on your reputation."

"All right—then why am I here. And you? Aren't you with the Hamburg-Bergedorft Sterwarte?"

"For many years now, but there we have no Schmidt. I have been here for the past month." Carl raised a hand as Spragg opened his mouth. "No, my friend, no more questions. Work can wait until tomorrow. Tonight a party has been arranged in your honour. You are hungry, I hope?"

"I could eat," admitted Spragg. "But why the party? I'm not a celebrity."

"No?" Carl shrugged. "Others would not agree. After all you are the one who—how do you say it? Ah, yes, you are the one who put the cat among the pigeons. So get yourself ready, my friend. Hilda will call for you."

* * * *

She had changed and now wore a long dress of some shimmering dark material that accentuated the curve of her breasts and the swell of hips and thighs. Dark stones shone dully in the golden hair and thin-strapped sandals graced the delicate feet.

"Herr Professor? Are you ready?"

"A moment." Spragg moved into the bathroom and dashed cold weather against his face, conscious of the need to appear calm and dignified. Conscious too of the effect the girl was having on him, one enhanced by his previous erotic imaginings. "Where are we going? The canteen?"

"No, the village. A room has been hired in the Gasthams. A car will take us."

It waited outside, long and dark and gleaming, a fit conveyance for the girl who slipped into the rear compartment after she had made sure Spragg was settled. As the driver moved the vehicle down the road he could feel the pressure of her thigh against his own, smell the sweet odour of her perfume.

"You have worked here long, Frauline?"

"A year. I like it very much, but I shall not be here for much longer. When married I shall move to America."

"Is your fiancé in America now?"

"No, Belgrade. He is waiting for the appointment to be verified then I shall join him at the Kitt Peak National Observatory at Tucson, Arizona. You know it?"

"I know of it but I've never been there."

"A pity. I have photographs, of course, but it is better to have an eye-witness account." The pressure of her thigh increased as the car swung around a curve. "Heinrich is certain that I will like it."

Spragg stared at his reflection in the window. "How much further have we to go?"

"Not long now, Herr Professor. See? There lies the village."

It nestled in the heart of the valley, small houses dominated by the looming pine-covered hills. The car halted before a timbered house with a steeply pitched roof the eaves ornamented with elaborate carvings in time-stained wood. Inside the party was being held in a back room.

Spragg found himself with a drink in his hand surrounded by strangers all of whom in deference to his ignorance, spoke English. Carl Waldemar attended to the introductions.

"Professor Malcolm Spragg. Mal, meet Doctor Elsa Braun."

Spragg nodded, smiling at a short, plump, red-cheeked woman with sparse grey hair and a mouth that looked as if she had just tasted a lemon. At Carl's urging he turned to beam at a group of technicians and astronomers. At a buxom wench with dark eyes and hair to match—to be told she was the niece of the landlord on duty filling glasses. At a blonde who caught his arm.

"Tell me, Professor Spragg, have you had any experience with the latest model Cominetti computer? The Z5081?"

"No." Spragg freed his arm and tasted his drink. It was aquavite and did things to his empty stomach.

"Which model do you use at Althene?" She pursed her lips as he told her. "You find it satisfactory?"

"No, but it's all we have, Frau—?"

"Frieda Osten. I know of your work, Professor, and you have my admiration. Such painstaking labour."

He looked around the room, his eyes settling on Hilda where she stood talking to a tall man with a grizzled beard. He wore a gaudy sports jacket over a polo-necked sweater with flared slacks and elevated shoes and stood very close to the girl, one hand resting on her hip, a knee almost touching her own. Heinrich? No, it couldn't be, the man was in Belgrade. An old friend, perhaps, but if she allowed such familiarity he could have wasted an opportunity while in the car.

"Professor?"

"Sorry." He returned his attention to the woman at his side. Against Hilda she wasn't much, her face betraying wear beneath the cosmetics but she was better than nothing. "So you're a computer expert."

"No, I am a mathematician. A computer is simply a tool. Of course we have technicians to keep them in repair and to programme them if necessary but I am not one of them."

"I see." Spragg sensed that he had offended her pride. "I must apologise for my error."

"No need for that, Professor Spragg. You were not to know. Of course you have given us all a lot of work."

"I have? How?"

"Surely you must be—" She broke off as Carl came thrusting his way through the crowd towards them. "I am sorry. It is my turn to apologise. It was agreed we should not talk shop. Instead we must do something else."

"What?"

Carl answered for her, his voice rising, booming as he pushed a fresh drink into Spragg's hand. "What else but to follow the most sensible advice ever given? To enjoy ourselves while we still have the chance. You remember that poem you quoted that night in Carlisle?"

And, suddenly, it was back; the warm comfort of the pub and the smiling face of the young girl standing beside him.

"Gather ye rosebuds while ye may," said Spragg, remembering. "For time is a-flying. And the rose which blooms here today tomorrow will be dying." He lifted his glass and drank. "I don't know if I got it right."

"It doesn't matter. It's good enough reason to throw a party!" Carl lifted his own glass. "A toast, my friends. Let us eat, drink and be merry, for tomorrow—"

"We die," said Spragg. "So what else is new?"

CHAPTER 6

Spragg lay moaning softly. He had died and gone to Hell and had there suffered the torments of the damned. In detailed procession had come all the wasted opportunities of his life, the errors, the embarrassments. The girls who had rejected him, each refusal a wound to his ego. The child he had insisted be aborted losing his sole chance at parenthood. The jobs refused because of his dedication to the skies. His marriage. This present trip to Germany. The party.

Spragg moaned again, feeling daylight beat against the closed lids of his eyes. Drink, of course, the initial schnapps drunk before leaving, the aquavite, the wine, the whisky, the vodka, the toasts and laughter and cheering—and there had been a poisonous green substance called vergutz which evaporated on the lips and held the kick of a rocket-engine. Hilda had served it to him, smiling as he sipped, her eyes holding all the wanton promise of Lilith.

And Carl singing and shouting as the food had been served; sucking pig with all the trimmings and cakes and bread and succulent sausages. Later there had been a display by a local troupe of dancers and, later still, the girls had circulated, mellow and smiling and deft as they escaped from groping hands. Somehow, about then, he had put his arms around Hilda and made lying promises about using his influence to help her fiancé…then there had been the touch of chill night air and...

Spragg turned away from the window to face the other side of the bed. Cautiously he reached out, his hand touching the warm, rounded softness of naked flesh. Hilda?

It was possible and, lying in shadowed darkness, he felt a mounting excitement. They had been close. He had made her a promise and she had been grateful enough to come to bed with him.

If so, it had been a waste—he couldn't remember. Details were lost but concentrating he vaguely remembered another in the room, a time of staggering and almost falling, of hands tugging at his clothing and then darkness followed by warmth and softness as the bed had begun to spin and Hell had opened its jaws.

Another wasted opportunity but all was not yet lost. He turned to wards her, then hesitated as he saw the blonde hair spread over the pillow. The blonde hair and the smiling face of Frieda Osten.

* * * *

Breakfast was black coffee and rolls served with butter and a conserve. He ate well, noting that sex after a debauch could have a lot to commend it. That and the clear mountain air and the shower he had taken; ice-cold water that had stung like whips and cured if it didn't kill. Now, seated in the warm comfort of the canteen, Spragg sipped at his coffee.

It had been an interesting morning. He had expected to find Hilda and the shock had thrown him but, as if understanding, Frieda had repaired the damage and carried the affair to mutually satisfying conclusion. And had then, with quiet competence, slipped from his room as he had used the shower. Would Hilda have done that? Would Myrna? Leaving without a word, with no opportunity given for recriminations or regrets. No demands made, no promises extracted.

It was a mistake for a man to yearn after a young girl the more so if he was of advanced years. Aside from the boost to his ego resulting from the illusion of recaptured youth and the envy of his male friends there was little he could gain but trouble. As Shaw had said youth was wasted on the young.

Frieda hadn't been Hilda and that was the sum of it. Did it matter what bottle he drank from as long as there was something to drink?

But it wasn't the same and no amount of philosophical meandering could make it so. He had been a fool to have left Myrna behind. Reilly would be after her with his soft, Irish charm and even Hammond could be tempted. And even if she said nothing the fact would remain, the new relationship waiting to break out again in secret meeting and arranged coincidences until, again, he would know the pain of a collapsing world.

Irene—for God's sake why had she done it? Why had she betrayed him with that bastard Arkwright?

"Professor?

"What?" Spragg blinked, starting in his chair, aware that he must have sat, dozing as his mind had drifted in the past.

"You looked a little strained." The man was one Spragg vaguely remembered as having seen at the party. "The schnapps, ja?"

"I guess so. I'll just take a walk to clear my head."

Outside the air was balmy, a faint breeze carrying the scent of the trees clothing the surrounding terrain. In the distance he spotted movement; a beast of some kind running and leaving a trail of nodding fronds. Birds rose above it, wheeling before again settling to rest. A quiet, calm and peaceful scene, idyllic in its pastoral charm. Spragg stood enjoying it for a few minutes then turned and headed down the path winding around the observatory.

It led to the garden, an area cleared and set with flowers and shrubs, benches set in alcoves and obsolete astronomical instruments decorating the lawns. He halted by a quadrant and then again at a marked dial set with astrological symbols. Kepler stared at him with blind, bronze eyes, the bust set on a plinth of lichened stone, and Copernicus and Tycho faced each other frozen in a mosaic of coloured chips set in an upright concrete slab. Turning from it he saw Hilda Brandt.

She stood at the far side of the garden, searching, smiling as she saw him.

"Good morning, Herr Professor!"

"Good morning, Frauline Brandt. Did your friend enjoy the party?"

"Friend?"

"The man you were with at the party. Tall and with a beard."

"That's Otto. Otto Papen." She shrugged, dismissing him. "An old friend, but I explained that to you last night. Don't you remember? When you said that you would help Heinrich to get the appointment."

"Yes," he lied. "Yes, of course. I've a friend at Kitt Peak. He could even arrange to find a place for you."

"That would be nice." She handed Spragg a scrap of paper. "Heinrich's address," she explained. "You will need it if you are to help. I have added his telephone number and other relevant information."

"Thanks." Spragg tucked the paper into a pocket. "Hilda will you—"

"Herr Professor?"

"Nothing." Instinct warned him not to press his luck. To ask for a date now would be to smack too much of a demanded bribe. "We can talk about it later." He hurried on before she could ask questions. "Now I'd like to see the Schmidt."

It was housed in a dome that held the attributes of a cathedral and it was the ultimate of its kind. Basically it was just a mirror, a camera and a lens, but Spragg looked at it with the respect it deserved knowing the technology that had gone into it. Light entering the upper end of the telescope tube was refracted slightly by a correcting lens and was then reflected from a spherical mirror with a short focus. The camera, placed inside the telescope at the focus of the mirror, photographed large sections of the sky without distortion at the edges of the film. It was big, the correcting lens 54 inches in diameter, the mirror 80. Beating even the one at Palomar which was 48-72.

A magnificent tool but one that could already be obsolete. Advances in electronics had made image intensifiers relatively cheap and superior alternative and if McGregor's analogue system could be perfected it would put even the giant to shame.

Spragg stepped back, looking at the telescope, the dome about. It was closed now but tonight it would open and the instrument aligned. The drive would hold it aimed at the selected portion of the sky while the exposed plate recorded the received images. Tiny dots and points that burned like beacons throughout the dark immensity of the universe. Millions of stars depicted as a scatter of dusty motes.

Work they had down at Althene but there he had been forced to work with primitive equipment.

"Impressive, isn't it? But a little frightening."

Spragg turned to see Carl Waldemar standing close. "Frightening?"

"To study the mystery of creation and to realise that you are, in a sense, peering into the face of God. That out there, so very far away from us, could be other intelligent creatures who could be looking towards us with instruments of their own. What else is space but a great darkness from which could come all kinds of terror?"

Spragg said, dryly, "Do you really want me to answer that? I've had enough sensationalism to last me a lifetime."

"Of course!" Carl quickly changed the subject. "Did you enjoy the party? I must admit I didn't think you'd be up so early."

"Why not?" Spragg met the other's bland stare. "You know?"

"About Frieda? Yes, but you can rely on my discretion. I am pleased for you both. She is a very accomplished woman, no?" Waldemar smiled at Spragg's expression. "She has her doctorate and an enviable reputation in her field. She mentioned it, perhaps?"

"Only that she was a mathematician." Spragg frowned as he strove to remember. "That was just before you came over to join us and made that stupid toast."

"Not so stupid, my friend." Carl was solemn.

"I wasn't invited here just to have fun, surely?"

"No, Mal, you weren't. But Otto can explain better than I can."

"Otto Papen?"

"Yes, he's in charge of the plate processing and examining department. You know him?"

"No," said Spragg dryly, "but it seems we have a mutual interest."

* * * *

His office was in a corner of the big examination chamber; a large room fitted with wide desks, lights, scanning equipment, stools on which sat figures in deep concentration. He rose as they entered, extending his hand.

"Herr Professor! I am honoured!"

He was as Spragg remembered, dressed now in a shirt and pants of dark material, sombre colours, which would normally have been relieved by the light jacket and bright cravat now hanging on a peg behind the desk. His hair, like his beard, was grizzled and Spragg realised the man must be as old if not older than himself.

His grip was firm. As he released Spragg's hand he said, "It is not often we have the chance to entertains a celebrity. You enjoyed the party?"

"Yes, but I'd rather you didn't remind me of my recent exposure in the press."

Papen shrugged. "The penalty of fame, I suppose, and it has to be borne with patience." He glanced at Waldemar then back at Spragg. "You are curious as to the invitation, of course. Naturally it has to do with your discovery. You would, perhaps, like to study the evidence?"

"You've verified? When?"

"I think, Professor Spragg," said Papen, "that you had better study the plates."

They were from the Schmidt, negatives as large as newspapers, the stars depicted as black motes on the transparent film. But, from most of them, positives had been made together with enlargements of selected areas—treatments which lost definition but which clarified and exaggerated certain images. Spragg riffled though them, noting dates and regions of the sky they covered.

Papen said, "We were following a programme of study dealing with the spiral nebulae in order to run a comparison check on distribution and magnitude. Also, in that region, are several variables and binaries of major interest."

"Yes," said Spragg dryly. "I know."

"Of course, Professor. I mention it only to explain why little interest was taken at the time in what later became most obvious. If you will study the first plate?" He grunted as Spragg set it over the illuminated surface. "Now here, you see?"

Spragg followed the tip of the pencil-eraser Papen used a pointer.

"See what?"

"Use the magnifier. Are you familiar with the region?"

"Familiar, yes, but you have far higher detail than I normally work with." Spragg frowned as he stared through the glass. No astronomer could possibly memorise all the millions of dots that the plate revealed. To compare them one with another taken at a later date would require long and painstaking effort. But surely there was something? "A moment! You have an earlier plate?"

He found it, set it over the other, concentrated again as he studied the superimposed images with the glass, searching the indicated region Papen had indicated. Removing the added plate he stared again then finally leaned back in his chair.

Waldemar said, quietly, "Well, Mal, did you see it?"

A black dot, which had appeared where no dot had been before. A tiny but unmistakable disc on the negative—a minute flare on the positive, which Papen fed into a projector. One that had blossomed and died—or had apparently died.

"We missed it," said Waldemar. "Or rather the staff here did—I was still at Hamburg. You noticed the date?"

Five months ago and Spragg remembered what Gulvain had written in his notes. A bright flare that he had spotted and which, to him, had meant more than it had to those in the observatory. But they were not to be blamed. Such a flare could be easily missed by those looking for other objects on the plate. As it had been missed. As the significance of the minute disc had escaped immediate attention.

"It had to be close," said Spragg. "A nova could have looked as large and a supernova larger but neither would have died so quickly. It did die?"

"Nothing could be seen on the next plate," said Papen. "It diminished the urgency but a watch was maintained and, later, something was discovered."

"Thor? And you said nothing?"

"At the time we could not be certain. There were checks to be made, computations and observations, all the usual precautions against error. Before we could be sure you had made your announcement."

Opening his mouth and making himself a fool who saw death and destruction coming from the sky and who had rushed to cash in on his find. That, at least, was how it must have looked to the public and his colleagues. Damn Eagan! And damn Hammond for his greed and impatience!

Spragg said, "Why didn't you announce the verification?"

"We couldn't—there are other reasons." Papen glanced at his watch. "I have a telephone call to make. I will order some coffee to be brought here to you, Professor. Carl, I suggest we leave Herr Spragg to study the plates."

A challenge, Spragg knew it as they left, and felt a wry amusement at how badly they had manipulated it. Carl, obviously was here to guide him the way they wanted him to go. It was no accident he had ended in this office—if he hadn't made the suggestion it would have been arranged in some other way. But why? What was so important about a scrap of planetary rubbish way out in space?

The flare, he thought. Why had it flared? If the planetoid had an amazing high albedo, if it's surface was like that of a mirror then reflection could account for the sudden blaze of brilliance as a mirror flared when struck by a beam of sunlight. But space wasn't filled with either mirrors or directed beams of brilliance so the theory was untenable. What then? If light had been reflected at all it must have come from a nearby source and there was no sign of any other spread of brilliance on the negative. But if the planetoid had hit something?

Matter, hurtling through space on opposed paths, meeting in the void. Energy could not be lost only transformed and the speeds that would have been diminished would have resulted in an eruption of light and heat as kinetic forces were released. If one of the pieces had been relatively small and if the velocities had been high then complete vaporisation of the smaller mass could have resulted. A cloud of incandescence blooming, expanding, cooling as it expanded to fade almost as quickly as it had been created. A theory only but it would do until a better one came along.

Spragg resumed his study of the plates, checking, scanning, fitting one over the other, frowning, finally stepping form the office to gesture to an assistant.

"Have you a blink comparator?"

"Ja, Herr Professor. It is old but—"

"Get it for me, please."

The coffee arrived as it was being installed and Spragg sipped, not tasting, setting aside the cup and turning to the sheaf of positive prints a the technicians left. They were of equal size and scale so that the bright points exactly matched those on another print. Projecting a pair of them on a screen resulted in a perfectly matched picture. But if between taking one picture and another something had moved then, by rapid alternation of the projection, the object which had moved would seem to 'blink'

An old piece of equipment as the assistant had said but with it, back in 1930, Clyde William Tombaugh had spotted he motion of Pluto announcing the discovery a month later on March 13th.

Now Spragg tensed as he saw the tell-tale blink.

It was small but it was there and it could not have signalled the presence of a planet or any known asteroid. It was new and was what the Reverend Aird Gulvain must have seen before writing to Althene. A check of the dates confirmed the suspicion. But what had happened afterwards?

Long hours spent in a lonely vigil cooped up in his little observatory. Chilled, aching, numbed but determined. Using every scrap of his mathematical skill to predict where the object would be, finding it, predicting again and so plotting a course.

Spragg fed more prints into the comparator. The coffee grew and he neither saw nor heard the girl who came to remove the cup. All his attention was on the screen, the heap of positive prints, the projected images, which, unaccountably, remained steady.

Then he remembered the television interview when he had laboriously explained the impossibility of determining the speed or mass of an object seen head-on. But since then the Earth had moved on its journey around the sun and so away from the flight-path of the stranger. Later prints would show that movement and Spragg relaxed as the imaged blinked. The blink became more prominent as he fed in the last of the prints.

Again stepping outside the office he gestured to the assistant, speaking quickly before the other could voice the routine salutation. "Have you the most recent plates taken of Thor?"

"I can get them, Herr Professor."

"Please hurry."

Back in the office Spragg checked dates and fitted the latest print available to the illuminated viewing surface. Thor, as he had known, was no longer a small disc but a thread of brightness. The camera had been held motionless relative to the stars during its long exposure but the planetoid had been moving and had left its trail on the emulsion.

Spragg measured it with a pair of dividers. He turned as the assistant arrived with the latest plate, took it, fitted it and found the trail he had expected, measuring that too. Collating the dates he found the exact times between exposures. From the relative appearance of Thor against the star field and knowing the base-line of Earth's movement he had data to find the planetoid's distance by triangulation. Knowing the distance he could determine the size from apparent diameter. The difference in trail-length coupled with known distance would yield the velocity. Those factors added to angular observation would give the course.

Taking a point of light and giving it a name and direction, mass and speed, fitting it into a complex pattern governed by immutable rules. He had done it before and would do it again.

Rising he straightened his back then stepped towards to door of the office. The assistant, he noticed, still lurked outside apparently engrossed in studying a list of some kind. He looked up as Spragg stepped towards him.

"Have you finished with the plates, Herr Professor? Can I return them to the files?"

"Yes, of course. Can you tell me where I can find the mathematical department?" He saw the other frown. "Computers," Spragg added then, remembering, "Doctor Frieda Osten?"

"Ja, Herr Professor. I understand. Doctor Osten. I will guide you."

She came to meet him as they entered her domain, a cool, rustling place in which machines whispered and displays blinked. In her white coat she looked like any of the other technicians working at their places but there was an assurance in her stride and the gesture as she put out her hand.

"Professor! It is good of you to have come. You are interested in what I do, yes?"

"Yes." He touched her hand and found it cold and wondered at her calm. "I need your help Doctor. The use of a computer to be exact."

"May I ask why?" She nodded as he told her. "I understand. But, Professor, it is not necessary. All the work has been done. Did I not tell you that you have given us a lot to do?"

"Thor?"

"What else? Take a chair, Professor," she waved towards a desk. "I'll have the figures for you in a moment."

They came neat and cold and utterly impersonal and even as he began to study them Spragg felt again the odd sensation he had known twice before. The feeling of utter and complete certainty that his hand was on the future. That, like some visionary of old, he knew just what was to be. The first time he had felt it had been just prior to discovering the asteroid which had built his reputation. The second was when he had felt the irresistible impulse to leave what he was doing and to get back home where he had found Irene with Arkwright. The first time had given him fame, the second had cost him a wife and a friend, and now?

The figures gave the answer and he had a vision of implacable forces moving towards each other. Of a planet orbiting its sun and of a wanderer from space rushing blindly to a destructive rendezvous. Thor had been well-named.

Spragg leaned back, closing his eyes, feeling the papers between his hands, the figures he would check and recheck again and again. The figures which, deep in his bones, he knew did not lie.

Carl had been wrong in his toast and knew it. Eat, drink and be merry, he'd said, for tomorrow we die. Not tomorrow. The Hammer of God would strike in exactly nine months and thirteen days.

CHAPTER 7

Beneath him Myrna struggled, fighting. "For God's sake! What the hell are you doing? Mal! Mal!"

He rolled off and swung his legs over the edge of the bed and rose to pad on naked feet towards the curtained window. It was dawn and beyond the panes a new day was coming to life. In the trees birds made their raucous sounds and, from the motorway, came the muted thunder of traffic. In the village, the town, all over England, the young would be waking eager for the new day, the lovers would be lost in passionate embraces, the old lost in dreams of past achievements.

"Mal?" Sitting up in the bed Myrna stared at him with a puzzled expression. "Mal, are you all right?"

He said nothing, standing before the window, drawing the curtains with a sudden gesture so that the light illuminated his naked body. His hair, she noticed, seemed thinner than before and a little fuzz on his shoulders caught the light and accentuated their slope. His waist was hardly distinguishable from chest and hips. The bluish traces of mottled veins showed on the calves and back of his knees.

A man no longer young and yet with him she had found a comfort unknown with others.

He crossed the room and, catching sight of himself in a mirror, snatched up his dressing gown. Tying the cord he went downstairs and into the living room heading towards the low table, the bottle it carried, the glasses. The first slug burned like fire. The second lit a beacon in the pit of his stomach. The third was halfway to his mouth when Myrna stepped into the room.

"For God's sake, Mal! You'll be stoned before breakfast."

"Would it matter?"

"I thought you had to see Hammond. The drive's been repaired and he was talking about setting up a viewing schedule."

"To hell with him!"

"You're crazy," she said with cold detachment. "Ever since you came back from Germany you've been acting strange. And what kept you there so long? Three weeks and you didn't write or phone once, you could have been dead for all I knew! Now put that glass down and come and talk to me while I make some coffee."

As he ignored her and lifted the glass to his mouth she added, sharply, "You can't hide in a bottle. Believe me I know."

"How?"

She stared at him, tempted to answer, seeing again her father as she had seen him just before he died, standing in the dawn light, swaying, vomit staining his shirt, a drink in his hand. A drunk who has thrown away the last vestige of his self respect.

Then, as she made no answer, Spragg said, lightly, "Don't worry about me, darling. I'm just taking a drink to greet the dawn."

"I don't want you to get drunk."

"I won't." Spragg looked at the glass and set it down beside the bottle. "It's a habit, I guess. The Russians like to hit the vodka and—"

"The Russians?" Myrna frowned. "I thought you went to Germany?"

"I did, and later to Potsdam, then on to Pulkova. They've some nice equipment at the Academy of Sciences."

"Russia? You went to Russia? But why, Mal? Why?"

"To discuss the end of the world."

He remembered the uniforms, the flat, Mongolian faces, the hard, suspicious eyes. The guns and the men the guards had protected, those with neatly trimmed beards some young, others old, a few who had seen too much war, too much blood. And the conferences, the endless conferences when the figures had been checked and rechecked and questions had poured through the earphones in the calm and detached voices of the translators.

Ernst Kassel had arranged it even before he had invited Spragg to Germany and Carl Waldemar had steered him the way they wanted to go. To sit and talk and tell his story. To emphasise the reality of the coming doom.

They'd known, of course. All at the observatory had known, at least those connected with the Schmidt and the computers and the communications network. Carl and Frieda and Papen and most of the rest he'd met at the party. Perhaps even Hilda though he doubted it, her concern with her future had been too genuine. And they had all seemed too calm.

How long had the bastards known?

She said, uncertainly, "You're teasing me aren't you?"

"Yes. I'm getting my own back for this morning."

"You startled me. I don't like waking up like that."

"I'm sorry." He added, lightly, "Did you do anything interesting while I was away? See much of Reilly, for example?"

"Of course. We've been working. Hammond set us to work checking the lines of the solar spectrum. The spectroscope doesn't need long exposures so the faulty drive didn't matter that much."

"But it's repaired now?"

"Yes, but he's still keeping us on the same programme. It's boring but has advantages. For one thing we can live normal hours. I've even been to Carlisle a few times."

"With Reilly?"

"He drove me. We went to the cinema and had a few drinks after in a club he knows. One night we went to a disco. It was fun."

She didn't, he noticed, ask if he objected but it would never occur to her that he might.

"I won't go with him now you're back," she said. "But I saw no point in sitting around twiddling my thumbs. Are you going to report to Hammond? He probably expected to see you on your return."

"He probably did." Spragg glanced towards the bottle, the empty glass. "What about that coffee?"

She made it as always, water boiled, a spoonful of powder dumped into the cup, mild added. Instant coffee, which he had never learned to like, but they had no beans and even if they had she wouldn't have known what to do with them.

Sipping he said, casually, "I wasn't really joking, you know. It's really going to happen. The end of the world. And soon."

"How soon?" She blinked when he told her, "You're mad!"

"Why do you say that? You're an astronomer. You know how implacable mathematics are when applied to the movement of spatial bodies. Thor is moving towards us. It's going to hit us. It's a simple as that!"

"Simple?" She slammed down her cup. "What you're saying is that even if I wanted to have a baby by you I couldn't do it. There wouldn't be time. Right?"

"Right." He wondered why she had chosen that example. "I'm not lying Myrna. Why the hell should I lie?"

She rose with a flash of thighs. "There's such a thing as human error. And I remember you on the TV a few weeks ago telling everyone that such a thing couldn't possibly happen. Am I to believe you then or now? When you decide, let me know."

She left and he heard the scurry of her movements a she dressed, the rapid thud of booted heels as she came down the stairs, the slam of the door as she left the house.

Why had she mentioned a baby?

The coffee held a sour taint and he rose and crossed to the whisky and poured and lifted the glass, sipping as he looked through the window at the brightening day. Could Myrna be pregnant? Had her anger and disbelief stemmed from a natural fear for the unborn child?

The glass empty he went upstairs and bathed and dressed then wandered restlessly about the house conscious of old ghosts, old memories.

Irene had chosen that picture and he had laughed when she had hammered her thumb while hanging it.

Ghosts and memories from which, suddenly, he had to escape.

* * * *

The distance from his house to the observatory was short but Spragg took two hours to cover it, making a long, winding detour before heading towards the dome. It was, he noticed, open, the instrument within probably aimed at the sun, which shone bright and clear in an azure sky. Easy seeing; with such a target it was hard not to get good resolution and city haze, glow and reflections had no chance against the furnace-brightness. Even vibration became a minor hazard.

The door was ajar and Spragg pushed his way inside blinking in the relative dimness. Beyond lay the dome itself with the interior now illuminated by the sun but here in this section of the building only reflected light served to dispel the gloom. Spragg paused as he reached the little room that served to hold clothing and supply modest comforts. It was empty. He lengthened his stride as he heard Reilly's voice.

"Careful on the setting, there! And watch your step! Watch it, I said! Damn it, now it has to be done over!"

A tone he wouldn't have used to Myrna and Spragg wasn't surprised to find her absent. Reilly, standing at the drive controls, turned as he approached.

"Mal! Good to see you! How was the trip?"

"Fine. What are you doing?"

"Setting this thing for corona-photograph. Fred's giving a hand."

Fred, a youngster from the laboratory, smiled in awed humility at the noted astronomer. "Good to have you back, sir."

"We'll try it again, Fred." Reilly, intent on the job at hand, wanted to waste no time in empty greetings.

Spragg watched as the telescope moved, halted, moved again. The usual eyepiece had been removed and an arrangement of lenses and mirrors caught the magnified image of the solar disc and sent it through filters to where a glass screen rested beside the lattice. Spragg blinked as it flared with sudden brilliance, retinal images dancing, turning away as Reilly made further adjustments.

"There! That should do it. Want to look, Mal?"

The brilliance was masked now by a circle of blackness, which, covering the exact orb of the sun, allowed the flaring corona to be seen in all its majestic splendour. Great tongues and gouts on flame reared like inverted waterfalls of incandescence, taking odd shapes and proportions, falling to rise against new and more entrancing configurations.

"You've got it, Sean. Hammond order this?"

"Who else?" Reilly's voice carried his disgust. "Make work for idiots. Right, Fred, it's all yours. Get some good pictures and you may find yourself hanging in the Royal Academy."

"Would they consider it to be art, sir?"

"These days you could piss on porridge and they'd call it art. But let's not get ambitious. Just take some decent snaps—we can always sell prints to the visitors."

"Would I get a royalty, sir?"

"You'll get the door if I have any more of your lip!" Reilly turned to Spragg as the youngster set to work. "I can't really blame him. Any fool would know he's doing work which is being done a dozen times better by others."

"But it gives him experience."

"True." Reilly glanced at him then led the way from the dome. Outside he leaned back against the wall, found and lit a cigarette. "What's with Myrna? Sick?"

"In a way, yes."

"I'm not surprised. She's been as tense as a spring these last few days. No trouble, I hope? No? Good." Casually he added, "How was it in Germany? Make any friends at the observatory?"

"A few." Spragg remembered the other had tried to get a job there and would have a particular interest. "I met Carl Waldemar—I think he was before your time here. And Ernst Kassel."

"The Director?"

"Yes." Lying Spragg added, "I mentioned you and he seemed interested but said they had no vacancies. But you could stand a chance later. Next year, maybe."

"Too long to wait." Reilly studied the tip of his cigarette. "I've irons in the fire in the States but thanks for trying anyway. Seen Hammond yet?"

"No."

"When you do try and find out what's going on. First the trouble with the drive and now this solar crap—hell, what more can we discover about the sun with this junk equipment? Can't you get him to put us back on the Jovian Project?"

"What more could we discover if he did?"

"Maybe nothing but at least I'd feel like an astronomer again." Reilly dropped the cigarette and trod on it. "Well, I'd better see how our young friend is getting on. We can't have him wasting film."

He went back into the building, an irritated man and, thought Spragg, one shrewd enough to know that he had been lying. Well, everyone lied for social convenience and there had been no point in telling him that he'd been too busy to push his case. As Reilly had said nothing about his jaunts with Myrna. As Hammond said nothing about his delay in reporting.

"Mal! It's good to see you!" Hammond smiled, his grip firm. A mask Spragg assessed at its true value. "Drink?"

"Why not?" Spragg glanced around the office as the Director busied himself with a bottle and glasses. Fresh flowers stood in the bowl, the windows sparkled in the sun and the wood held the scent of newly applied wax. Someone had been busy. Dowton?

"He insisted," said Hammond when Spragg asked. "A dedicated man— there are so few of them now. He said he wanted to feel more a part of the observatory and volunteered to polish the wood. Not strictly his job, of course, but how could I refuse? Cheers!"

Spragg lifted his glass, sipped, lowered it half-empty. Hammond was cautious with his generosity. He was also curious.

"Not much," said Spragg when the Director asked him what had happened during his trip. "We talked and checked some plates and I gave a talk on rogue bodies in space with particular reference to those within the solar system. Not that we have many rogues, of course, everything follows an orbit of some kind but now and again we do get the odd mass which is new."

"Like Thor?"

"Yes." Spragg finished his drink and stood with the glass held suggestively in his hand. "They'd spotted it before we did."

"And didn't announce?"

"They wanted to be sure."

"Which shows how important it is to get in first." Hammond ignored the empty glass. "If I followed your advice we'd have missed the boat. As it is you, and the observatory, have achieved a measure of fame."

Notoriety that he could have done without. Spragg said, "Why the new Solar programme?"

"We have a commission from the Admiralty for a complete check and correlation of all coronal and sunspot activity over a three-month period. It has something to do with weather prediction."

"Three months? What about my own work?"

"Surely, Mal, such observations are your work. Primarily you are needed here to do what has to be done. You're thinking of your discovery, perhaps? Well, surely other observatories will be studying Thor. Of course, if you feel restricted—" Hammond broke off, smiling, but the message was plain. "You understand the situation I am sure."

Play along or get out and he'd made it clear. Althene now had its reputation and wouldn't want for staff. His own position could be used as a bribe or as a reward to the son of a generous patron. In fact, now, he could even be an embarrassment to the observatory. No scientific institution could afford to be associated with an apparently irresponsible glory-hound.

Pressure which Spragg recognised and which he suddenly found hilarious.

"You find it funny?" Hammond frowned as Spragg straightened, gasping for breath, tears of mirth wetting his cheeks. "What's the matter with you, man? Are you drunk or mad, or what?"

"No, I'm sane," said Spragg, sobering. "Saner than I've ever been in my life before and you know why? Because nothing matters now. Nothing at all. You, your job, the observatory, your stinking little affectations—God, what a creep you are! You really think I'm going to jump when you give the word? Dance to your tune? Not on your life. Stuff you, Hammond—and your job!"

* * * *

He woke from a dream in which he was a bee crawling desperately across a flat surface, legs broken, wings torn, while from high above a clenched fist descended to squash out his life. The fist vanished, the table, the dragging legs and only the buzz remained; the thin, strident hum of the doorbell.

Spragg rolled, gasping, staring at the flickering dance of coloured shadows. He lay on the floor in a gloom broken only by the swathes of coloured light, which streamed from the silent television. An empty bottle rolled under his hand and he stared at it, remembering his farewell to the Director, the walk afterwards, the return to the empty house. He had turned on the TV, killing the sound because of its inane babble, sitting to watch the mouthing off po-faced pundits as he had sipped at twelve- year old Scotch. Now it was dark and the doorbell was a dragging irritation and he swore as, painfully, he climbed to his feet.

Eagan stood outside. "You look like hell," he said dryly.

"I was asleep." Spragg wiped his mouth with the back of his hand. "Come on in. Make some tea while I have a wash."

Upstairs Spragg studied his face. His eyes were puffed and his cheeks looked bloated. The whisky must have hit him with sudden force, he guessed. He had sprawled from the couch to the floor where he had wakened. Hours ago now and he was sober again even if he did ache all over.

"Here." Eagan had come upstairs and now handed him a steaming cup. "And here." He'd found a bottle of aspirins. "Take four, drink the tea, have a wash and I'll fix you something downstairs. Need any help?"

"No. I can manage, but thanks."

Alone Spragg sipped the tea and dutifully swallowed the tablets. The aspirin would take care of the head as the tea would take care of the stomach. A shower and a change and he'd be almost as good as new.

Eagan grinned as Spragg finally joined him in the kitchen. He waved to a chair and held out a tumbler half-full of assorted ingredients.

"My version of a Bombay Oyster," said Eagan cheerfully. "You swallow it straight down." He waited as Spragg obeyed. "Better?"

"I will be... What are you doing here, anyway?"

"I dropped by to see how you were getting on. I'd hoped you'd get in touch with me when you got back from Germany to put me in the picture." Eagan took out a cigarettes and lit it. Through a haze of smoke he said, quietly, "Why the binge, Mal? Had a row with your girl?"

"That's my business not yours." Spragg coughed. "Do you have to smoke that rubbish in here?"

"Sorry." Eagan stubbed out the cigarette. "I bumped into Myrna in town earlier," he said casually. "She was going into the Church of the Holy Rosary to pray and light a candle. Didn't you know she was a Catholic?"

If she was Spragg hadn't guessed it. Not once while he'd been with her had she ever spoken of attending Mass or of believing in the tenets of any faith. The act had been a gesture, he decided. A return to childish conditioning or a form or coin-in-the-fountain insurance.

"Funny how some people do without religion all their lives," mused Eagan. "and then, when trouble hits, they turn to God. Others, of course, hit the bottle."

"Like me? Damn it, Eagan, what the hell are you after?"

"Answers—the truth! Why, for example, is Althene suddenly interested in the sun? Why other private observatories are busy on government contracts? Why all the big installations haven't the time to answer a simple question. I think there's a big cover-up operation going on. Take Althene— why the contract? Why else but to keep the telescope away from Thor?" Eagan was shrewd and it wasn't difficult to figure out his source of information. Dowton, of course, Spragg remembered the polished office and guessed why the man had volunteered. Bribed by Eagan he'd wanted the opportunity to snoop and report what he'd found or heard. The thought of the janitor acting the spy made him smile.

Eagan scowled. "You find that amusing?"

"It's ludicrous! You're looking for an answer you already have."

"Thor," Eagan mused. "The hullabaloo. You going to Germany. The conference—yes, the press picked it up, but no statement was issued. Thor," he repeated. "Mal?"

"You broke the story, remember? The Hammer of God coming to crush us all. Vengeance from the skies. The doom from outer space. Well, it's all going to happen."

"When?"

Eagan drew in his breath when Spragg told him.

"You're thinking there could be the possibility of error," said Spragg. "That's what they thought at the conference. They refused to believe what they were told despite the evidence and ordered a clamp down on the news while appropriate observatories made careful checks. But no matter how you add the figures the answer comes out the same."

"Death," said Eagan. "The End. There's no hope?"

"None." Spragg added, "If you want a drink it's in the other room."

He watched as the other poured himself five ounces of old Scotch, refusing a similar measure.

Eagan lifted the glass. "To life! May it be short and merry!"

"You're like Myrna," Spragg said. "You don't really believe you're going to die."

"Does anyone? Go out into the streets and tell anyone you meet they've only eight months to live and they'd laugh in your face. We can't face the prospect of extinction. That's why the whole damned world is insane. We know death will come, we watch it happen, we see it—but always it happens to someone else. So we all live our lives as if they will last forever."

"We could tell them. You did it once."

"To sell papers," explained Eagan patiently. "This is different. Can you guess what would happen if people really believed everything was coming to an end in a few months time? Whenever there's a shortage of anything people go wild. They turn to animals and grab whatever's going—what the hell would they do for life itself?"

Spragg could guess. He crossed to face the window as Eagan poured himself another drink. Outside it was raining heavily, the panes running with a shimmering waterfall, wind gushing in the trees. It would be chill and wet and yet never again might he have the chance to walk in this exact combination of circumstances. Each day now was precious for none could ever be repeated.

Spragg tensed and turned as the phone rang. Quickly he crossed the room and snatched up the instrument. "Myrna?"

The voice was a man's. Spragg heard him out then lowered the phone.

Eagan was curious "Something wrong?"

"No, nothing wrong. I've just been invited to America."

CHAPTER 8

The man was tall, slim, neatly dressed, his expression masking the fact he was performing a tiresome duty. He came forward as Spragg entered the VIP lounge, hand extended, teeth displayed in a smile.

"Professor Spragg? I'm from the Embassy, Rodger Harcourt-Smythe. Welcome to Washington. Have a good flight?"

"Fine." It had been first class all the way. "This is Miss Parkin, my confidential assistant. You'll take care of the bags?"

"Of course." Harcourt-Smythe beamed at Myrna.

She deserved his attention. The jeans were gone as were the boots and uniform-style shirt, all replaced by neat shoes, sheer tights, a business-like skirt, blouse and jacket. Her perfume was one of the most expensive money could buy, her hair had been set by an expert, cosmetics accentuated her golden tan. Spragg had insisted and, to his surprise, she had not objected. She was now a picture of elegance, worthy of her new position.

She returned his smile. "Have you been here long?"

"My second year with the Embassy but before that I was attached to the liaison department of the Ministry of Defence. Your first visit?"

"Yes."

"You must permit me to show you around. There is so much to see and enjoy here in Washington."

Spragg said, impatiently, "Miss Parkin will be happy to take advantage of your offer should time permit. However we are not here on holiday. You are aware of the situation?"

"Of course, Professor. You are here at the request of the American Government to take part in the scientific exposition arranged to determine the distribution and origin of the asteroids with particular reference to the Apollo-objects." He added, a little vaguely, "Something to do with using them as sources of minerals, I understand."

Myrna looked from him to Spragg. "They want to mine the asteroids?"

"An extrapolation based on the present run-down of easily available minerals here on Earth," explained Spragg. "The asteroids could offer an alternative supply."

As the story offered a perfect cover for what he knew would form the core of the discussions. Any genuine leaks could be explained away under the guise of speculative interest. But the mere fact that such a story had been devised and the exposition arranged was clear proof the Americans were worried.

As were the British.

Leaning back in the car Spragg remembered the short, sharp hassle he'd had with the authorities. First to gain VIP treatment, then to insist that Myrna be allowed to accompany him, then to delay his leaving until it suited them both. Concessions grudgingly conceded.

"Mal!" Myrna stared eagerly through the windows at the slender shape of the Monument rising like an ancient obelisk on the horizon. "Do we pass the White House?"

Rodger turned from where he sat beside the driver. "No, but you'll see it later. The White House, the Senate Building, the Jefferson Memorial—Washington is full of things to see. A pity it isn't earlier—you've missed the celebrations, but autumn has its own charm."

Maybe, but late summer had its own hell. Spragg dabbed at his face and neck, conscious of the humidity despite the air-conditioning built into the car. He hoped the hotel selected for them had better equipment.

Rodger blinked when he fired the question. "Your hotel, Professor? It's the Clairmont. One of the best. We have rooms reserved for visiting dignitaries and I'm sure you'll find them comfortable."

"Rooms? Why not a suite?"

"Impossible to arrange at such short notice, Professor. But of course your rooms are adjoining."

"And we're going there now?"

"Not exactly. The Ambassador would like a few words with you first."

Sir Edgar Waring was an older version of the attaché. He came forward to greet them as they entered his office, smiling, nodding dismissal at Harcourt-Smythe, turning to a table bearing glasses and a decanter as the young man discretely vanished.

"Some sherry? Or perhaps you are already Americanised and would prefer something with ice?"

"Sherry will do nicely, thank you Sir Edgar." Spragg lifted his own glass towards Myrna before taking a delicate sip.

Sir Edgar decided on the direct approach. "Were you briefed in London? I mean as to your duties here?"

"Duties?" Spragg raised his eyebrows. "I am here at the invitation of the American Government."

"Yes, of course. They seem to regard you as some kind of expert on the catastrophe that appears to threaten us and, naturally, we were more than pleased to aid them in obtaining your services. A mutual arrangement, I trust. As you must be aware Her Majesty's Government is deeply interested in any recommendations or decisions that may be clarified at the Exposition. Especially in items which may affect the National Interest."

"Of course."

"I knew you would understand. We all have to pull together in times like these, what? And there is so much you could do to guide things along the correct path—a word in the right ear, a suggestion, the use of your reputation to emphasise a point. Wars are not always won on the battlefield, eh?"

"War?" Myrna looked puzzled.

"A metaphor, my dear, don't let it worry your pretty little head." He beamed at Myrna. "I must say Spragg is a fortunate devil to have such a charming assistant. I'm sure you will enjoy your stay in Washington. Our hosts are always hospitable—especially to a young and lovely girl."

After Rodger had finally dropped them at their hotel and they were alone in one of the adjoining rooms Myrna said, "God, what a fool! No wonder we lost the Empire!"

"Don't underestimate him." Spragg watched as she kicked off her shoes and removed her jacket, skirt and blouse. "If he wasn't clever he wouldn't have the job he does."

"Crap!" She turned to face him her eyes furious and Spragg remembered the rebellious nature of his own student days. "He's where he is because he was born to the right family, went to the right school, married the right woman and didn't step on the wrong toes. What's so clever about that?"

"He's a success in his own world which is the only way he can really be judged. At least he's learned to survive." Then, changing the subject, he asked, "You know why he wanted to see us, of course?"

"Sure." Myrna sat on the edge of the bed and took off her tights, making the awkward operation seem somehow graceful. "He wants us to act the spy. The damned fool—any reporter could tell him as much as we could."

"Wrong. He was talking about the things that never get reported—smoke-filled-room stuff when arrangements and deals are made. From that he can assess weakness and gain advantages." Use betrayals and bribes to make friends and create enemies—the normal tools of diplomacy. "And you got the hint he dropped at the end?

"That I should do the Mata Hari bit? What the hell does the old fool think I am?"

She stepped past him, vanishing into the bathroom, water gushing form the shower as he reached the door.

Sitting on the edge of the tub he said, "So you don't want to cooperate? Not even for the good of the National Interest?" He grinned as she told him what to do with it. "Did you notice how incurious he was? The world coming to an end and he didn't seem to care a damn."

"His class," she shouted. "Stiff upper lip and all that jazz. Anyway, nothing ever happens to the Establishment. They've got it made."

"Not this time."

"I hope not." The sound of water died and she stepped from the shower, her body dewed with pearls, the golden skin pimpled from the final, icy deluge. She said, "He knew all about it before we got here. He must have received the checked verification of Thor's approach direct form the Royal Astronomer himself."

"Maybe," agreed Spragg, "but the Americans must have had it before that. It took time to arrange this Exposition. They must have begun to set it up as soon as they'd heard from Germany. Or," he mused, "they could have had prior knowledge. God knows what they've got up in space but it's more than we know about. Or one of their spy-satellites could have been adapted in some way. And if they knew then the Russians knew also."

"Which puts us right smack in the minor league." Myrna looked over the edge of the fluffy towel covering her nudity. "The last to be told—so much for past glories. Well, to hell with it. What's the programme for tonight?"

"We eat then go to bed."

"So early?"

"You're forgetting the jet-lag. We're five hours ahead of local time. Anyway I want to bone up on my notes in case I'm called on to speak tomorrow. I'm the expert, remember?" He laughed at the thought of it. "How the hell can anyone be an expert on the end of the world?"

"You discovered Thor."

And was here on the strength of it. The wrong man—it should have been the Reverend Aird Gulvain. He, at least, would have had all the answers.

* * * *

Thomas Clottery was convinced he had one. He stood on the podium, legs straddled, head thrust forward over his notes, his voice an irritating drone.

"...so it seems incontrovertible that most of the cratering of the Moon and Mars as well as those sites clearly delineated on Earth must have been caused by an intense bombardment of matter expelled from the area of space known as the asteroidal zone. This matter was probably produced by the break-up of the planet that held an orbit between Earth and Mars in eons past. The catastrophe that destroyed it can only be a matter of speculation and for our purposes, is immaterial. The facts, however, are plain. The

Moon has something like 300,000 craters of a kilometre or more. Mars, larger and closer to the asteroidal zone, should have 25 times as many craters but, in fact, appears to have only 4 times as many. This discrepancy is more apparent than real when it is borne in mind that the planet would have had an atmosphere and water in past ages—a combination which, aided by winds, would have erased most large and all small craters. Earth, of course, is a larger target than the Moon with 14 times the cross-sectional area and 80 times the gravity attraction. Some of these impacts must have left marks, which still remain despite the action of the elements and many of these have been mapped as highly probable sites. I mention only the Aral Sea and the Great Barringer Meteor Crater near Winslow, Arizona..."

At his side Myrna whispered, "Mal, how can a sea be a crater?"

"It filled with water after it had been made," he whispered back. "There are a lot of sites like that; any coast which looks as if it is the part of a circle or any lake which looks neatly round."

"Like Hudson's Bay or the Gulf of Mexico?"

"Yes."

Clottery was coming to the end. After painting the picture of a tremendous explosion in space which had shattered a planet to fragments and sent those fragments hurtling against the inner worlds he ended "...seems to be obvious that the object known as Thor must be a part of the original mass which managed to avoid being drawn into the gravity well of the sun and has been following a wide-flung orbit ever since the initial holocaust."

"Thank you, Doctor Clottery," said the president quickly. "A most interesting dissertation. Has anyone any questions?"

They had but they were voiced over coffee and doughnuts during the morning break.

"The man's a fool!" A thin-faced, balding professor from California left no doubt as to his feelings. "So we have one big bang which wrecks a planet. All right—did all the stuff hit Mars, Earth and the Moon? Venus too from what we've found lately. All of it? We've checked on what was left—and why was any left? Counted what we can find in the asteroidal zone and if the planet was about Earth size, eighty percent of it is missing. Now spray that out in a widening sphere and how much would hit and how much would miss. Give me a while and I'll tell you if I can find my god-amned calculator."

And:

"Blew up, he said, but what made it do that in the first place? Maybe something like Thor came along and did it. So we get a kind of chain-reaction—something breaks up the planet which blasts us with debris and forms the asteroidal zone and now another comes along to do the same thing to us—say, what's the time-element in all this? Maybe we can find a pattern."

And, more to the point:

"Who gives a damn where the thing comes from? What the hell is it going to do to us?"

Donald Lauter discussed that after lunch. He was a tall, slim, hawk-faced man, neat in his uniform, the insignia of a colonel bright on his shoulders. A military scientist attached to NASA and engaged in the space programme. One whom, Spragg guessed, would have walked on the Moon if the money hadn't run out. He stood quietly on the podium, a long pointer in his hand, waiting until all had settled.

"Your attention, thank you. Slide on, please."

The lights dimmed as the wall behind him flared to brilliance. A crater taken from one of the orbiting vessels scanning Earth's satellite. It looked dusty, frayed, as old as time.

Lauter said, "Note the streaks which run like rays form the edges. This is unusual and not as yet fully explained but comparison tests on simulated materials reveal they must have been created by an intensely high velocity. Next!"

Another crater, wide, deep, monstrous, peaked in the centre, the rim-wall jagged as if gnawed by rodent teeth.

"Kepler. You will not there are no rays such as are visible in the Tycho areas. Next!"

More slides, all depicting craters, giant pits driven into the lunar surface as if some lunatic had been at work with a ball-hammer, striking at random, one crater overlapping another, some with central peaks, others without, all bearing the indefinable stamp of age.

"As I mentioned comparisons have been made with various materials in order to try and emulate the appearance of the Lunar craters," said Lauter as the screen glowed white and featureless. "We used a base of talc and dropped various materials on it from differing heights. The results were interesting."

The white screen blurred, steadied to show what seemed to be more lunar craters then, as the illuminated area widened, the true scale became apparent. The craters were in a box a few feet on a side, the craters were miniatures created by artifice.

"Under high-velocity impact solid materials tend to act as if they are liquid. The action of the talc proved that and these following slides, taken as water was dropped into water, shows the formation of the crater-pattern." A click and pictures shone on the screen in rapid succession; water, a drop falling, hitting, walls rising, an inner peak forming, the whole gently subsiding, time stretched by the magic of the camera. "Now this is film taken to show the stress and yield patterns of various substances when affected by high-velocity impact. First a boulder of granite weighing some ten tons when hit by a cannon ball weighing two pounds and travelling at fifteen hundred feet a second."

Colours writhed on the screen as special film traced the threads of stress from the point of impact, creating a mesh of conflicting forces and energies. More film, other substances, other forces, all spelling out a story of relative strengths and weaknesses.

"As you can see the critical point is relatively low in that an applied force of small capability can result in unexpected devastation especially when applied to non-homogenous materials." He added, dryly, "I have no need to remind you that our planet is far from homogenous. The edges of the tectonic plates alone present an in-built weakness as do all volcanic sites either active or quiescent. We are also extremely vulnerable in respect of the polar ice caps. Next!"

Earth shone on the screen. Not the planet as seen from space but a Mercator projection familiar to every schoolboy, inaccurate but useful and ideal for the colonel's purpose. The pointer in his hand tapped at various regions.

"From aerial surveys it is obvious that the Earth has been struck many times in the past by masses of considerable dimensions. These impacts have left recognisable configurations, which, together with geological examination, remove any doubt as to their extra-terrestrial origin. One of the most obvious is the Barringer Crater, which has earlier been mentioned. It is roughly circular with an average diameter of over 4,000 feet. It is 570 feet deep and the bottom is filled with rubble to a depth of about 600 feet. It is surrounded by a wall of between 130 to 160 feet higher than the outside plain. Its age, as far as can be assessed, is in the region of 50,000 years. This, of course, makes it comparatively recent but not as much as the fall in Siberia in 1908 which, together with the one in 1947, also in Siberia, fortunately missed inhabited areas. The point I am making, ladies and gentlemen, is that our planet is no stranger to bombardment from space and some of the missiles have been responsible for altering our terrain. Here, for example," the pointer moved and steadied. "The area known as the Michigan Basin. You will note the near circle formed by the Lakes Huron and Michigan, a circle, which, if completed, would result in a crater some 300 miles in diameter. And here," the pointer halted on the Atlantic coast of the United States. "Kelly Crater—the arc of a circle which would be more than 1200 miles in diameter. And here we have the significant curvature of the northern boundary of the Black Sea, Lake Victoria in Africa, the Gulf of Carpentaria in Northern Australia—possible impact sites are scattered over the entire globe."

The butt of the pointer rapped on the floor and the projection changed, the same Mercator depiction of the planet but this time the areas mentioned together with a host more were delineated with scarlet circles. More rested on the oceans.

"Submarine trenches have been plotted which could be the remains of tremendous impacts in the distant past," continued Lauter. "Tidal flow and currents would have eroded the original craters but their residue remains. The effect of such an impact on the nearby shores can best be imagined by considering the known effects of the tsunami following an earthquake. A wall of water would sweep from the sea and destroy everything in its path for a distance of perhaps several hundred miles. There would also be steam from the superheated water and scalding rains—an added ingredient to the normal tsunami." The pointer rose and tapped a point on the map. "I mentioned the Barringer Crater in detail and for a reason. According to the revised estimates the mass that caused it must have been in the region of 70 to 100 feet in diameter. Large, but it would have lost mass through atmospheric burning and we can assume that the actual size of the mass on impact was about 50 feet in diameter. A ratio, you observe, of 1 to 8. However, in the Michigan Basin, the mass responsible has been estimated at being 30 miles in diameter, which makes the enhancing ratio 1 to 10. And here," the pointer moved to Kelly Crater, "the object must have been in the region of a 100 miles in diameter which gives us a ratio of 1 to 12."

A pause and then with an air of finality Donald Lauter said, "the most recent estimate of the diameter of Thor, plus or minus 10 percent, is 550 miles."

* * * *

The dining room of the Clairmont was discrete, the classical music from the five-piece combo muted so as not to interfere with conversation. Facing him Myrna sat toying with a steak far too large and around him, smiling, talking, engaged in the communal eating, other couples occupied about half the tables. Later all would be full but now, so early in the evening, there was time for the neatly uniformed waitresses to relax.

Myrna said, abruptly, "Mal, I wish I hadn't come to America." She pushed aside her plate. "I feel numb."

"Ill?"

"Sick. That man in there—if he was trying to scare the hell out of me he did a good job."

Her and the others in the auditorium. Spragg remembered the silence which had followed the bald announcement, lengthening while all had made their mental computations, then the sudden extinguishing of the lights and Lauder's absence when they had brightened again. Showmanship, of course, but performed with a calculated dexterity. The rattle of figures and then, like the blast of a gun, the final shock.

Spragg said, "You knew, Myrna. I told you."

"You told me," she admitted. "But I guess I didn't want to believe you. Christ, Mal, how can you be so calm?"

Hysteria tinged her voice as she almost shouted the question and an attentive waitress took a step towards them halting to retreat as Spragg shook his head.

She took a sip of water, regaining her composure. "Sorry."

"No need to apologise." Spragg recalled his own experience. First the numbness, the sick horror, the frantic rejection and then, the intellect rising above the primitive emotive need to survive, the acceptance. Or perhaps it wasn't an intellectual acceptance but a passive resignation. Death was coming, a little earlier than anticipated, but that was all. And, as a bonus, it brought freedom.

"Mal?"

"I was thinking," he said. "Remembering Hammond's face when I told him what he could do with his job." He added, casually, "That was the day Sam Eagan saw you going into church."

"The day you told me about Thor. I didn't want to believe you. I thought you were being cruel for some reason. I—found help." She looked at the glass of water in her hands. "Obviously it didn't last."

The music died, resumed after a moment, a new arrangement that tweaked at his memory. When had he heard it before? In Carlisle when he and Irene had gone on one of their little excursions? Damn it, why did he have to think of Irene?

The waitress came forward at his signal and took his order for Scotch on the rocks, glancing at Myrna who shook her head. She shook it again as he downed half the drink at a swallow.

"Trying to drown memories?"

She was too damned shrewd at times and Spragg felt the heat of a violent resentment. What he did was his business, not hers; she was the girl he slept with not the woman who shared his life. But he had no woman to share his life, not now and maybe not ever. He had only thought he had.

"Sir!" The waitress was at his side again, and this time a familiar figure stood behind her, one who stepped forward, smiling.

"Glad to have found you, Professor. Miss Parkin." Rodger Harcourt-Smythe nodded in her direction. To Spragg he said, "We're having a sort of function at the Embassy and Sir Edgar hopes you'll both be able to drop in. Cocktails at eight-thirty. I'll send a car."

Spragg said, coldly, "What if we don't choose to come?"

"Sir Edgar would be most upset." The blue eyes were suddenly hard. "He's the Ambassador, you know. It's almost a royal summons, what? Wouldn't do to let the side down now, would it?"

A means of making contact, nationals invited to their Embassy for drinks and snacks, time found for him to make his report. Spragg met Myrna's eyes and knew that, like himself, she was fighting the desire to laugh.

"We'll be there," she said. "Formal dress?"

"Just something dark, Professor and for you, my dear, something long and not too revealing." Rodger's smile was brittle. "No need to make all the old biddies envious, what?"

Later when they were changing and he caught sight of her tall, slender silhouette against the pale oblong of the curtained window, Spragg blurted without conscious intention, "God, Myrna, how I love you!"

She made no reply and he wondered if she thought him a fool.

CHAPTER 9

The car was the same that had carried them from the airport and it glided through the streets of Washington, still bright but with the hint of coming dusk, the later darkness in which muggers and rapists and murderers would do their work. The secret, hidden life of the city which made a mockery of the neo-Grecian buildings, the white pillars and domes and carefully tended sward. The fester that lurked at the heart of every city, and, one day, would explode in a savage and bloody frenzy.

Myrna turned towards him, her eyes still bearing a haunted expression.

"I was thinking," she said. "You know a few hundred years ago all this was nothing but wilderness. Animals and a few natives living quietly in their own way. And then the Europeans came—and that particular paradise came to an end."

"But was it ever a paradise in the first place? Those natives suffered death and disease and ignorance and the vagaries of climate. They had all the tribulations we have and many we've forgotten."

"They were ignorant," she admitted. "But isn't ignorance sometimes a blessing?"

"You're thinking about Thor."

"How can I forget it? We can't make it go away by ignoring it. That tree, that building, this car, this city even—in a few months it will all be gone."

"A few months or a few years, what does it matter?" He strove to give her his own, detached viewpoint, the one he had had time to gain. "When we die a universe dies with us—our own. And we all know we're going to die. The only difference is we now know just when it will happen so we have the chance to do all the things we meant to do but kept putting off to a later occasion."

* * * *

Sir Edgar greeted them as they were announced, very stiff and correct in his evening dress, medals gracing the sombre fabric with miniature touches of colour. His smile was automatic as was the touch of his hand, a dismissal and they passed on, Spragg lifting drinks from a tray carried by a waiter, passing one to Myrna, sipping at his own.

He stood with it in his hand as he surveyed the assembly. They were as he'd expected; notables, wives of influential merchants, politicians, members of other embassies, a scatter of nationals from the United Nations—the usual crowd. Rodger, beaming, pushed his way to where Myrna stood regal in a long gown of shimmering black touched with silver. More silver shone in the aureole of her hair. Both gown and jewellery had been a last-minute purchase from a shop in the Clairmont and, thought Spragg looking at her, it had been money well-spent.

"Miss Parkin! You look positively enchanting. Come and meet the Spanish Minister of War. Juan Hose Rodgego Nova De Gaia—a bit of a mouthful but he's quite nice and has an aide who acts almost human aside from his love of bullfighting. You like to watch the bulls, Miss Parkin? Or may I call you Myrna? Professor?"

"Go ahead." Spragg waved with his empty hand. "She's on her own time."

And the attention and flattery and party-atmosphere would serve to banish the ghosts from her mind and enable her to laugh and enjoy her youth and beauty. As for himself there was always the anodyne of drink and he drained his glass and replenished it with another, wondering why it should taste like water and be having almost the same effect.

"Professor Malcolm Spragg! Well, I never! After all this time!"

She was short, broad, with a face lined and flaked with cosmetics, extra chins lying in steps to her jewelled throat. Her dress was too young and too tight.

"Don't you recognise me? Shelia Vaslow. We met years ago at a conference held in Paris. You read a paper on the asteroids. Afterwards we were introduced and we had some drinks and—surely you must remember!"

He said, "Shelia! Of course! I just hadn't expected meeting you. And you've changed," The curves now sagging mounds of ungovernable fat, Things he knew better than to mention saying instead, "I guess we've both changed. It was a long time ago and I used to have a waist then." He patted his paunch. "Who would want me now?"

"Your assistant, perhaps?" Her eyes were sharp. "She's a beautiful girl."

"Yes, I suppose she is. Rodger seems to think so."

"And so does every man in the room." She sighed with envy. "Well, Mal, have you come for the Exposition? It's in your field but do you honestly think we'll ever be able to mine the asteroids successfully? The prohibitive cost, the weight-fuel ratio, and that isn't taking into account crew problems and the need to refine in vacuo not to mention the danger of solar flares and other radiation hazards unavoidable unless extra-heavy shielding is used which again adds a greater burden on…"

Spragg smiled as her voice droned on, nodding, but not really listening.

As she paused he said, "You've obviously given the matter a lot of thought, Shelia. Are you also attending the Exposition?"

"No. I'm working for the Air and Space museum, next to the old Smithsonian. You must know it. They've got me creating panoramas depicting alien-world conditions." She added. "I had to do something after Harry died."

"Harry?"

"My husband. You wouldn't know him. We met five years ago and he died last year. A coronary. He was attached to the museum and they offered me a job. Before that I was with the UN but Harry made me quit. He hoped for children. I guess we both did."

A year, he thought. A year of compulsive eating to ease the hurt of her loss. Of working too hard to fill the waking hours. Did she lie awake at night wondering where she had gone wrong? Brooding over what she would do had she the chance to live her life over again?

"Shelia! I'm sorry!"

If she guessed his expression of sympathy was for more than her bereavement she gave no sign. Instead she said, unintentionally cruel, "And you, Mal? Are you married?"

"Divorced. It didn't work out. But I'm over it."

"That's a relief, anyway. Sometimes I think divorce is worse than death if you're in love with the one that's gone…" She shook her head then said, hopefully, "Maybe we could get together soon. Talk over the old times and have a few drinks. Old friends shouldn't grow into strangers."

But they already had and he was grateful to the waiter who came to discretely pluck at his sleeve and to whisper that Sir Edgar would appreciate his company in the study.

* * * *

It was a snug room lined with old books, the heavy desk an antiquarian's delight with its elaborate carving and the silver accessories that caught and reflected the light.

"You like it?" Sir Edgar had noticed his interest. "I collect such things. I hope to recreate an office such as would have been used by my predecessor almost two hundred years ago."

Spragg crossed the room to finger the frame of a sombre painting, to touch a brass set of scales, to move onto where a globe of the world stood on a stand at the side of the window. Idly he spun it.

"A nice collection, Sir Edgar."

"Are you interested in old things? If so I've some maps from the sixteenth century, which might interest you and a set of duelling pistols from the seventeenth... But I forget myself. Professor Spragg, meet Charles Pyne."

The man sitting in the deep chair nursing a glass of sherry, though in civilian dress, had the unmistakable stamp of the services. The Navy, Spragg guessed, looking at the grey eyes deep-set beneath bushy brows, the thin, no-nonsense mouth. A man who carried all the outward attributes of someone accustomed to being obeyed.

"Spragg." He nodded, waving his free hand. "What's it like out there?"

"Noisy."

"Better off in here then. A busy day, I understand."

"Sherry?" Sir Edgar lifted the decanter. He poured at Spragg's nod and handed over the delicate glass. "I'm glad you managed to drop in, Professor. I didn't expect us to meet again so soon, but trust the Americans not to waste time." He paused, sipping at his own sherry. "Anything to tell me?"

"Nothing you don't already know, Sir Edgar."

From the chair Pyne made a snorting sound then rose to pace the floor, head stooped, hands clasped behind his back. Small steps, Spragg noticed, the turns sharp, A trait learned in the confined quarters of a submarine. Halting he snapped, "We're not here to play games, Spragg!"

Spragg's glass rang a little as he set it down on the desk. Flatly he said, "I'm not one of your uniformed puppets to jump when you snap your fingers, Commander. Or should it be Admiral?"

"You are impertinent, sir!"

"I don't think so. I am simply independent. Spragg glanced at the Ambassador. "And now, Sir Edgar, if you will excuse me?"

"Please!" Sir Edgar held his arm. "Charles, I think you owe the Professor an apology. Professor, the Admiral—yes, Charles is an Admiral—is both tired and worried. Now pick up your drink like a good fellow."

Gruffly Pyne said, "I've got reason to be irritable. Still, no need to act the boor, though."

"Professor?"

"All right, let's forget it. But what can I tell you that your other informants haven't?" He added, dryly, "I assure you there were no secret discussions or resolutions or anything affecting the National Interest. Aside, of course, from what we already know."

"And that is?" Pyne prompted. "You're a scientist and could be taking things which are obvious to you as being obvious to everyone. We haven't your specialised knowledge. Sir Edgar is a diplomat. He relies on advisors. Well—be one."

Spragg said, impatiently, "All astronomers agree Thor will hit the Earth in 226 days. The Exposition, so far, has merely verified what we already know. As far as—" He broke off as he looked at the two men's faces, their eyes.

He remembered Eagan and what he'd said. "Tell a man he's going to die and he won't believe you."

Pyne said, slowly, "We get hit all the time. Dust particles, meteors— isn't there a big shower due soon?"

"The Leonids in October," agreed Spragg. "But we aren't talking about the same thing. Thor is 550 miles in diameter. It is heading towards us at a velocity of 5 miles a second—18,000 miles an hour. Can't either of you imagine what will happen when it hits? Admiral, you've used guns. A .45 bullet weighs an ounce but when fired it hits with the impact of a ton. That's because of kinetic energy created and stored by motion. The faster a thing is moving the harder it is to stop and Thor is moving damned fast."

Sir Edgar said, "But won't the atmosphere protect us?"

"As it does against the meteoroids? No. The trails you see in the sky, the 'shooting starts' are caused by tiny scraps of interstellar debris. Dust. They hit and are heated by atmospheric friction, burning as they fall and, burning, are destroyed while still in the air. A few are sometimes large enough to reach the surface and you can see many of them in museums. The largest weighs only a few tons. But this time the atmosphere is going to work against us."

"How?"

"It's a gas and therefore it can be compressed. When Thor hits that's just what it will do. And when it does..."

The tremendous mass of the striking planetoid plunging down, the air unable to escape from beneath it because of the speed of its descent, that same air heated by compression spreading to either side below so as to form a near-solid ram, carrying the shock-wave of initial impact to flatten all beneath. A ghastly harbinger of what was to come—the colossal bulk of Thor itself slamming into the surface, turning liquid into steam, rock into liquid, splitting the crust and releasing the inner magma—killing, burning, destroying until nothing was left but the shattered debris of a broken world.

* * * *

Standing at the open window of his room in the Washington hotel Spragg looked at the massed buildings lying sweltering beneath the blanket of late-summer heat. Coloured lights glowed like land-locked stars, winking, blinking, gaudy invitations to sophisticated delights mixed with advertisements of various poisons, traffic signals, the illuminated oblongs of windows; the beacons of the sleepless, the lonely, the bored. Like mournful ghosts the wail of police sirens cut the air either to warn the criminals or to assure their victims help was on the way. From the airport, a coruscation of lights painted the clouds a dusty orange.

A man alone standing at a window watching the teeming activity of which he was not a part—an ant barely aware of the forces that affected his world. And yet, now, he sensed the interplay of powerful interests, the influences always present but rarely displayed.

Behind him he heard the opening of the connecting door, the rustle of clothing, the soft tread of feet on the thick carpet. The scent of perfume became strong in his nostrils.

Without turning he said, "Not tired?"

Myrna halted beside him. "No more than you are, Mal."

He doubted it; his body was tired if his mind was not. It was three in the morning and he had drunk and talked and danced a little and smiled even as he fought the screaming desire to run and hid and pray to something larger than himself for ease and comfort. The anodyne of religion, which he had never known.

"Enjoy yourself?"

"Mostly I was bored. That damned Spaniard! The only way I could get rid of him was to tell him that I considered that anyone who enjoy the spectacle of an animal being tortured had to be mentally and morally sick. He didn't like me saying that."

"He has his pride."

"And regards all women as creatures created by God for the personal comfort of males. If ever there was a chauvinistic pig it's that Spaniard!"

She took a step forward and breathed deeply of the sultry air. "Who was that woman you were talking to? The fat cow who grabbed hold of you when we parted."

"Shelia Vaslow? We knew each other years ago. Before I was married. She never met Irene." He added, in defence, "She's altered a lot since then. Put on a lot of weight and I think she must have a diabetic condition." From defence he moved to the attack. "You seemed to be pretty engrossed with that Brazilian."

"You noticed?" She smiled like a contented child. "Santos is nice. He invited me to spend a week—or longer—at his home, Should I accept?"

She was playing with him, he thought, a game in which he had no interest. An aging jealous man was pathetic. He remembered her recent escort, tall, young, vital, a thick mass of dark hair and flashing teeth. To him she would be merely another conquest. But did it matter? Had it ever mattered?

She said, as if guessing his thoughts, "Don't worry, Mal, I'm not going to become a part of his collection. That kind of man nauseates me. But I do have an invitation to visit New York. Madam Kuluva has asked me to be her guest for a few days. She is attached to the United Nations. It could be interesting." She added, casually, "We leave tomorrow, that is today, at noon."

She offered no apology at not having consulted him. "I want to see the place and I guess you'll be busy."

"Not today. Nor tomorrow."

"You can't be sure of that. Sir Edgar might send for you again. What happened, anyway?"

"We talked about Thor. Admiral Charles Pyne was with him."

"A Sea Lord," she said. "Chief of Naval Intelligence and the man who will fire the atomic missiles if ever they have to be fired." Seeing his expression she explained, "I was interested in such things at University. I joined a group that wanted to stage a series of anti-nuclear demonstrations and I was involved for a while. My job was research—it's surprising what you can find out by studying the official listings. What did he want?"

"I'm not sure. My guess is that he is to report back to London on the seriousness of the situation." Spragg looked at the city and saw the pale gleam of the dome of the Senate building in the distance. Understanding came like a kick in the groin. "The cunning bastards!"

"Mal?"

"The Yanks! The Exposition! The whole damned thing was staged!" He felt his initial anger transform to a grudging admiration. "I'd just thought they had arranged the Exposition to make sure we astronomers realised the true nature of the threat and could relay that information back to those in authority. It didn't occur to me to wonder why. Now I'm beginning to understand."

She said. "I wish I could, damn you. Mal, tell me!"

"The world's going to end," he said. "You know it and I know it and now every damned government must know it. Know it beyond any question of doubt. That's what the Exposition was for." He fell silent, thinking, remembering the rows of attentive figures, the translating machines, the scheduled repetitions. A programme designed to ensure that none attending would be left in any doubt as to the true extent of the coming catastrophe. "But why?" He demanded. "What do the Americans hope to get out of it?"

The question every government would be asking. Myrna had another.

"How do they hope to keep the news from the public?"

"Old news is dead news," said Spragg. "The story will be buried or laughed off by the media or it won't be allowed to appear at all."

"Censorship?" Myrna looked doubtful. "Back home, yes, and in most European countries, but here in the States? You think it possible?"

"One way or another, certainly. Read the papers during the next few days and you'll see how it can be done." He added, quietly, "Do you really want to go to New York? I'll miss you."

"And I'll miss you." Her hand found his own and pressed with warm intimacy. "But I'd like to see it, Mal. The buildings, the streets, everything."

And it would be selfish and wrong for him to try and dissuade her. Life consisted of the sum total of experience and for him to deny her novelty would be to limit her existence.

"You go," he said. "Say hello to Central Park for me and don't forget to visit Staten Island. Go and enjoy yourself, Myrna—enjoy yourself!"

As the whole world should now be enjoying itself with all thoughts of future needs put aside, all doubts, all cares and worries, all rigid disciplines. Looking down at the city Myrna thought of what could be done.

"The government could open the warehouses," she murmured. "Free food, power, gas, liquor, transportation. Free housing. Free clothing. Freedom to do and say what anyone damn well pleased. Why not? They've paid for it. Taxed and milked and robbed and exploited all along the line. Food destroyed so as to keep up the price when the public have paid for it in the first place. An army of bureaucrats riding like lice on the back of the populace. Politicians, civil servants, aristocrats, petty dictators—the whole stinking mess. Now, for God's sake, everyone could have a holiday. For Christ's sake, why not?"

A question he couldn't answer then or later when, after a blindly passionate coupling, she had retired to her own room to leave him lying, drained, tired and aching to stare at the window until it began to pale with the coming of a new dawn.

CHAPTER 10

It was late when he woke. Myrna had left and Spragg ate a lonely brunch in the near-deserted dining room of the hotel. He'd bought a newspaper and read it over his coffee, amused to find screaming headlines announcing the discovery of a ring which supplied complaisant partners of either sex to Senators, Judges and visiting dignitaries. The opening shots of the smokescreen he'd anticipated. Presented with such juicy items of tantalising filth what editor would be interested in the reports of a dry-as-dust astronomical Exposition?

Spragg left the newspaper beside his empty cup and left the dining room. He was already missing Myrna, wondering if she had left Madam Kuluva's address so he could follow her. She hadn't and he was saved from the temptation of making a nuisance of himself.

The girl at the desk said, "If you're alone, sir, and wondering what to do then why not see the sights? We have a guided tour leaving in thirty minutes. Shall I book you a place?"

"No thank you. But you can give me a map and call a cab to drop me at the Lincoln Memorial."

He had seen it before but it was as good a place as any to start and after looking at the solemn, brooding figure Spragg hesitated between visiting Arlington cemetery or walking over the carefully tended sward towards the Washington Monument and the buildings flanking the Mall. He decided he was in no mood for the company of the dead so turned to face the soaring dome of the Capitol beyond the slender obelisk.

At length he entered the natural history Museum. Spragg liked museums. Here was displayed the endless panorama of life in all its ramifications and adaptations, its blind-alleys and triumphant progression. He wandered the galleries looking at fossils, skeletons, reconstructions of plants and creatures long dead and vanished from the face of the planet. An ape-man glowered at him, a stone gripped in one hairy paw. A weapon that had been unable to save him and his kind from extinction. Another peered from beneath jutting brows but Neanderthal Man had also been unable to survive. That had been left to Homo Sapiens who stood in a simulated group, startling in his modernity.

Homo Sap—doomed to join the other relics of the past. Just another life form destined to become extinct. He, his wife, his children, everything he had known and all he had built soon to be less than dust.

"Mister?" A woman looked at Spragg as he turned, sweating. "Is anything wrong?"

"No." He forced a smile. "Just a touch of vertigo, I guess. I must have overdone things a little."

"There's a cafeteria in the building. You could get some coffee and rest up for a while."

"Thank you—I'll do that."

He needed something stronger than coffee. Outside the afternoon sun held all the smouldering fury of a banked furnace and he paused, squinting, staring at the buildings almost facing him across the broad, green expanse of the Mall. The Air and Space museum and he remembered that Shelia Vaslow worked there. She could have a bottle or be able to guide him to a bar. In any case she would be company of a sort.

The cathedral-like interior was refreshingly cool, galleries running around an open area in which reared the slender shapes of early rockets. Spragg passed them, riding an elevator to the upper floors, searching for someone who could guide him to the department he wanted. A guard looked blank when he asked but sent him down a passage. Another was more helpful. A woman, her face daubed with paint, her smock covered with a smeared rainbow, grinned as she invited him into her domain.

"Shelia didn't make it in today. She called up with a sick headache. I guess that reception she went to was more than she could handle. Known her long?"

"Years, but we haven't seen each other for a long time. She told me what she did here. Alien—" He frowned.

"Depictions of alien worlds. Panoramas, really, backdrops with way-out vegetation and creatures and skies." She waved to where sheets of thin board stood against the walls, the mounds of foam, coiled plastic of various sizes, sheets and balls and oddly convoluted fragments. "We take a load of junk, some paint, a wad of imagination and the best extrapolations we can get. That's what Shelia does—extrapolate."

"Design?"

"In a way. You know the kind of thing—what would life be like on a planet with a white dwarf for a sun and a methane atmosphere? No one knows, really, but we try to keep things as scientifically accurate as we can. What's your line?" She nodded as he told her then said, dryly, "I guess you don't think much of what we do here?"

"Then you guess wrong. Space needs to be understood and young minds need to be stimulated to the possibility of a broader scheme of existence. Get a kid interested and he'll want to learn more." Spragg remembered his own early days, the brightly coloured comics, the stories, the magazines—all triggers which had fired his imagination. "The young need something to reach out for and what better than new worlds?"

"Sure, and when they grow up they'll want to back to space programme," she said. "That's what this is all about really. NASA is building a lobby, which will have real muscle in a few years time. Every kid we can hook now will be willing for us to spend his dollars when he's old enough to vote."

"You're a cynic."

"I'm a realist," she corrected. "We could have had an observatory on the Moon by now, and even a colony orbiting the Earth. We've the technical knowledge—all we need is the money. And once we get some real clout the politicians won't be able to dump us down the tubes as they did before."

Spragg said, "I'm sorry Shelia isn't here. Maybe I'll drop in again before I leave."

"You want her number?" The woman scribbled on a scrap of paper. "Here. If you can give her a boost I'd be grateful. Sometimes she gets awful low."

She and all of us, thought Spragg as he left. The paper he slipped into a pocket, unread, forgotten as soon as his fingers had driven it from sight. Already he felt light relief that Shelia had been absent; had she been at work he would have been lumbered with her for the evening and probably longer.

He followed the signs that led him to the cafeteria. Food and drink was dispensed from a rotation carousel and he selected iced tea and a hot dog together with mustard. The food was bland, but the other visitors busy taking nourishment provided an amusing diversion. Spragg listened to a babble of French, German, some Hebrew and what he guessed to be Swedish. A party of youngsters from the south shrilled like birds and a matron, her round black face dewed with perspiration, eased her shoes off aching feet.

Leaving the cafeteria Spragg wandered the galleries looking at ancient aircraft, modern rockets, Apollo nosecones, the recently obsolete space shuttles—the history of a century compressed into an hour of fast walking. Spragg didn't walk fast. He was tired after a restless night and he had time to kill. He reached the planetarium as a performance was about to commence, paid, passed into cooled darkness and sat looking at an artificial sky. One better than most astronomers had had the good fortune ever to know; the depicted stars neatly arrayed, the bowl clear, all distracting annoyances absent.

The programme, probably to tie in with the supposed reason for the Exposition, was about the possibility of mining the asteroids and he watched as ships reached out like hungry bees to settle and return with holds stuffed with rare and precious metals.

"Albert," murmured the mellifluous voice from the speakers. "Discovered in 1911 it has an estimated diameter of 3 miles and its closest approach to the Earth is something like 20 million miles." A bleak, jagged scrap of rock swelled on the dome to recede as another took its place. "Apollo, discovered much later in 1932, smaller but it does come closer. At its nearest approach it is barely 7 million miles distant which should not be too far for mining ships to travel." Another image. "Vesta," said the voice. "One of the so-called 'big four' the other three being Juno, Pallas and Ceres. These are the most promising sources of minerals and their size would make it feasible to set up permanent installations on and below their surfaces. Living quarters would be dug from the rock, sealed, supplied with air and all other essentials to normal living and viable colonies established. Pallas, for example, discovered in 1802, has a diameter of 300 miles and a surface area larger than that of France. Ceres, the largest of the known asteroids, discovered in 1801, has a diameter of 470 miles and a surface area three times larger than that of Pallas. The low gravity on these asteroids would also be an advantage. On Ceres a 180-pound man would weigh only 6. However the distances of these large masses are far greater than those of Albert and Apollo, Icarus and Hermes and..."

Spragg closed his eyes, imagination replacing the depicted scene. Ships reaching out to serve colonies which had never known what it was to stand with the wind blowing against faces of the touch of rain on the skin. Men, women and children living like moles in an artificial environment, needing suits to protect them whenever they left their quarters to venture to the surface. To stare at a naked sky and a naked sun. To be strangers to bird-song, to clouds, to rainbows, to mist, to the awesome hush before dawn, to the wonder of mountains, the poetry of seas.

But to live. To be safe against destruction by a jagged mass of rock which would smash into them and turn them into a bloody pulp and ash and broken fragments which would drift in emptiness for eternity...

He jerked awake, sweating, aware of staring eyes, conscious that he must have cried out in his tormented dream. Rising he stumbled towards and exit, muttering apologies, thankful to get outside the darkened auditorium.

He was thirsty but not for coffee of tea. He craved a long, strong drink of whisky loaded with ice and smoothed with dry ginger ale. He wanted a cold shower and a bed to lie on and a bottle to hand. He needed to sleep and not to dream.

The stairs were to hand and he took them, running down the flights to the ground floor. The building had two main entrances and he headed for the one opposite to that he had used to gain entrance. One side of the hall was flanked by a counter and display and he slowed, coming to a halt as he recognised familiar items; the plastic assemblies of the Voyagers, the books, posters, pictures and badges of the probes which had recently passed on a new mission through the moons of Jupiter. The same items they had offered for sale at Althene and now, as then, they reminded him of Irene.

He lingered, vaguely hopeful, looking at those standing behind the counter; a tall, middle-aged man with sparse hair and gold-rimmed spectacles and two girls, both younger, with rich, coffee-coloured skins. If Irene was attached to the display she wasn't present and it had been idiotic to even imagine she could be. Her job would necessitate more than serving or talking people into buying souvenirs. Even to enquire about her would be a waste of time. Then, as Spragg turned away, he saw her.

She came towards him from the doors, sunlight behind the transparent panels haloing her with golden brilliance so that for a moment she seemed to be frozen in an icon-like depiction of grace, an illusion shattered a she took another step and halted as he called her name. "Irene!"

Her eyes widened, moved to glance at the man behind the counter before returning to his face.

"Hello, Mal. Here for the Exposition?"

"Yes."

"I thought you would be invited—you've earned the right."

"By appearing on the front pages?"

"By being at the top of your profession." She changed the subject. "What do you think of our display?"

She hadn't changed. Her voice was still as he remembered, soft, deeply resonant, music to his ears. Her hair was a little shorter and had lost its russet sheen either because of age or artifice, but it was still thick, still framing her neatly-shaped head with a golden halo. He looked at it, at the eyes, the nose, the mouth, the lips with their familiar pout, the chin, the line of her throat. Softness met his fingers as he touched her cheek, velvet riding beneath them as he traced the line of her jaw. He lowered his trembling hand as she stepped backwards from the caress.

"I'm sorry." He added, lamely. "It's been a long time."

But not long enough to dull the memory of her entrancing figure and it was still the same. The body he had known, did know, so well. Eight years, he thought bleakly, and was shaken by the waste, the criminal, stupid waste.

"You're looking tired," she said. "You should watch yourself at these get-togethers. You drink too much and sleep too little."

Was she really concerned or was she just making polite noises? But how could she be indifferent? They had been married. They had been lovers. How could she think of him as a stranger?

He said, "This is an amazing coincidence. I never thought it would happen but I'm glad it did. I've often wondered how you were getting on. How are things?"

"Fine."

"I'm glad to hear it," he lied. "I'm not doing to badly myself. You're looking well. You live in Washington?"

"Yes."

"Good." He was, he realised, babbling like an idiot. He said, more slowly, "I'd like to take you to dinner. Tonight, perhaps? Tomorrow?"

"Sorry, Mal. I just don't think it would be a good idea for us to be together."

He fought to calm himself. "Just a meal together. Who could object?"

"Did I say anyone would object?" Again her eyes moved in a glance to the man behind the counter. "I just can't see any point to it. Eight years is a long time, Mal, and when we parted it wasn't on the best of terms."

She shouldn't have reminded him because, suddenly, it all came back. He felt again the tension, the conviction that something was wrong, the overwhelming need to drop everything and go home, only to find...

He said, quietly, "You can learn a lot in eight years, Irene. The fact that you've made a mistake, for example. That it's stupid to cut off your nose to spite your face. Please come to dinner."

"No."

"I miss you," he said. "Surely you can spare me a little time? We have things to talk about. There are still things in the house—"

"Which no longer interest me. And now—" She broke off looking down at the hand he had rested on her arm. "Mal?"

Reluctantly he dropped the detaining hand. If she went now it could be to pass completely out of his life but if he tried too hard to hold her he would only drive her away. How to persuade her that she would want to see him again?

"Irene?"

Spragg turned at the sound of the strange voice at his side. The tall man with the gold-rimmed spectacles had joined them from behind the counter. "Is everything all right?"

"Yes, Paul—I'll be with you in a moment." To Spragg, as the man returned to his position, she said, "Paul Sellar. A friend of mine."

"So I see." Spragg forced a smile. "Close?"

"Is that any of your business?"

"No of course not." Another mistake which he did his best to rectify. "I'm sorry, I spoke without thinking. I must be more tired than I thought—it must be the heat." He dabbed at his face and neck with a handkerchief. "Let me see you again when I'm at my best. I'm staying at the Clairmont and you could come to dinner. Your friend too if you want. I won't embarrass you. We could just talk and share a few drinks and I'll tell you what's going on at the Exposition. You've heard about it?"

"Rumours only, but—"

"Think about it," he urged, giving her no time to refuse. "The Clairmont, remember? I'll be looking forward to hearing from you."

He left it at that, walking directly towards the doors, not looking back and doing his best to appear casual. A cab took him to his hotel where he ordered a bottle, took a shower and then lay on the bed, sipping whisky and looking at the bright oblong of the window. As the drink took effect he relaxed, reliving their meeting.

Would she phone? Had he appeared too jealous? Should he have managed things to as to talk to her friend? Should he have spoken to her at all?

That would have been impossible. They had met and his reaction had startled him. He wanted her but, even more, he wanted her to want him. Once she did that he would have everything.

He dozed at last, waking with a start to the jangle of the phone. The window framed darkness and he fumbled before finding the instrument.

"Yes?" He listened to the voice of someone on duty downstairs, interrupting after the first few words. "A lady to see me? Send her up!"

It had to be Irene and he rose, dressing with feverish haste, shipping a comb through his hair as the doorbell chimed. Running to the panel he opened it.

"Good evening, Herr Professor." Frieda Osten stood smiling at him from the passage. "This is a surprise for you, no?"

* * * *

She had arrived that morning together with Carl Waldemar and they were staying at a hotel nearby. Finding him had been simple as Carl explained.

"I knew you were in Washington and had attended the Exposition. The rest was just a matter of phoning around." He lifted the glass in his hand. "To a happy meeting!

Mechanically Spragg responded to the toast. It had been Carl's idea, of course, to have sent Frieda to get him to share a dinner he didn't want and then to join a party he could have done without. But the man meant well and couldn't possible know of his chance meeting with Irene. If she called now he would be out but if she called he would know about it and could track her down.

"You look glum, my friend." Waldemar said. "A little lonely here in the big city? Why, when there are so many nubile young girls eager to ease your tensions for the sake of a few dollars? Or, of course—" He eyes moved to where Frieda stood at the far side of the room talking to a podgy man with a close-cropped hair style.

Spragg said, "Carl, I'm not here alone."

"You have a companion? That is good. Where is she?"

"She's staying with friends in New York." Spragg caught the ironic lift of the other's eyebrows. "She left at noon."

"Do I know her?"

"No. She's my assistant."

"And so she attended the Exposition with you?" Waldemar looked thoughtful. "Which means she knows what is going to happen if she has any brains at all. How did she take it?"

"How did you?"

"At first, badly. I felt numb, sick, unable to accept what I knew to be true. Then I got very drunk and, afterwards, things didn't seem so bad. What is the use of worrying? Thor is coming. Not all the burning candles and fervent prayers in the world can stop it. Not even joy and laughter but they, at least, ease the time of waiting." Waldemar finished his drink. "Let me get you another, Mal, then come and talk to Harry."

Harry Frazer was the podgy man with Frieda. Like her he was a mathematician. Unlike her he was a trifle drunk. A state he claimed to be the best for the clear working of his mind.

"It's a matter of the synapses," he explained after Spragg had been introduced. "You know how the impulses jump along the nerves. Alcohol slows them down a little. Now the same thing happens in the brain. The thoughts jump too damned fast and get all mixed up but after a few drinks they slow down and you can catch and corral the bastards and detach them to jump through hoops. Catch?"

"I catch."

"Good. That makes you one of the fraternity. You with NASA?"

"No."

"I am. Attached to them, that is. My real line is atomics. I'm an advisor to CALNED, you've heard of them? No? Constructional Application of Limited Nuclear Devices. We haven't done much as yet but when we get the work just watch our smoke! A new Atlantic-Pacific canal cut through Mexico. Mines in the Antarctic. Deserts irrigated, mountains levelled, tunnels fashioned, bores—you name it and we'll do it. Given time we'll change the whole damned face of the planet."

"With atomic bombs?"

"Atomic devices. They blow up, sure, but the explosion is controlled. Like dynamite. Once we lick the residue problem and get the nuts off our back who keep screaming about pollution and get a few politicians to see sense we'll be on our way. Can you realise what it would mean to Australia to have the Great Desert irrigated? To India to solve the drought problem? To Argentina to have a tunnel cut through the Andes?" Frazer looked at his glass. "The damned thing's empty!"

Spragg refilled it and moved on to talk to others. He answered them absently, resenting the intrusion into his privacy. Waldemar came to rescue him finally, thrusting a drink into his hand, shooing away the woman who was haranguing him with her religious beliefs.

Smiling he said, "Well, Mal, what do you think of her?"

"Very little. She's like all Jesus-freaks—worshipping the signpost instead of following the directions. A friend of yours?"

"She came with Bud Aldcock. They arrived early and he left her here while he went off to settle some other business. You may have seen him at the Exposition—tall, thin mouth, stooped, eyes too close together. No? Well, he was there. What did you think of it the Exposition? Did you find it interesting?"

"Frightening would be a better word. But they were preaching to the converted as far as I'm concerned. But it wasn't a waste of time."

"Why?" Waldemar nodded as Spragg gave his reasons. "You are shrewd, my friend. If the nations are to work together they must first be convinced there is no other hope of salvation. If necessary they—" He broke off looking at Spragg. "Is something wrong?"

"Hope—you said hope."

"So? There is always hope."

But not unless backed with a plan. Spragg turned to look across the room to where Harry Frazer expanded his theory of quietened synapses to a pale-faced young woman who held degrees in chemistry. To where Frieda was engaged in conversation with a physicist. To a man who had helped train pilots for the space shuttle who smiled at a female meteorologist. At the others all trained in allied skills. All attached to NASA. All, he guessed, heading for Cape Canaveral.

He said, bleakly, "Will it work? You're thinking of blowing Thor to hell and gone with atomics. Will it work?"

"So you guessed—I wondered how long it would take you. A drink now to celebrate." He returned with full glasses, smiling as always, "Prosit!"

"Cheers!"

"It depends on the math," said Waldemar as they lowered their glasses. "That and on the material available and the ships to carry it in. The Americans ran all manner of situations through their war-games and constructed analogues of almost all conceivable events. Some of the answers we can adapt to present needs, especially those concerned with logistics and the movement of men and machines. The Russians too—the project would be impossible without their cooperation, but it's mutual—they have an equal interest in survival."

Spragg said, dryly, "We all have an equal interest in survival."

"Maybe, but you know what they say about equality—some are born more equal than others." Waldemar took a sip of his vodka. "I'm not actually in charge of the operation. It's a combined effort, naturally, but I was connected with the European conference and was asked to arrange the initial stages. Also I'm a civilian, which helps. The military are reluctant to trust each other especially those of the major powers. Well, Mal, there it is. Naturally you're involved."

"As the scientific advisor to Sir Edgar Waring?"

"I know what you are—I suggested you be given the job. And there's more to it than you think. Don't undersell yourself—Thor is basically your baby. That makes you important. And I need to have a friend I can trust. One who will help me celebrate afterwards if nothing else. After we've shown whoever runs this damned universe that we can't be pushed around."

Waldemar swayed and caught at Spragg's shoulder for support. His breath reeked of whisky. "When we've smashed the Hammer of God with the Fires of Satan. God, Mal, what a night that will be!"

CHAPTER II

Spragg said, patiently, "There are only three ways of dealing with Thor, to dodge, deflect or destroy. Obviously we can't dodge and the thing is far too massive to destroy. Our only hope lies in managing to deflect it in such a way that it will miss Earth instead of colliding with it."

He looked from one to the other feeling like a schoolmaster facing intractable children: Sir Edgar, Admiral Pyne, Rodger Harcourt-Smythe, elevated to the inner councils and looking a little green, and a stranger who said little but whose eyes were never still. Peter Ogden, a recent addition to the Embassy and obviously a man of some importance.

He said, "When you say we can't dodge, Spragg, are we to take that at face value?"

"Unless you know a way to move the Earth bodily through space, yes."

"I wasn't thinking of the entire Earth but of the point of impact. Do you know exactly where that will be?"

"As yet, no."

"But, once ascertained, would it be possible to change it by, for example, slowing down the advance of Thor?"

Spragg looked at the man with new interest. Not a fool, certainly, his grasp of the situation proved that. Not, apparently, a product of the usual public school system, at least he lacked the accents and ties of Eton or Harrow. A military man, perhaps, but if so one connected with intelligence.

From his chair Admiral Pyne snapped, "Well, Spragg, would it?"

"Theoretically, yes, but in practice no." They had assembled in the study of the Embassy and Spragg moved to where the globe stood in its frame beside the window. Spinning it he said, "The surface of the Earth at the equator moves at a speed of approximately 1000 miles an hour. If Thor were to hit here, for example," he rested his finger on Borneo, "and we wanted it to hit here instead," he moved his finger to Zaire in Central Africa, "we would need to delay the strike by 6 hours."

"Could the time of impact be advanced?" The suggestion came from Ogden. "I'm not talking about it hitting a specific target, you understand, but of avoiding a certain area."

Such as Great Britain, naturally. Spragg shook his head. "Impossible. To do that we would have to transport explosives beyond the mass, turn, send them against it faster than its present velocity and maintain the barrage until the desired increase is attained. It simply cannot be done."

"Then the slowing—"

"Is, as I've said, theoretical. You must bear in mind that the Earth, aside from rotation, is also moving in orbit around the sun. If we could slow Thor down sufficiently it would, of course, miss us, but the energy necessary to do that is beyond us. It would be like trying to slow down a thrown brick by shooting at it with peas. We don't have enough peas and we don't have enough time."

And more was being wasted every moment. It was a week now since the party. Carl had gone and Frieda with him. Irene had stayed out of sight. Myrna had dropped a line to say she was going to take a look at the Niagara Falls. And still he was trying to drive sense into the blockheads!

He said, "Gentlemen, we are faced with a cosmic threat. Thor isn't a bubble, which can be blown away. It can't be slowed. It can't be speeded. It can't be guided in any way. A pity, no doubt—Russia would probably be pleased if it hit the United States and some Americans would cheer if it were to hit Russia. Others would be happy to see it strike Africa, or India, or Australia, or China—anywhere other than on their own doorstep. But wherever it strikes the Earth is doomed. The impact will be worldwide. One entire quarter of the planetary surface will be directly affected. One quarter! Think about it." The globe spun beneath his fingers. "Europe and Africa—all of North America including Canada and Greenland. All China and Japan. Australia and Indonesia. South America and most of Antarctica. The axis will be disturbed, the crust—there can and will be no escape!"

Facts he had stated before with little apparent result. The inertia of planetary masses was nothing when compared to the inertia of bureaucracy.

Irritably, he said, "This is the last time I shall explain all this. Either you believe me or not. If not there is no point in my continuing to waste my time."

From his chair Pyne rapped, "No need to take that attitude, Spragg. We have to be sure."

"No one is calling you a liar," soothed Sir Edgar. "But certain details have to be clarified, what?" He glanced at Ogden. "For example, do you know the exact time of impact?"

"Not as yet. Nor the time nor the place. I can give you the day but not the second." Spragg added, bitterly, "If you're thinking of making contingency plans to safeguard a few selected individuals forget them. When we go we all go together. There is no escape for anyone once Thor hits."

"If it hits." Ogden was on his feet smoothly taking charge of the situation. "I think that is all for now, gentlemen. Obviously the Professor is a little upset and, personally, I can't blame him. Like me he could probably use a drink. Rodger? If you would be so kind?" He waited until the others had left and a tray had been set on the desk. "Scotch or vodka?"

"Scotch." Spragg accepted the proffered glass. "Which department are you? M16? Special Branch? Something I haven't heard of yet?"

"You guessed?"

"You must be here for some reason and in our modern democracy Security takes precedence even over staid diplomats. Why on earth are you wasting your time?"

"It's a job."

"And you like doing it. Have you been watching me long?" Spragg didn't expect an answer. "And Myrna? Is she really at Niagara Falls?"

"Yes. With Madam Kuluva—a woman with quite a reputation in certain fields. You can guess who she works for."

"Does it matter? Myrna can only tell her what she already knows."

"You're missing the point, Professor. It doesn't matter what you tell each other as long as you don't try to alarm the public. We're handling that pretty well at the moment as I think you'll agree."

Spragg nodded, the papers now carried an exposé of corruption in government circles together with hints of allegations more startling than Watergate.

"You can't keep it up," he pointed out. "Soon anyone with a cheap pair of binoculars will be able to see Thor bright and clear if they know where to look. Later it'll be visible to the naked eye."

"And by that time everyone will be certain that it's going to miss by a wide margin. You'll tell them that as you did before." Ogden smiled and lifted his glass. "How are you on imagination?"

"What?"

"Most scientists suffer from a strange blindness—they often fail to see what's under their nose. This threat, for instance. To you and to most of your colleagues it is the end. We either divert Thor or it's the finish. But what if we do manage to divert it?"

"We go on," said Spragg. "We survive."

"And?" Ogden shrugged as Spragg made no answer. "You see? That's the blindness I was talking about. Diplomats look at things in a different way and those connected with National Security—"

Spragg said, "When a house is burning you don't argue who is to get what—you just get together to put it out."

"You think so?" Ogden shook his head. "Those days are long gone. Now it's a matter of greed—who is to pay for the water, the labour to carry it, the buckets?" He added, without change of tone. "You don't seem to get on well with Admiral Pyne."

"I just can't stand his authoritarian attitude. Just what gives him the right to give the orders?"

"He and his class?" Odgen smiled when Spragg made no answer. "You're a bit of a rebel, aren't you? You had quite a reputation for kicking against the traces at University and you weren't too kind to Director Hammond."

"Because I told him what to do with himself and his job? Is that a crime?"

"No, but sometimes it can be foolish."

"The price of liberty," said Spragg. "Be yourself and you lose everthing. So much for democracy."

"A dream. We haven't got it and never had. It's a word used by politicians to gull fools." Ogden shrugged at Spragg's expression. "I'm a realist. Because I work for those who hold the reins I don't have to be deaf and dumb and blind. But, equally so, I don't have to be daft. It pays to be on the winning side. My job is to make sure we stay on it."

"In a few months there won't be any sides."

"If Thor hits, no," agreed Ogden. "But we have to take the long-term view and make plans in the event it can be deflected with the use of atomic missiles. That's why I want you to come to New York to attend the Special Emergency Session of the United Nations Security Council."

New York? It would take him from Washington and Irene but also from the temptation of haunting the museum and NASA building in the hope of seeing her. But, on the other hand, it would take him closer to Myrna. She wouldn't stay long at Niagara Falls—what the hell was there aside from water?

He said, "Let's get one thing clear. I'm not going to stay away from Miss Parkin. Not even if she continues to see Madam Kulova."

"Of course not." Ogden was bland. "I wouldn't even think of asking you to ignore her. And I'm certain that Madam Kulova will see that you have the opportunity to meet. Representative Extraordinary to the UN."

* * * *

The seats were covered with red leather, the desks were of polished spruce, the carpet, like the chairs, held a sombre warmth. Little plaques; gold letters on light backgrounds, gave names and titles and country of origin. Notepads, bottles of water, ballpoint pens, completed the furnishings. At their places in the chairs the Council sat like rows of mummified corpses, earphones dangling from ears, spectacles flashing like blank windows, some apparently sleeping, all trapped in an artificial stasis of strained ritual.

Spragg leaned back, looking at the painted ceiling of the chamber, the depiction of an idealised figure pouring out a stream of good things to the clamouring masses of the world. The cost of the work would have fed a thousand for a decade—an irony that had apparently escaped those responsible for the commission. In his ears a smoothly detached voice enunciated better English than he possessed.

Since taking his place in the Council Spragg had learned something of the rules; it wasn't so much what you said but how and when you said it. The current speaker, for example, couldn't really believe in the rubbish he was saying but was saying it in order to strengthen the value of the cards in his hand. He finally came to an end to be replaced by Madam Chandi from India. Bright in her sari she spoke in English; presumably she wanted what she said to be free of all ambiguity.

Spragg yawned as once again he listened to a capsulated history of early struggles, striving, sacrifices and national destinies all of which seemed a mandatory preliminary to the newly emerged powers. Then came the real meat of the discussion.

"...Larger powers such as the United States and Russia, which have a high nuclear capacity. My own country has few atomic plants and missiles. To place our entire capability into the common pool would be to make a sacrifice far in excess of our stronger partners. Therefore I cannot agree to operate on a basis of percentages or of yielded numbers either of which would place my country at a tremendous disadvantage. India will retain only two nuclear missiles if all other countries will follow her example."

Spragg heard the sigh of released breath when she sat down and felt a grudging admiration for the woman's cunning. She had made a good case and if she pulled it off it would mean that India would be as strong as any other nation on the Earth in the event the Earth survived.

Israel, as usual quick to grasp the implications, next demanded the floor. Moshe Abishua, like Madam Chandi, spoke in English and didn't pull his punches. If his country was to donate all its missiles he demanded assurances from the large powers that the national boundaries, indeed the very existence of Israel itself, should be guaranteed. The boundaries he specified would increase the overall area of present dimensions by a healthy amount and would settle the West Bank, Gaza Strip, Golan Heights and the Syrian and Lebanese problem for all time. Those who stood to lose naturally objected or others did it on their behalf.

Spragg, careless of who might be watching, produced his flask, poured whisky into the glass provided and added water from the decanter. He was, he knew, offending the dignity of the assembly and upsetting all concepts of formalised procedure but he was bored and didn't care who the hell knew it. He was also more than a little afraid. This was poker as Ogden had warned him it would be but he hadn't realised then that it was suicide-poker—a game in which none could win and all were doomed to lose.

Days had slipped into weeks and, outside, the October dusk would be falling over the East River, turning the normal appearance of the man-made sewer into the enchanting mystery it had been in the time of the early settlers. A time of argument and discussion and of beating his head against brick walls. Of speaking again and again of what would happen when Thor smashed into the Earth. Of letting himself be used to aid the common good.

The house was burning—but they argued over who was to provide the water to put out the blaze. God alone knew how long it would take to thrash out the cost and who was to meet it.

He was drinking too much, he knew, but could see no reason for cutting it out. Life was full of miseries; Irene apparently lost and Myrna coming to New York a week ago to almost immediately leave again on a jaunt to Florida and the magic of Orlando. They had made brief love and he had waited for her to question him but she had surprised him by her lack of interest in what he was doing.

And Ogden, feeding him instructions, wanting reports, smiling that damned, bland smile as if the title he now carried had made him a creature of the Establishment. Which, in a way it did. It provided him with position, and expense account, good accommodation and the entry into circles that would normally have been closed.

A bell and the session ended with nothing apparently accomplished.

* * * *

The girl with the pompadour hairstyle and the high, yellow boots said, "And you can assure our readers, Professor, there is absolutely nothing to worry about?"

"Nothing at all." Spragg lied and smiled as he lied, the result of long practice and the growing conviction that no matter what he said it wouldn't make a damned bit of difference. "In fact it will make the most exciting spectacle anyone has ever seen."

Thor was back in the news, deliberately so, those involved deciding it was time for the cork to be drawn from the bottle. Deciding too not only that the news should be released but how it should be handled. As Ogden had warned Spragg was in the forefront of those handing out platitudes.

Thor was real, it was coming, but it would miss by a big margin. In fact the nations acting in concert were going to reap a bonanza from the cosmic visitor. Again Spragg explained.

"As you may have been informed from the recent Exposition on the possibility of mining the asteroids the project is viable. Thor provides us with a magnificent opportunity. It will pass close which means it can be easily reached. With the calculated use of atomic devices we will split off a large section and swing it into orbit around the Earth. In a sense we will fashion a second Moon and one with several advantages over the old. It will be closer and so easier to reach and—"

"How's that Professor?" The interruption came from a young man with an earnest face. Surely once we reach escape velocity it doesn't really matter how close the captured fragment will be?"

A wise guy and right. Spragg retained his smile.

"The proposed orbit will be approximately 80,000 miles as against 250,000 of our Moon. A saving that I'm sure most will think of as worth having. But more than that is the potential composition of the planetoid itself. We know that the majority of meteors are of a nickel-iron basis and so there is no reason to doubt that Thor is of the same composition. The proposed fragment will be in the region of 50 miles in diameter. A solid mass of rare and precious metal, which we can tap at our leisure. Once established in orbit our fears as to the exhaustion of raw materials will be over. Ladies? Gentlemen? If there are no more questions?"

Spragg waited until the last reporter had left the hall before making his way from the chamber towards the reception area of the hotel. As usual it was a scene of apparent chaos. Two men whom he knew to be security guards stood watching—the hotel had many UN representatives as guests. Against one wall he saw a new splash of colour where a poster had been hung that very evening. A familiar poster depicting a ebon background spattered with stars, the glow of a massive planet and, against it, the frail vanes and extensions of a Voyager.

Coincidence?

He felt the interior of his mouth go dry at the possibility that she had followed him to New York and was here at this very moment. To the receptionist he said, "The woman who hung that poster. Where is she?"

"Sir?"

"For God's sake, man!" He found money and pressed crumpled bills into a ready hand. "Now think. Is she staying in the hotel? Room 753. Thank you."

He had no doubt that it would be Irene and when the door opened to his knock he stepped forward and took her in his arms.

"Mal!"

"No!" He fought her attempt to escape from his embrace. "No, Irene, no!"

"What is it, Mal? What do you want?"

"To talk. For God's sake, Irene, can't you understand that? Just to talk." He eased the constriction of his arms, conscious of the pounding of his heart, his rising desire. "Why didn't you contact me in Washington?"

"There was no point."

"Then why follow me here?"

"I didn't." She stepped away from him, one hand lifting to adjust her hair. She was, he noted, flushed and breathing fast. "I came to set up a display. Once it's arranged I move on. Since seeing you in Washington I've been to Chicago, Cleveland. Boston and, oh, lots of places."

"With that man? Paul—whatever his name is?"

"Paul Sellar. We work together, yes."

And slept together? Jealousy tore at his stomach and drummed at his brain.

He said, "Let's leave here. We could have dinner." Get her out before Paul could appear and ruin things. "Please," he urged. "You know I hate eating alone."

"Are you alone?"

"Of course!" Could she be jealous? "All alone. I guess you've heard the news."

"About Thor?" She nodded. "The truth this time or more lies?"

"What makes you say that?"

"I was married to an astronomer once." She gave him a rueful smile. "Some of what he knew rubbed off. Lies, Mal?"

He nodded. "I'll tell you the truth over dinner."

But he didn't, conscious of those sitting close, delaying the moment until they had finished their desert and sat lingering over coffee and brandy. Conscious too that the truth was a trump card and not to be played too soon or too lightly. Irene had always been curious—now he could use that trait to his advantage.

He said, forcing himself to sound casual, "Why not go up to my room and have a drink? We can talk there. Incidentally, I've a wonderful view."

"So have I."

I, not we, and his spirits soared to be as quickly flattened. Even if she didn't share a room with Paul he could be an all-night visitor.

Still striving to appear casual he said, "I've a lot to tell you and it's best done over cognac and champagne. Remember that time in Spain when we used to sit on the balcony at night and watch the lights way out at sea and drink sparkling white wine and local brandy?"

"And smuggle out the bottles for fear the hotel would charge us corkage." She smiled, remembering. "Our first real holiday together. We could hardly afford it."

"Good times," he said. And added, with naked sincerity, "I miss them, Irene. The walks and the searching for bargains in little shops, the markets and the rest of it. Christ, how I miss them!" He bit at his lips, aware that he had betrayed himself. Quietly he said, "I guess you've no taste for cognac and champagne now?"

"No, Mal—it wouldn't be the same."

As nothing would ever be the same, he thought bleakly. Not now and not ever. Too much had happened between them and, like a fool, he had realised the value of what he had lost only after losing it. Yet he could still act in a civilised manner.

"Of course. Another drink?"

"Thank you, no." She dabbed at her lips with a paper towel. "But you can take me for a walk."

CHAPTER 12

The night held magic. Even though it was late October the summer still lingered and the air held the trapped warmth of the city, relieved only slightly by the breeze from the East river. Spragg led the way, stepping along the terrace fronting the UN building, aware of the lights still glowing in the offices; lights that would burn until dawn as they burned elsewhere in other offices where real work was being done.

"The heart of the world," she murmured looking up at the sheer facade. "Or it should be. Why does it take a catastrophe for people to remember their common humanity?"

And why did they so quickly forget? Spragg followed her eyes then lowered his own to where the dim bulk of a statue stood limned against the reflected glow of lights edging the water. Frozen in perpetual labour an idealised man strove to turn a sword into a ploughshare.

"Mal?" Irene had paused and was tracing a finger over the bronze leaving a line of wetness as the tip caught and spread the patina of condensation. "Are you ever—I mean do you ever get afraid?"

"Too often."

"Is that why you hate to be alone?"

"Yes." He added, "You know?"

"Of your affairs? Of course. They're no secret, Mal, not when you've the kind of friends who love to spread gossip and stick in their knives. Don't tell me you never realised what they were like."

He said, flatly, "I lost all illusions concerning the value of friendship when I found Arkwright in your bed. In our bed." He paused, trying not to remember. "Do you remember Ian McGregor?"

"Of course. How is he?"

"He's working for Rand now. Before he left he said that you and Bob had split up."

"He was right. It happened some time ago now. We'd drifted for years before making the final break. We just didn't get along."

She offered no further explanation, Scragg watched intently as she stood limned against the glow of lights from the river. Brilliance caught her hair and turned it into a golden nimbus framing a face which seemed to have lost years, the lines of time erased, the scars of emotional battle voided.

"Irene! I love you! I love you!"

She sighed and moved a little closer to where he stood, halting as he lifted his hands. The magic of the night wasn't strong enough, his protestations had been too weak, the barrier between them remained.

Tasting defeat he said, quietly, "Maybe I shouldn't have said that but I just wanted you to know. Now, I guess, you'd like to go back. I mean, if someone is waiting?"

She smiled and shook her head, reflected light dancing in her hair. "Paul is a very happily married man. He has three children and talks about them all the time. He phones his wife every day when away from home. I doubt if the thought of being unfaithful has ever crossed his mind."

"Three children, eh? Good for him."

"Two boys and a girl." Her voice held a poignant yearning. "A nice family."

"Yes," said Spragg. "Let's get back."

He heard the scrape of shoes after they had begun their journey along the terrace and, at the same moment, caught the silhouette of a hulking shape. More sounds came from behind and he acted without thinking, pushing Irene to one side as the man ahead stepped into view, a cigarette in on brown hand.

"Gimme a light, mister?"

The old ploy of muggers, to hold the attention of the victim while the man's companion attacked from the rear. Spragg jumped to one side and felt the wind of the sap as it grazed his head and numbed his shoulder. His foot, lifting, kicked out to land on something soft. He spun as the man doubled, gasping, to see the other stagger back, screaming, hands to his eyes.

"Run!" Irene stood, an aerosol can in her hand. "Quickly, Mal! Run!"

Their shoes thudded on the flags as they raced along the terrace, emerging in a brilliantly lit area, seeing the familiar uniforms of lounging police.

"No!" Irene caught and dragged at his arm as Spragg headed towards them. "No, Mal, it will do no good. Those men are gone by now. We'll have to answer a lot of questions and look at endless photographs in an attempt to identify them. It will all be a waste of time."

"The bastards! What happened?"

"I used this." She lifted the can before slipping it back into her handbag. "Hairspray. I always carry it." Her tone changed as they reached an area of brighter light. "Mal, your head! You're bleeding!"

* * * *

From where she sat facing him Irene said, "How's the head and shoulder now, Mal?"

"I'll live." The blood had come from a graze, now patched and his padded jacket had saved him from more than a nasty bruise on the shoulder. Irene had helped to ease it, holding ice to his naked flesh, seemingly unaware of the effect of her propinquity. "How's your drink?"

"Nice. A little too cold, perhaps."

"That's due to the national love of ice." Spragg held his glass between his palms, warming it. Even though he had specified it the hotel had been unable to provide unchilled champagne. "I'll mix a brew and stand it in hot water for a while."

He switched off the lights as he returned from the bathroom and moved towards the window, the room now illuminated only by the dusky glow from the external city. It was bright enough for him to see her profile, the halo of her hair, the lines of her body.

She said, "You were going to talk to me, Mal. Tell me something. Have you changed your mind?"

"Perhaps." The attack had changed things, brought them closer together, awakened in him a more tender regard. Would it be a kindness to tell her the truth? To gain time he said, "The drink should be warmed by now. Give me your glass and I'll get you some."

She smiled as he returned, taking the glass, sipping, nodding her approval. "That's better. Now tell me about Thor."

"You know?"

"I guessed. It has to be that. The first time it appeared on the news was the truth, wasn't it? It's going to hit."

It was a relief to admit it. "Yes."

"When?" She sucked in her breath when he told her. "So soon? But—"

"There's a chance," he said quickly. At least he could relay that comfort. "We might be able to deflect it given enough men and missiles." And time and transport and skill—things he didn't mention. "That's what all the stuff in the media is about—to block any awkward questions."

"To prevent panic." She nodded, frowning. "Is it going to work, Mal? Can it?"

"There's a chance."

"What kind of an answer is that? I could jump out of this window and there's a chance I might live. I could land in a load of feather mattresses or get caught up in a dangling line or something. I could even learn how to fly or—" She broke off, swallowing, her anger vanishing as quickly as it had come. "Such a short while," she whispered, "So very short."

"Six months," he said. "A little less. Thor will hit on April the 11th of next year."

"Is that a Sunday?"

"I don't know. Why?"

"It would be appropriate in a way. The Sun—Sunday—but Thor isn't the sun, is it? It's the Hammer of God. But Sunday would be a good day for it to strike." Her laugh was shaky, devoid of humour. "I'm sorry. You must think me a fool for babbling on like that. It's the shock, I guess. It isn't every day you learn just how long you have to live."

"There's still a chance."

"The chance you mentioned? Do you expect me to believe it can succeed?" She shrugged at his silence. "So that's it then. Finish. We all pack up and go home. Pick up out toys and...and..."

He waited as the tears came, wanting to hold her but resisting the temptation. This was a moment she had to face alone. Nothing he or anyone could do or say could ease that isolation. The moment of truth, he thought, how well the Spaniards had put it. The moment when nothing stood between yourself and the ultimate reality. But she would learn to live with it as he had done, as others, as those who even now were doing their best to save the world. Working even as they doubted—but anything was better than just to wait.

Taking her glass he threw the contents out of the window filling it with neat cognac.

"Here." He placed it in her hand. "Drink this. It will help."

Like a child she obeyed. Quietly she said, "You know, I've often wondered what I'd do if a doctor told me I had only six months to live. At first I thought I'll eat every kind of food in the world and taste every drink and see every monument and tomb and ancient building and painting and sculptor ever made. A glorified tour of the entire world. Then I thought, no, that would really accomplish nothing. It would be better to sit and read all the books I'd never had time to read before. And look at a flower, really look at it, And to get close to a pet, an animal of some kind, to try and understand the way it felt and lived. And then, at last, I thought even that was wrong. The thing to do, the only thing, would be to get close to God."

"So as to thank Him?"

"Mal?"

"Nothing." He shouldn't mock, she was entitled to her beliefs and what comfort they could give. "I didn't think you were a strong believer."

"I'm not. It's just that, at times, there is a need." She looked at the glass in her hand. "People shouldn't have to live alone. They should never have to do that."

Tiny flecks of consciousness locked in individual prisons—Spragg knew all too well the pain of a solitary existence when to be in a crowd was to be more alone than to dwell on the summit of a mountain. But Irene? As he remembered she had been sparkling and vivacious and full of gaiety. At first, anyway, when they had met and were busy discovering each other.

Finding new and more entrancing facts of personality as they found new and more exciting depths of physical attraction.

She had changed—they both had changed. He said, abruptly, "Are you happy Irene?"

"Happy?" The glass in her hand glittered as she lifted it to sip and lower it again. "At times perhaps. Can anyone ever be more than that? To be truly happy is to understand what the Greeks meant when they spoke of ecstasy. It's like...like..."

"Being in love?"

She said nothing, apparently lost in contemplation of her glass, the soft reflections which glowed and died to glow again in the facets of the crystal. Spragg resisted the impulse to smash it from her hand, to grab her by the shoulders, to shake her, to force her to recognise his need. Defeated he turned away.

"Mal!"

She rose to face him and was suddenly in his arms, soft, warm, wonderful—and the universe sang in echo of his joy.

* * * *

October died with masks and witches and all the baroque of Halloween. Mist drifted from the rivers to cast a kindly veil over rotting tenements and mouldering Brownstones, adding a touch of enchantment to the more ornate piles of the fashionable quarter, clothing the UN building in draperies of gossamer. On All Souls the churches droned with prayers for the departed and the stores, cleared of the grotesque paraphernalia of the festival, readied for Thanksgiving.

A time of cool evenings and pleasant days when the air held the smoke of burning leaves and the sky showed drifting masses of cloud by day and the dulled orb of the moon at night. Soon there would be snow and ice and all the discomforts of winter but, for now, it was enough to enjoy the changing face of the city.

"Look!" Irene halted before a store window looking at the heaps of turkeys within, the jars of cranberry sauce, the pumpkins. A display model had been dressed as an old-time woodsman complete with skin cap and long rifle, "They must have been good days," she said. "A man worked and slept and lived by the seasons."

"And suffered from bad teeth, stomach ulcers, sores, vermin and vitamin-deficiency-diseases. If that man cut himself badly with that knife in his belt he could have died from infection. The good old days weren't all that good for those who had to live in them."

"But they managed," she said. "It was the same for everyone and, at least, a man had a sense of freedom. If he didn't like things where he was he could get up and go."

"I guess he could." Spragg didn't want to argue to point. "How about it?"

"Doing what?"

"Going to the hotel. Don't you have to phone your boss and tell him you're quitting." He caught her expression. "You are going to phone?"

"No." She met his eyes, her own determined. "Not yet. The programme has to be completed and it's only a few more weeks. To leave now would be to upset the arrangements made by others. Surely you can see that."

"Of course, but—"

"In any case, Mal, you have your own work to take care of."

Was she telling him that she had tried and it hadn't worked out but, damn it, they had been happy enough during the past few days. Or he had been happy and she had seemed contented enough. He trembled on the brink of asking her if it was all over, that he had failed.

Before he could speak she said, "No, Mal, it isn't that. I just feel as if I want to be alone for a while. Finishing the programme will let me do that."

"If that's what you want, Irene." He managed to smile. "I guess there's a lot I've still got to learn. But—"

"I know." She matched his smile. "I think we both have a lot to learn. Now I want to do some shopping at Macey's, then to the hotel, then to the museum to wrap up the display. I'll be gone before you get back from the UN."

"To hell with them!" But it was easier to say than do. Ogden would be relying on him and Irene, he knew, would want him to attend. She had always been considerate and expected others to be the same. "Will I see you before you leave?"

"I doubt it. You'll probably be late and there won't by time unless—" she glanced at her watch. "I'll try. If Paul can finish up at the museum I'll come back to the hotel for a farewell drink. But I'll have to be gone by eight."

He said, "Must you leave so soon?"

"We've a long way to go." She leaned forward, rising on her toes. "Goodbye for now, Mal."

Her kiss was the touch of a butterfly then she was gone, golden hair bright as she stepped towards the curb and hailed a cab. Spragg stood looking after it, feeling numb, shaken by the sudden turn of events. She was his wife and—no, she was not his wife. She was a woman he had met again after a lapse of years and they had spent some time together and had made love and now she was gone about her business as he must go about his.

Thoughts that gave him no comfort as he headed towards the UN building.

Lamont was speaking in his own language when he entered the chamber. Spragg sat, adjusted the earphones, listened to a spate of national pride. France was perfectly capable of taking an equal share in Operation Thor. Her technicians and scientists were equal to any in the world. Willing as she was to donate her atomic capability yet she still retained the right to fire her own missiles from her own soil. A position he wanted to make clear.

Spragg glanced around the chamber. The American met his eyes as did the Russian. Both were waiting for him to speak and he realised Ogden's strategy. Great Britain, now not so great in world affairs, would act as the middle-man.

Rising he said, "May I make the situation quite clear? It isn't enough that we have all agreed to pool our nuclear capability for the sake of the common good—that capability must be used with the utmost care and discretion if a successful conclusion is to be achieved. Thor is approaching us at 5 miles a second. To hit an object at a distance of millions of miles which is only a few hundred miles in diameter requires a fantastic ability as any marksman here will acknowledge. But things are not as simple as that. Thor is moving but so is the Earth; it revolves once each 24 hours. It also circles the sun at a speed of 20 miles a second. And the entire solar system is moving towards the constellation Hercules at a speed almost as great. So we are in the position of trying to hit a moving target while standing on a firing platform which not only also is moving but is moving in three vectors at the same time."

He took a sip of water, pausing for the facts to sink in. Lecture-room experience now put to a more profitable use. The American, he noted, seemed satisfied, the Russian was frowning a little; briefed he must be impatient at the repetition of the obvious. Raoul Lamont sat looking bland; he had probably been acting a part and was satisfied with his performance. Madam Chandi sat like a Buddha. Others rested in their chairs—people to be convinced, manipulated, threatened if the need arose.

Spragg continued, "In view of these facts my own government, after long and careful deliberation, has reached the conclusion that it would be in the best interest of the project and of all those concerned if the nations with the greatest experience in the skills and technology needed in space flight should be the ones to manage the affair. In the light of that decision we have not only donated our entire nuclear capacity together with firm assurances that all supplies of plutonium produced in the near future will also be donated but that all our scientists and computer-capacity will be directed to the same end. We place ourselves and our destiny in the hands of those who, in the past, have not only been our allies in time of war but have shown their good intentions in many ways since those dark and dreadful days when civilisation itself stood in danger as our entire world does now."

He sat to muted cheers. Many of the countries were only here by courtesy of charity. They had to know their bombs were Indian-gifts that were loaded with strings. Set and guarded by the nationals of those who had donated them, useless as a source of real attack or defence.

Algeria, for example, their bomb had come from Libya who had probably got it originally from Russia. If they tried to fire it they would try in vain. If they tried to take it over by force they would lose it and several square miles of terrain as its self-destruct mechanism was operated.

And others, nursing gifts from China or other self-seeking friends. Gifts which now had been placed in the common pool with promises of their return. Promises which would be ignored if Spragg knew his politics. The real power would once again lie in the hands of the original Big Five.

A man from Zaire wanted to know why the missiles couldn't be fired from within the borders of his own country.

"Have you the facilities?" Spragg asked patiently. To hurry now would be to offend and that would mean more wasted time. "I am aware the representative from Zaire comes of a race of noted warriors and can both understand and appreciate his desire to take an active part in this battle for survival. But, sometimes, the best part we can play is to step back and let others do the work. We must use existing installations—we lack the time to build new ones. We must use existing vehicles and fuel depots and control-points. We have no choice but to take advantage of the skills of those accustomed to sending vessels into space."

Ireland rose to back him up, Italy the same. China said nothing but sat in watchful contemplation. Sweden agreed as did Denmark that Russia and the United States should take full charge of the project. Madam Chandri objected.

She was thinking of the riches to be won if a firing point could be set up in India; the flow of money, men and supplies, the buildings left after the thing was over. A big boost to the economy and a few steps up the ladder to industrial independence.

Spragg used the same arguments he had before, this time lengthened and scattered with figures, coupled with an appeal to intelligent appreciation and ended with the hint of special consideration given for complaisance. A mistake, the next few hours were spent in market-place haggling, and it was past seven when he finally left the building. A cab took him to the hotel and he was panting as he ran into the foyer.

"Has she left? The lady in Room 755? Irene Spragg—no, Fiander." She had reverted to her maiden name. He fumed at the slowness of the receptionist. "Well?"

"Yes, sir, Madam Fiander left the hotel more than an hour ago. I saw her myself. She took a yellow cab but I couldn't tell you her destination." He added, "She left no message."

Why hadn't she waited for him as arranged? And why, if there had been an emergency, had she left no message? The answer waited for him in his room.

* * * *

"Hello, Mal," said Myrna. "It's been a long time."

She lay sprawled on the bed wearing a thin robe of shimmering black edged with scarlet. Her feet were bare as, he guessed, was the rest of her beneath the robe. The thick mane of black hair was bound in a towel and her face held the scrubbed look of the freshly-bathed.

Smiling she said, "What's wrong, lover? You look as if you'd seen a ghost."

One from his past, whom he had, incredibly, managed to forget. The sight of her shocked him as if he'd walked into a door. "Why didn't you phone? Warn me you were coming?"

"I tried, no answer, so I thought I'd give you a surprise." She added, dryly, "It was me that got the surprise."

He said, knowing the answer, "How did you get in here?"

"Your wife let me in. We had quite a talk. You know, Mal, she's much younger then I'd imagined. Ten years older than me? Twelve?"

"Ten."

"You like to get them young, don't you?"

"Never mind that. What did you talk about?"

"Things. She wanted to know what I'd been doing so I told her all about the trip to Niagara and then down to Orlando. She's been there herself. And after when I took off into the West, the Grand Canyon and the Painted Desert. Just a tourist you might say with my friend Boris paying my way. Madam Kuluva thinks the world of him. She thinks he's seduced me to the cause. Now I'm supposed to discover all your hidden secrets. Amusing, isn't it?"

Patiently he said, "Stick to the point."

"I will." She reached for her bag and produced a tin and from it took a yellow-paper cigarette. Her hands, he noticed, were trembling a little. The lighter she used was new and sprang into flame as she touched a button. Blue-grey smoke roiled from the cigarette, her nose, from between her lips. "Join me?"

He shook his head, recognising the smell, the sickly-sweet odour he had known when young and it had been the thing to smoke pot in defiance of authority. A habit he'd given up long ago.

"Do you need that stuff?"

"Need?" She looked at him, the joint forgotten. "What is 'need', Mal? I needed you, remember?"

"So much so that you left as soon as you could to go sightseeing."

"Can't you guess what drove me? I needed things to see and people to laugh with and a way to forget. This was one." She gestured with the reefer then, with sudden irritation, flung it to one side where it lay shouldering on the carpet until Spragg crushed it beneath his heel. "Why, Mal? Damn you, why?"

"Why not?" He met her eyes. "One law for you and a different one for me, is that it? You to have lovers and me to remain pure?"

She looked at her hands and clenched them to hide their trembling. "She was more than just a casual affair, Mal. She was your wife."

Was and maybe would be again. Then he looked at Myrna and saw what Irene must have seen, the dream of every middle-aged man such as himself. No wonder she had left so soon.

He said, tightly, "Damn you, Myrna, tell me what you talked about!"

"You, me, and life in general. She asked how close we were and I told her. Then I told her something else. I told her I thought I was pregnant."

"You did what!"

"Told her I thought I was pregnant. She can't have children, can she?"

He was at the side of the bed before he knew it, fists raised, feeling a raw, primitive desire to hurt, to kill. Myrna rolled as he struck at her, falling from the bed as he drove fists into the pillow. Eyes wide she stared at his distorted face.

"Mal! For God's sake!"

He lunged towards her and tripped as his foot caught in the trailing covers, falling to hit his nose on the floor. Blood stained his lips and chin, dappled his shirt and jacket as he rose. "You liar!" he yelled. "You damned liar!"

"Am I?" She faced him, breathing deeply, hands lifted in a judo defence learned many years before. But now she wasn't protecting herself against a would-be rapist and, watching him, she realised there was no need for defence now. The moment of fury had passed. "What makes you so sure?"

A question he couldn't answer. He had made love to her with the usual indifference of a man confident that she had taken all necessary precautions. Perhaps he'd had a secret wish to get her with child and so bind her closer to him. But that had been before finding Irene. Now—

"Are you?" He moved closer, careless of the blood running from his nose. "For Christ's sake, Myrna! Are you?"

"No."

"Then why lie to her?"

"I love you, you bastard, isn't that answer enough? We were at war." Her voice rose. "War, blast you. I hated her for having had you and she wanted to see me burn. So I fought dirty—is there any other way if you want to win?"

"Shut up!"

"You think you can forget me? Just throw me aside so as to make room for her?"

"Shut up, damn you!" Spragg wiped at his mouth and looked at the blood on his hand. "Get out! Get dressed and get out! Out! Out!"

Shaking he went into the bathroom and stripped off his ruined jacket and shirt. Filling the bowl with water he ducked his head. The bleeding was slow to stop and Myrna had gone by the time he left the bathroom. Probably to take another room, he thought, or to stay with her new-found friends. The hell with her—why couldn't she have stayed away another day?

Scotch stood on a table and he helped himself to a drink before reaching for the phone. Which museum had held the display?

He rang the desk, obtained the number, punched it and waited listening to the soft barring of the phone at the other end. Either the place was closed or no incoming calls were being received. NASA? This time someone answered.

"Yes?"

"I'm Professor Malcolm Spragg attached to the UN. I need to contact Mrs. Irene Fiander on an important matter. She works for you arranging Voyager displays in museums and such. She was here in New York but has moved on. Where can I find her?"

A pause then, "I'm sorry, mister, but the office staff has all left. Why not try again tomorrow?"

A click and his life was over. It had been over since Myrna had met Irene and hit her where it hurt the most. No matter what he said now it would be impossible to repair the damage. She would expect him to remain with his mistress and the coming child.

The liar!

Crystal shattered as he flung the glass at the wall wishing it had landed in Myrna's face so as to ruin her scheming, deceptive beauty.

The phone demanded attention.

It was Ogden and Spragg listened as the man congratulated him on his performance at the UN. "Now, tomorrow I want—"

"No. You don't need me and I'm sick of facing all those pimp-politicians. I'm a scientist and I want to get to work. Send me to Cape Canaveral. That's where the action is. I want to go there. I mean it." Spragg listened, frowning, "All right, I'll be your eyes and ears. When do I leave?"

He hung up and sat sipping from the bottle and looking at the mark his glass had made against the wall. After a while it began to look like a face, a series of faces.

Someone knocked twice at his door during the night but he ignored it both times.

CHAPTER 13

After the siren came a moment of silence then out on the sands a giant bellowed into life. Its voice was thunder and its breath was flame; a spouting fire lengthening as it rose to challenge the sun.

From the box of the speaker the comptroller's voice held a mechanical flatness. "Launch Charlie 4B7 a hit."

Spragg relaxed, sharing in the victory. Another one on its way into orbit there to be robbed of its load and maybe cannibalised for materials. Or maybe not, the coding system used was meaningless to any not closely involved with the launching. Charlie could be of the series designed for re-entry, salvage and further use. As Baker could have been the now obsolete space shuttles and therefore expendable.

"Area clear!"

The area, maybe, but not the ether. Spragg frowned at the screen set before him on the desk. The original image relayed down from the International Space Station was distorted by a mass of flecks and wavering lines caused by the electronic 'noise' of the launch. Given time it would clear but it was a gamble whether or not another crew could get another launch readied before it did. Not that it mattered—his work was done.

Spragg leaned back, palming his eyes. Figures danced on his retinas, the imaginary notations made a thousand times by his subconscious even as they were forwarded to be fed into the computers. The machines could do the sums but it took eyes and a brain to determine the original elements of the equations. But to continue now with his dulled vision and concentration would be to do more harm than good. It was time for him to quit.

Rising he went to the toilet where he washed face and hands, drying both on a paper towel as he studied his ravaged reflection in a mirror. The past weeks had left their mark. Work, he thought. Once I could take it. Now resiliency had vanished with his youth.

He made his way outside. The air struck chill after the warmed interior of the bunker. Drawing a deep breath he looked around.

Cape Canaveral was a madhouse of men and machines, a scene of frantic, non-stop activity, which had swallowed him as water does a stone. Provided with accommodation, a place to work and duties to perform he had become a part of an army fighting a war against time with progress marked by the vessels that rose into space. And, if not all his duties were concerned with astronomy, then who was he to complain?

He turned as sirens wailed to see a convoy of chemical-carriers heading to where a slender shape stood silhouetted against the sky. Adorned with flashing lights and wreathed in vapour from their frozen, liquid contents the vehicles looked like strange and alien beasts from a fevered delirium. As did the teams already cooling down the area of the recent launch. As did the others, armed and protected who stood beside ominous containers set on low-slung carriers bearing flaring symbols of universal recognition.

Unconsciously Spragg glanced up at the sky. If atomic material was being sent up then the basic programme was keeping to schedule. Or, perhaps, to save time a little was being sent up with each load. That made sense in a way providing all precautions were being taken and he felt a sharp sympathy for those above and the work they had to do. Compared to it Hell itself would have been a playground.

"Mal!"

Spragg turned, smiling as he saw Bud Aldcock. The man belied his appearance and had turned out to be a good companion and friend. His association with the religious fanatic had, he'd explained, been the result of a false line of logic.

"She kept preaching love, so I thought I'd give it a try. Well, maybe I moved too fast—she damned near took out an eye! Hell, no woman's worth that kind of grief."

Now he said, "How many is that to date, Mal?"

"God knows." Spragg glanced towards the telemetering section of the bunkers. "Why not ask the boys who should know?"

The section was never idle, always there were men monitoring the launches from other sites; New Mexico, the three in Russia and now, it appeared, one in China.

"They're firing from Wenchow," explained a man with a dark face seamed with scars. "Making good time, too, but they insist on playing it cagey. I guess they don't want us to know if they lose a few in the Pacific. The big worry is the way they're going at it. Two at a time and three launches last week. Why the hell can't they tie in with the general pattern?"

"Probably a matter of face," said one of the others. "I read a book about it once. It's all to do with honour or something."

"That was before the revolution." The dark man turned to check his screen. "They don't put so much stock in it now. Even so—" His voice broke into a shout. "Christ! Fred! Joe! Get on the boards! Max—get in touch with general control. The Chinese have got a wild one!"

A vessel off-course, its telemetry unbalanced or absent for the sake of fuel economy. Spragg watched as the technicians ran to their stations, voices rapping as they swept into action.

"Check the original flight plan. Find initial thrust, duration of burn, shedding of boosters if any." A moment while voices blurred from the speakers as questions reached across the globe. "Anyone know what a Mao is?"

"Which model?" The first was a converted ICBM. They ripped out the telemetry, added boosters and settled for a small payload." The speaker added, dryly, "I guess they must have improved things since then."

"Not enough." The dark man frowned as he studied his board. "It's heading towards sector 14."

"That's right. Check on ETA and get hold of the poor bastard in charge of that sector and warn him trouble is on the way."

* * * *

His name was Gus Easton and he was an Angel. He had wanted to be a pilot but events had moved faster than anticipated and, suddenly, he found himself circling the Earth in free fall. Others were with him, living in a circular tin can that revolved fast enough to draw vomit down to the floor and supplied enough artificial gravity to dispense with the need for air-circulators. A bunch of raw kids half of whom would die before they had learned how to live in their new environment. And learning, of necessity, had to be fast.

They slept to wake and ride up to the long axis and pass out through the airlock to where their ships hung waiting. But first they had to suit up and check seals and tanks and radios, lifelines and reaction pistols and filters, magnetic grapnels and internal plumbing. All with good reason. It was distracting and therefore dangerous to work in a suit awash with waste products. It was hard to manoeuvre without a reaction pistol or the grapnels. It was more than hard to see with eyes seared by unshielded sunlight and impossible to breathe without air. Things they learned if they hoped to live.

Gus Easton was a veteran of nine solid weeks and was oldest in terms of experience of his bunch. That put him in charge until he died or went plain crazy when the next senior in experience would take over. It was a system that offered no hope and no reward but it was one they were stuck with. As they were stuck in space until the job was done.

"Let's get on with it." Gus spoke into his radio. "Let's hear you check." He listened to the babble of a dozen voices. They were open shells fitted with powerful rocket engines, buffers, electro-magnets, lines hooks and eyes. Three men sat in each. Two of each of the three were operating hands while the third guided the craft. He was also in command of the squad. Gus was the exception in that he had delegated the driving seat to another and thus was free to concentrate on the overall situation.

Now he said over the radio, "Right. Spread out in normal pattern. Don't move until I give the word."

The first time in space he had almost died because he had trusted his eyes. Against the background of space things lost their relation to each other and distances became confused. Against the blue-white orb of the planet it wasn't so bad but the Earth itself held a strange and hypnotic charm. With the sun in the background things came darkened by the shields and could hit before anticipated.

And yet the environment held a strange charm and eerie majesty. Bright and harshly clear with the stars like jewels and the drifting motion of free-fall giving the impression of utter freedom of movement. A poetic image over which those on Earth could muse knowing nothing of the ache and pain of muscles and joints trying to adapt to zero gravity while subjected to sudden and relatively tremendous strains. Of the raw sores caused by the chafing of the suits. The general discomfort of life as an Angel.

"Is that it, Gus?"

"Where?" Gus narrowed his eyes as his driver pointed. "Maybe. Keep it under observation." Then, remembering, he added to the third man, "You too, Sam."

Sam Meillion, young, eager, too careless for his own good. As yet he still woke with a smile, cracked jokes, could pass urine without pain and enjoyed regular bowel-movements. Another few days, a couple of weeks, say, and that would change. He'd learn he had kidneys and that paste was a bad substitute for food. His eyes would play up and his skin get a scaly feel. He'd start to lose hair and he'd carry permanent bruises. But, if he managed to live long enough, he'd get promotion, extra pay and a medal.

"There, Gus! There!"

Hard against the blue-white swirl came a rising black shape. It lifted as if in a dream, rising, slowing as it rose, the markings now plain.

"In!" Gus rapped the order. "Steady! Fasten and withdraw!"

Orders repeated every time they made a catch. The slowness was deceptive, relative only to themselves, but the Charlie could be a little off and to ignore the possibility was dangerous.

"Wonder what it's carrying? Candy, I hope."

That was Hayes with his goddamned sweet tooth. He sent his ship in even as he spoke but he was both cautious and clever. He rode close, one of his crew attaching a line, the other waiting before springing abroad. A panel lifted and the others closed in.

"Any supplies?" They were getting low on water and air. They were always conscious of the air. "Move it!" Gus let his irritation show. "You think it's Christmas and this a gift from Daddy?"

An unwise remark and he regretted it. A thing like that could set a man off and trigger a lurking insanity. He could try and make it back home in the returning Charlie—one of the commonest ways Angels did a dutch.

"All right now," he said, mollifying his tone. "Let's get this stuff where it should go and get back to the sack."

Most of it went into orbit with the rest. The supplies were taken to where the drum-like living quarters revolved like a battered beer can. The stuff in orbit would circle where it was put aside from minor drifting which could which could be taken care of on regular inspections. Later the engineers would come to assemble it and build what the hell it was supposed to be. Certain items, clearly marked and both small and compact, were placed well apart from each other.

"That's it!" Sam Meillion was cheerful. "You want me to send it down, Gus?"

"Wait, I—" Gus broke off as his earphones jarred. "Jesus Christ! We've a wild one coming up! Scatter!"

The usual response to potential danger—if one went there was no need for others to follow. Gus waited, listening, grunting as he saw the uprising shape.

"I've got it. The rest of you stand by. I'll take this one myself."

The penalty of command as he understood it. To take on any unanticipated or unexpected danger. Hayes chuckled as the thing came closer.

"A Chinese, eh? They could have fortune cookies inside. Or some chow mein or maybe a couple of those Geisha girls."

"Shut up!" Gus roared into his mike. "Keep your traps shut or I'll gut you!" From his tone they knew he meant it. To his driver he said, "Watch it now, Ken."

"I'm watching." The ship moved a little as gas flared from its vent. The Chinese vessel, now close, came even closer. Another touch of the controls and the ship matched velocity then edged for contact. "How's that?"

"Too damned close!" Gus gauged distance, time, the vectors of relative motion. "Don't hit!"

Sam Meillion decided to take a hand. The ship was within reach of the Chinese vessel, running apparently neck and neck, and there was a convenient projection. It would be a simple matter to reach out, grab hold, and bring the two craft together.

He reached out, grabbed—and the discharge of opposed electrical potentials which Gus had feared arched to fuse the gloved hand to the projection. The relative motion had been deceptive and the Chinese vessel, travelling faster, ripped the arm from the socket and spilled both air from the suit and life from the body. In effect the dead Angel had tried to form a living bridge between a railway express and a not quite as fast automobile.

"Gus!"

"He's dead!" Easton swore as the body sprayed his helmet with globules of blood. He threw it aside and it hit the driver, who, trying to avoid it, hit the controls. The vent flared into life and sent the ship slamming into the body of the strange vessel. Weakened metal yielded and exposed familiar shapes. "Christ! Nukes!"

The detonation was a smear of light in the firmament, a touch of angry colour gone as soon as spotted. Spragg watched it from his place in the bunker and knew before the dark man spoke what must have happened.

"Easton's bought it. He tried to keep the Chinese nukes apart from the others but he couldn't manage it. A few got together and—" The flapping motions of his hands was expressive. "Critical mass and blooie!"

"The others?"

"The rest of his Angels escaped the initial blast. We asked them if they wanted anything and they said booze and blondes."

Consolations to men who knew they were doomed to die from the effects of the radiation that had blasted the area. The first they would get together with pills to make the ending painless, but Spragg doubted the second. Nor for want of mercy or a desire to please but a woman needed food, water and air. She needed fuel to lift her and could take the place of essential warheads. And even the most willing sacrifice would hesitate knowing it would have to be a one-way trip.

On the ground, here at Canaveral, it was different. Life had taken on the peculiar aspect of a city under siege rather like the camaraderie of the war years in London when the city had been the target of Nazi bombs. People had gained something then as now. A common purpose as strong as a common misfortune. Knowing the truth, realising the importance of time, they had shed reserve. Women, in particular, had reacted in a positive manner.

Spragg left the bunker thinking of Angels. Not the kind found in religious testimony but of those so aptly named young men circling the Earth in the zero gravity of free fall. Falling, always falling and yet never to land. As Lucifer had fallen for an eternity before claiming the world as his own. Those above would not fall as long and would never be in any physical condition to claim anything but a plot of ground and a headstone. And even for that they would have to rely on the good graces of the living.

A sombre thought he could have done without. His fatigue had returned with bone-aching force and yet he knew he wouldn't be able to sleep. Not until he'd taken something to quieten the teeming activity of his mind, the figures that danced to form equations that mocked every effort they could make.

To Bud Aldcock he said, "Coming for a drink?"

"Love to, but I'm on duty. See you later."

A wave and he was gone and, alone, Spragg made his way to the pre-fabricated hut that served to provide recreation to those in his category. It was set with a bar and typical tavern games. Tables and chairs were scattered about. A pretence had been made to give visiting politicians the impression that it catered to a high level of intelligence but, basically, what the club supplied and what the scientists did was drink.

Harry Frazer waved to Spragg as he entered the hut. The man was another of those he had met at Waldemar's party but Carl himself was not to be seen and neither was Frieda. Both were probably engaged in their own ways; Carl busy with his liaison duties and Frieda tending her computers.

"Hi, Mal, have a drink?"

"Thanks—a big one."

Harry carried the glass to a table and sat down with his own drink. "A bad thing up there. You know about it?"

"I was in the bunker when it happened."

"Those poor bastards!" Harry drank deeply.

Spragg took a swallow of his own drink. The hut had been decorated with scraps of green and silver, some paper-chains, bunches of dyed grass, fronds and shreds of cooking foil—all the traditional garnish of the Christmas Festival. At the far end a group of women in WAC uniform were busy setting up a wire and paper tree. Others wearing civilian clothing mingled with the scientists. One of them, a striking blonde, smiled as she looked at Spragg.

"Anne Roberts," said Frazer. "A nurse over at the hospital. She's off duty. A nice girl—she does her best to help out in any way she can. You're lucky. She seems to like you."

Spragg looked at her with new interest. He knew of the new morality that many women had adopted and the advantages it gave to those who needed to relax after arduous spells of duty. As a nurse Anne would recognise the signs sooner than most. Was that why she had smiled? Did his face bear the reflection of the torment of his mind?

His eyes followed her as she moved on to stand and talk to a balding technician seated with two computer-men.

He drank and set down the empty glass and called for more then, because the bartender was busy, rose to fetch his own.

Pete blinked at his demand. "A bottle? Hell, Professor, you know it's against the regulations to take booze out of the club."

"Army regulations. Forget them. I'm a civilian."

"I'm not. And this is government property. And we're all under military jurisdiction."

"NASA too?"

"Everyone and everything." Pete leaned forward. "If I slip you a pint will you keep it under cover?" He grinned as Spragg nodded. "It'll cost."

"So you make a profit. Pass it over." Spragg tucked the flat bottle inside his belt, loaded a couple of glasses with ice and carried them back to the table where Frazer was sitting staring gloomily at the WAC's setting up the tree. "Here, Harry! Help yourself."

"Thanks." Frazer poured himself a stiff drink, held it, still looking at the group. "We go on, Mal," he mused. "At least some of us do."

The lucky ones, those not drifting in space or lying in hospital wards muttering under masking bandages, bodies scarred with oozing sores. The Angels and the heroes burned by leaking chemicals, seared by the chill of frozen gases; the oxygen and hydrogen, the nitric acid vapour, the fluorine and other products of the Devil's laboratory.

The hospital was filled with the technicians who primed the vessels and those who handled the stores and equipment, men broken, bruised, crushed, blinded—sacrifices to the need for speed which forced the cutting of corners and the neglecting of safety precautions. And others who had also lost their gambles; men with falling hair and wasting blood, dead and knowing it but still aware, still able to feel. Companions of the dying Angels and from the same cause but they, at least, wouldn't die alone.

Would they end it all with a pill? Would he? Would he drink himself stupid or would he just carry on until the moment came when he couldn't lift a hand or move a muscle?

"Professor Spragg?" Anne smiled down at him as he looked up. Introducing herself she said, "I've often wanted to meet you."

"Why? Because I'm the original Prophet of Doom?" He was being unfair. "Sorry, care for a drink?"

The bottle was empty and he stared at it as Frazer went to fetch drinks from the bar, setting them down to discretely vanish. A true friend.

Anne said, "You're thinking of those Angels, aren't you? You shouldn't."

"No," said Spragg. "You're right. Let the dead bury the dead—or is it dust to dust?" He blinked as he reached for his glass. "Are you a philosopher?"

"A nurse."

"Well, nurse, diagnose my condition."

"You're tired and suffering from toxin-poison due to accumulated fatigue. The tiredness is affecting your coordination and I'd take a bet your vision is blurred. You feel cold and yet have a tendency to sweat. When you close your eyes you see retinal flashes. You also experience an anxiety syndrome, affecting your mental concentration. You are beginning to doubt yourself and have a tendency to check things more than once. And you brood."

Over Irene and why he hadn't heard from her though it would be a miracle if he did. He must ask Carl to try and locate her. Or Ogden, the man had means at his disposal and should be able to find out exactly where she was and what she was doing—

"Angels," he said, and giggled. "Hundreds of them riding round and round the Earth. The Americans and the French and English and Russian and Chinese and the rest, all wheeling in an eternal circle. Dead eyes watching—always watching—" He straightened meeting her watchful blue eyes. "You forgot something in your diagnosis, nurse. You forgot to mention that I'm more than a little drunk…"

He fell, hitting the table, sending his glass to crash on the floor. He toppled and slowly fell after it, eyes open, fully aware, seeming to drift as he fell the journey extended by a peculiar slowing of time so that he could think of a scatter of things while suspended between chair and floor; Anne, the WACs and their tree, the faces looking down at him, the crack in the ceiling of the hut, the glare of the light which was like a sun. A sun that died as he landed.

CHAPTER 14

Christmas came with a plethora of useless gifts; stones wrapped in gay paper, pens, corks, empty bottles with lewd suggestions, a dead rat—all the rubbish available which could be wrapped and handed over and laughed at when unwrapped. A distortion of the festive motive matched by the atmosphere in the club, a grim, death-house humour reminiscent of the ancient Saturnalia when the world was turned upside down and the master became the slave as the slave aped the master.

"Hail!" Pete had been elected and stood by the tree dressed in red and white finery. A bowl of punch stood on a table and he greeted each man and woman as they came to partake of the libation. "Hail!"

Hail and farewell for we who meet today may never meet again. The unspoken meaning of the greeting and they drank and ate the little cakes and sandwiches and tried to ignore the throbbing of released giants.

Spragg had avoided the club since he had fallen down drunk to wake in his room with a throbbing head. He had remembered to eat and done his best to sleep. The following days had done little to restore his lost energy but, at least, he could close his eyes and not see the damned, dancing figures.

"Mal!" Waldemar came towards him. "Merry Christmas!" He beamed at the terse answer. "That's the trouble with you pagans you have no respect for orthodox festivals."

"Christmas is a pagan festival. The Christians stole it and adapted it to suit their own purposes."

Waldemar shrugged, smiling. "If you want to argue theology, my friend, you'll have to talk to the Chaplain. Me? I've other things to do."

Entertaining certain visitors who had come to bless the occasion with their presence. Spragg had seen them when they'd been given the guided tour; stars of the entertainment world eager for free publicity.

"You don't like them?" Waldemar had seen his expression. "Well, neither do I, but they have to be tolerated. The world goes on, Mal."

"I know." An election could be due and politicians had a liking for getting all the help they could in order to stay in power. The razzamatazz of show business was shared by entertainers and seekers after public office alike. "Trouble?"

"Nothing that can't be handled with a little assistance, Are you willing to give a hand?"

Spragg looked over the crowd assembled in the hut. Frieda was absent as was Frazer both probably with their heads together on some last-minute calculation. Bud Aldcock was standing with his head close to the dark curls of a vivacious WAC. Others with whom he had struck up an acquaintance were engrossed in their own pursuits. As good a time as any to leave.

"It won't take long," urged Waldemar. "They are to visit the hospital and get photographed and learn enough so to be able to make some more or less intelligent comments when questioned about Thor. You'll be free in plenty of time for dinner tonight." He added, "And you'll like Vivian."

Most men liked Vivian Dawn. She had cultivated a sensuous style, an air of subtle decadence.

Smiling she said, "So you are the great Professor Spragg. I've heard so much about you. You must be very religious to have summoned the Hammer of God."

"Did I?"

"That's what some people are saying. But people will say anything. They even hint that the President and I have an intimate relationship. Have you met him? A wonderful man, Mal. One of the world's greats. Tony, come and meet the Prophet of Doom."

Tony Inch, tall, dark, swarthy, a golden chain around his neck and heavy gold rings on his fingers. He stank of masculine perfume and his clothing was the latest thing in expensive bad taste. He nodded, scowling—it was a part of his public image.

Spragg nodded back and was introduced to the rest of the party. One of them, a pop singer with sunken cheeks, said, "Let's lay it on the line, Prof. Is this the real thing or is the public being ripped off? Come on, man, give it to us straight."

The man was high on something or had just taken too much Christmas spirit. Spragg looked at the hovering photographers all eager to get a few juicy shots.

"Krag, don't be rude." The other woman in the party gripped his arm. "He's got a thing about being robbed," she explained. "Ever since his first agent ran out and left him with a pile of bills and no money. But I guess we're all curious as to what's really going on. I mean, if all we need to do is to shoot atomic missiles at Thor why not do it from the ground?"

Patiently Spragg explained about the number of movement vectors involved ending, "Once we have completed the launching platform in space we will have eliminated the most troublesome part of the problem. We shall still be accompanying the Earth around the sun and still be affected by the galactic drift but we shall be free of the initial rotational spin together with all the problems associated with the atmosphere such as winds, storms, varying densities and so on. Think of the orbital launcher as a gun platform and you'll get a better grasp of what we need to do. Obviously the first thing is to build it."

"Which is why you're shooting all this stuff up into orbit?"

"Yes." Spragg remembered to smile. "Any missiles we fired from the ground would have to fight their way up through Earth's gravity well. That takes a lot of fuel, which means a smaller load, which means, in turn, more missiles. They would have to be aimed but any deflection would be great. They would simply miss the target. So we'd have to incorporate guidance systems in their construction—telemetry. That means more weight and so more fuel and so on. But the Earth is rotating so to keep the missiles under constant supervision we'd have to relay signals via an orbiting satellite. So why not just use the satellite in the first place?"

A question unanswered. Spragg wondered if they had understood anything of what he'd been saying. Vivian surprised him.

"I follow that, Mal, but Alex here has a point." She gestured to an attendant shadow. "Why not just adapt ICBM's?"

"They're simply not designed for the job. Intercontinental Ballistic Missiles are like giant artillery shells. They're obsolete now as it happens but most people remember them. They're aimed, fired, they rise until their fuel is exhausted then they reach the top if their trajectory and begin to fall on the target. To make them rise higher we must provide more fuel. That means extra tanks or engines—a booster system. We might just be able to get them into orbit but they wouldn't be able to carry a load."

"So they're useless?"

"On the contrary and it's another reason for building the launching platform. We can use them once they're in space. So we send them up and they're taken apart and adapted and fitted with warheads and made ready to go."

"When?" Krag had been silent for too long. "What the hell are we waiting for? If that damned rock is coming why not shoot at it now?"

"Yes, Mal," said Vivian. "Why not?"

She moved close to his side and he felt the soft touch of her hand on his arm and smelt her subtle perfume which hinted at depraved sophistication. "Is there a reason you can't shoot now?"

"Distance," said Spragg. "Thor is small and a long way away. Relatively small, that is, but still too far to be hit."

"Why?" The woman was shrewd. "If we could send the Voyagers out there and aim them then why not missiles?"

He said, "Those probes took years to reach the Jovian system. They were moving relatively slowly and there was plenty of time to relay instructions. This doesn't apply to the present situation. It is a matter of relative velocities and, well, there is really no comparison."

"Meaning it was a dumb question?" Krag glared his anger. "Listen, you egg-headed creep, no one is going to insult her while I'm around."

"Then piss off!"

"What?" The sunken cheeks flushed with anger. "Why, you—"

"Wait!" Spragg backed as the man advanced, fist raised. "I didn't—"

He went down as bunched knuckles slammed against his jaw.

* * * *

Outside the hospital a military band was determinedly playing Christmas carols as the nurse deftly treated Spragg's face. Watching her at work Carl Waldemar said, "What the hell came over you, Mal? Why insult the man? I can understand you not liking him but to tell him that in public was stupid—"

"I know." Spragg gingerly touched his jaw. The bone was unbroken but the flesh was bruised and a ring had lacerated the skin. "I didn't realise I'd spoken aloud." She had mentioned the Voyagers, which had reminded him of Irene and made him suddenly impatient with the whole stupid exercise in public relations. Well, Karg had got his publicity and Vivian her excitement.

Ann Roberts said, "The bone must be bruised and the blow could have triggered off a delicate tooth-nerve. I'll get you something to take care of the discomfort."

Spragg looked at Waldemar as she left the small treatment-room. Outside the band was still playing. Over the din he said, "Any news, Carl?"

"No."

"Damn it, man, she couldn't just vanish! Did you contact NASA?"

"Of course, but she has quit their employ." Waldemar shook his head, "Mal, my friend, I know what Irene means to you. But from what you told me I know how badly she has been hurt. People are like animals at such times, they want to run and hide and gain time for their injuries to heal. That, I think, is what she has done."

"And Myrna?"

"She has left Madam Luluva and is now under the protection of a colonel in the American Army who is giving her a conducted tour of the West Coast." Waldemar added, delicately, "He is far from being a young man."

Which could explain his attraction. She had always preferred the father-figure which was probably why she had left Boris. Now she was probably living high with her reefers and drugs and drinks and stimulating experiences.

"You'll keep looking?"

"For Irene? Of course, my friend." Waldemar rose from where he sat. "And now I must see to our honoured guests. They should be ready to leave now. Have you a word you wish me to convey to your adversary?" He smiled as he heard it.

As he left and the strains of 'Jingle Bells' played an accompaniment to the throb of Spragg's aching jaw. The nurse returned as it ended and he watched the neat movements of her body as she crossed to the faucet to fill a glass with water. He felt as if he knew her but couldn't remember having seen her before.

Approaching him, the glass in one hand pills in the other, she said, "Have you been drinking?"

"A little punch. No hard stuff."

"These don't go too well with alcohol." She placed three of the tablets in his hand. They were large; white flecked with green. Handing him the water she said, "Get them down."

He coughed when finally he had obeyed. "What were they?"

"Something strong we use for special cases. I guessed you wouldn't have enjoyed an aching jaw and teeth over Christmas."

"You were right, thanks." He relaxed, already the pain had almost vanished. "Can I drink later?"

"If you're careful but I'd advise you to go easy on the Scotch."

He caught the ironic tone and stared at her, really seeing her for the first time. She looked different in uniform.

"I know you," he said. "Anne Roberts, isn't it? We met at the club about a week ago when—"

"You were suffering from strain and accumulated tension."

"And I got drunk and passed out. What happened? Did you call for help and have me put to bed?" He frowned, trying to remember, but the entire incident was a blank.

"You just needed to forget, Mal. It's a common syndrome and nothing to worry about. In a sense your overloaded psyche blew a fuse in order to make you rest." Quietly she added, "Do you always blame yourself when anything goes wrong?"

He said, "You're talking about guilt."

"That accident wasn't your fault. You only announced the discovery of Thor. You didn't create it. You aren't really the Prophet of Doom announcing the coming of the Hammer of God."

He said, tightly, "I'm sick to the stomach with hearing that stupid title."

"I won't use it again. I promise. Feel better now?"

"Yes."

"Like to see where I work?"

Dutifully he followed her from the room and down the long passage to the wards and their contents of assorted misery.

* * * *

Night fell with a chill wind from the sea. Inside the club the debris of earlier festivities had been cleared away and the floor readied for dancing. The bar was fully stocked. Food was heaped on platters decorated with paper-lace fringes.

Spragg found himself a glass and, remembering Anne's warning, took only beer. Sipping it he thought of the nurse, wishing she was here with him now instead of having only half-promised to join him later.

Finishing the beer he rose to get another. Turning he bumped into a softly yielding figure.

"Herr Professor!" Frieda dabbed at her shoulder now wet with beer. She wore a party dress of some shimmering green material and what with skilfully applied make-up and neatly dressed hair looked far younger than her age. "Are you well?"

"I'm not drunk if that's what you mean." Spragg found his handkerchief and wiped at the damp patch. "Sorry about that. Can I get you something?"

"A large vodka and tonic please."

On impulse Spragg ordered two, dumping his beer and carrying both glasses high as he edged from the bar. Frieda took hers and sipped with the delicate precision of a cat.

"I looked for you earlier," said Spragg. "Harry too but I guess you were both busy. Cheers!"

They drank and she said, "Harry and I are working on flight computations. We are establishing various formulas based on a variety of load and velocity factors. As yet they are preliminary figures but will save time when we have access to more definitive data."

"And? Surely you haven't been working all the time?"

"No." She took another sip of her drink. "Herr Frazer is a very accomplished man."

In more ways than one, Spragg guessed, but kept the thought to himself. Frieda had dressed in her best for a purpose and he knew it wasn't himself.

"And you, Herr Professor? Have you anything new on our visitor?"

"A little. Velocity shows a slight increase as we anticipated. It has to be due to solar attraction but will fall as the conjunction of Mars and Jupiter takes effect. The latest determination of the diameter shows a slight increase over previous estimates—the figures are available when you want them."

"Later."

"Of course—I didn't mean right this minute. But Harry will need them in order to make his preliminary assessments. Is he coming to the party?"

"Yes. He will be here soon."

And would be certain of a welcome. Thinking about it made Spragg think of Anne. Waiting for her was becoming a strain. It would be best to walk down to the hospital and see if she'd managed to get free.

Spragg finished his drink and took his leave of Frieda as she was joined by other colleagues and admirers. Outside the chill stung face and hands and he stood a moment looking at the sky. Over the sea the stars hung in brilliant splendour accentuated by the misty fuzz of nebulae smeared like glowing curtains over the secret chambers of creation. A sight that always, caught at his heart.

"Mal?" The voice was low, familiar. "Mal, is that you?"

"Anne!" He turned and stepped towards her, closing the distance between them with quick, impatient strides to catch her hands and hold them as his eyes drank her face, her hair. Her perfume was of roses and she wore a long nurse's cape beneath which something white glimmered in the starlight. "I'm glad you could make it," he said. "So very glad.

She smiled at him then looked up at the sky. "You were watching," she said. "Thor?"

"It's too far away to be seen as yet."

"But you know where it its?" She followed his arm as, releasing her hands, he pointed at the sky. "And I could see it with a telescope?"

"Yes—if you knew just where to look."

Anne said, "Do you want to join the party?"

"Not really." What he wanted was to take her, to hold her and to find what happiness he could in the circle of her arms. A wish that grew to a need even as he thought of it. "I just want to be with you."

"And I with you," she said. "So why don't we go somewhere where we can be alone?"

So this was how it happened, he thought. The direct invitation divorced of any subterfuge. "Where?"

"I have a place—" She broke off as he shook his head. "No?"

"No." It would be full of the presence of others—the small things previous visitors would have left behind in a subconscious desire to stake territorial rights or to provide an excuse for a return visit. And even if the objects were out of sight the walls would know, the floor, the bed itself. "Let's use mine."

* * * *

"Mal?" She rose a little to look down into his face. "You asleep?"

"No."

"Good. Feel better now?"

"Thanks to you, yes."

"I'm glad." Relaxing she ran her hand over his chest. "Man! Were you all strung up!"

A nurse—was this how it was done? To take a man on the edge of nervous breakdown and stimulate him with the sight of pain and drug him and then give him the opportunity to release all his tensions in a furious burst of sexual activity?

Turning his head he looked into the face so close to his own. It was still beautiful but now something had been added to the eyes.

Abruptly, she said, "When, Mal?"

"Thor?" They had been talking of his discovery. He thought he knew what she wanted to know. "It will arrive in April. You know the date."

"The 11ᵗʰ, but that's not what I meant. When will you be certain whether it's going to hit or not?"

"I'm certain now. We're going to blast it into a deflected orbit with nuclear devices. You know that."

"I know that's what everyone keeps saying."

"Then believe it. Thor will be turned aside. We either defect it or blast it into dust and in either case it won't be able to harm us. You have absolutely—" He broke off as she rested her hand over his mouth. "Anne?"

"Don't lie to me, Mal, I'm too good at my job for that. Patients lie all the time. And I'm not a child. Now I'll ask you again—when? Not when Thor is due to hit but when will you be certain whether it will or not?"

"We can't be sure as yet," he admitted. "Maybe ten days."

"Ten days," she said thoughtfully. "Call it April 1ˢᵗ. All Fool's Day—and God help the poor fools if Thor can't be stopped. Mal!"

Her hands had begun to tremble, her body as, like a child she moved into his arms. And, now it was his turn to give comfort.

CHAPTER 15

New Year came and was over and the 100-day countdown began. As if flinching to an anticipated blow the Earth showed signs of unease; earthquakes created havoc in Turkey and China, a volcano erupted in Brazil and a tsunami inundated several islands of the Melanesian group. Items that provided up to the minute news for the media as did the spate of industrial unrest sweeping the more liberal countries.

A bell sounded the ending of the break and Spragg rose with the others as they filed from the room. It was a bleak enough place with its tables and chairs, dispensing machines serving a variety of non-alcoholic drinks and weary sandwiches and pastries, but it was a place of refuge in which all shoptalk was banned. A place to rest a while and sip apologies for coffee and tea and to pretend for a while that God was in his Heaven and all was right in the world.

In another chamber the figures were waiting.

They rested on sheaves of paper spilled from computer terminals, glowed on the displays, twined in elaborate patterns on pads but, most of all, they danced again in his mind. Endless figures, impact times and rendezvous times and the influence of solar and Lunar attraction and more.

Donald Lauter called them to order. He had recently joined the team and Spragg remembered him from when he had lectured at the Exposition. Now he stood at the end of the long table, tall and formal in his uniform, his tone quiet but penetrating. Behind him, on the wall, hung the pad of numbers they all hated to look at. Red on white and originally numbering 100 but now down to 94.

"Ladies! Gentlemen! Shall we proceed?" Lauter paused for a moment. "As you may have learned I am now in full charge of this section of the project and would like to be given the latest developments. Naturally I have read your reports but I would like to hear from you personally. Professor Spragg? Would you care to begin?"

From where he sat Spragg said, "Thor has displayed a slight oscillation revealed to us by a dark marking on the otherwise bright surface. The movement could be inherent in the mass, caused by gravitational influences, or more likely the result of residual forces gained from a previous impact. A flare was noted which, in a sense, signalled its arrival and this could have been caused by the impact of some small mass of debris from the asteroid belt or an unknown satellite of Jupiter. However the oscillation has no effect on either direction or velocity. Gravitational forces, which did combine to affect the velocity to a minor degree a few weeks ago have now levelled out. The alteration is minute but means that the previously estimated time of arrival must be advanced by 18 minutes 43 seconds."

Lauter nodded his thanks, "Doctor Osten?"

Frieda was little help. It all depended, as she pointed out, on her being given accurate data on which to work. The position of Thor was known together with its velocity. The position of Earth and the Moon also together with their speeds of motion. A relatively simple equation for her computers to solve. What wasn't so simple was to know the amount of nuclear material that would be needed to achieve the desired result, the time it should be launched, the velocity it needed to attain. A question of logistics, which Harry Frazer tried to answer.

"It's a question of maximum effectiveness," he said after Frieda had ended. "As yet we don't know the composition of Thor and we're only guessing when we say it's rock and nickel-iron. If it is, it's still one hell of a mass to deflect. The latest estimates put it at 585 miles in diameter and we haven't comparative figures to work with. The trick is to hit it just right and hard enough to do the job. The oscillation mentioned could help—we can time the blast so it will work in our favour. Frankly, Colonel, we can't tell you much more until you let us know how many ships you have and how much punch you can deliver. Tell us that and we'll tell you just when to leave, when to hit and when to duck."

Lauter said, "You'll have that information as soon as it's available. For now we need to agree on a target deadline. Any suggestions?"

The figures were familiar to them all. Thor would be 4,320,000 miles from Earth 10 days before the time of impact. To meet it at that distance missiles would have to be fired from the launching platform in good time to cover the distance before then just when depending on their velocity. There would also be a 24 second signal-delay due to the limitations of the speed of light. A long time between pressing a button and getting the desired response; double by the time it was relayed back to the operator. To allow Thor to approach closer would make the task of hitting it easier but of deflecting it harder. Somewhere there had to be an optimum time of attack.

Frazer said, "How fast can the missiles go? I've some preliminary figures based on various fuel-load ratios but they can't be applied until we know just what is to carry which. I assume there's no standardisation?"

"You assume correctly." Lauter was grim. "We've had to use what we could get. We are sure of the performance of some units, of course, ours and the Russians, the British and French, but many others like the adapted 1CBMs are something of a mystery. However we've a plan to take care of that. We intend to make up units of the same basic components. That means that all drives, fuel capacities and loads will be the same to the finest limits we can manage."

"Tests?"

"We've only built one unit as yet but it shows great promise."

Spragg said, "Multiple units? With multiple engines?" He drew in his breath as Lauter nodded. "That introduces a hell of a lot of variable factors. Get one venturis out of alignment and the whole unit will be thrown off course. The guidance problem will be too great."

Aldcock cleared his throat. "Couldn't we do something about that? What if we sent out relay-vessels so as to cut down transmission times? Use those nearest Thor to make the final adjustments. Possible?"

"It could be done," admitted Lauter. "And would be if we had the time."

But they had no time and they knew it. Even now the minutes were ticking away and tomorrow the numbers would be less on the wall and with the shrinking of time would come desperation.

"How then?" Aldcock wanted an answer. "Mal's right in what he says about those units. One lousy jet working wrong and the thing will be useless and don't tell me the engines are foolproof." His voice rose a little. "Figures. You ask for figures! Christ, we've worked on the figures until we're almost blind! What the hell are they good for without the men and machines?"

"We have them."

"The machines?"

"The machines and the men," said Lauter. "Volunteers."

* * * *

They had to be that and they had to be crazy with that particular type of lunacy which makes men run into burning houses to rescue strangers or to take a chance on an unknown drug because someone had to or to do any of the million and one things which turns a man into something more than a walking, talking animal. Madmen as the Angels were, the engineers and Spragg wishing he could be one of them.

"Kamikaze," said Aldcock. "That bastard Lauter knew about them all the time. Letting me rave on about guidance systems and making a fool of myself. Living computers—can you beat it?"

Not with things of micro chips and printed circuits and electronic blood. Not in the time available. Now flesh and bone and muscle had to take the place of snug but intricate components and men had one advantage instruments did not. They needed no 24-second response time. They would see and act with the speed of trained reflexes, which dispensed with the hampering need of thought. Young men, eager, dedicated—doomed to die and knowing it. Spragg wondered how they must feel.

Barry Dunne could have told him. Born in a black ghetto he had used brains and physical courage to fight his way from the dead end of drink and drugs and crime to gain a degree and a place in his country's army. Later he had gained officer status and then, quite deliberately, had chosen to throw away his future.

"On your feet!" The instructor was a man of middle-height, a wide streak of grey running through dark, curly hair. His eyes were narrowed as if he'd looked too long at the sun. His left hand was missing. As the class rose he lifted it. "Remember this. I lost it because I was stupid. I made a mistake. In space you usually make only one. That's why I'm teaching you. I'm lucky. Maybe some of it will rub off." He paused. "Any questions? No? Sit down!"

As they did the man beside him whispered, "Hey, Barry, listen to that guy. What makes him so special?"

Dunne could have told him. The engineer was an engineer who'd worked with the Angels. The mistake he'd mentioned was in letting his hand get trapped and crushed between two segments of metal. The courage he hadn't spoken of had been to cut free with the help of a laser; the beam cauterising the wound as it had sealed the suit with a mess of molten metal and plastic. The luck he wanted to pass on had been to successfully ride a Charlie back down to Earth.

"You've got courage," he said as the class settled. "But having guts isn't enough. You're going to have to live alone in conditions you haven't dreamed of as yet. To live and work for days in the most hostile environment you can imagine. Today I'm talking about it. Tomorrow you'll start doing it. Have any of you ever worn a suit?"

A hand rose. "I have, sir. Once when I volunteered for the Angels. They flunked me."

"Why?"

"I couldn't breathe. They didn't give me time to adapt. I'd have managed well enough given a chance."

"Out!" The instructor jerked his head. "Wait in the outer room." Thunder echoed as the man obeyed; the man-made roar of a rising vessel. As it died the instructor said, coldly, "I'm booking that guy on a charge of wasting time. The way things are he'll get a month in the stockade. If any of you want to follow him out do it now. No charge and no penalty—just go."

Dunne said, "Why the difference, sir?"

"He knew he was unfit for the job but still went ahead. If you can't breathe in a suit you're no dammed good for work in space. No crime and certainly nothing to be ashamed of but it has to be accepted. He wouldn't do that so I'm going to slap his wrist. Remember this. It isn't enough to be willing to die—you have to make dying worthwhile. Now let's talk about the basic components of a suit."

He gave it to them straight using language anyone could understand, words chosen for their direct punch and register.

"You get tubes shoved up your rear and into your pecker. You want to pass water you do it and it's collected in a bag. You want a crap and it's the same thing. You'll get cleared out before you get into the suit. You'll eat paste which contains almost no waste so there won't be any need for frequent motions."

And there'd be bromides and amphetamines to keep them cheerful and other drugs to keep them awake and alert and some hypnotism to indoctrinate them against a last-minute change of heart. All the devices which could be thought of to turn warm-blooded, virile young men into coldly calculating machines.

Spragg watched them a couple of weeks later. Now they were suited and would remain so for increasing periods of time. In them they trained, sitting at instrument panels and moving controls to match one bright point with another. Doing it over and over until their reflexes reacted without the need for calculation or delay. Moving like the automatons they were training to become.

But they had consolation.

"I have to, Mal." Anne stood unresisting in Spragg's arms as she explained. "They need me so much."

"So do I." He tried to hold her close but felt her resistance and knew it was hopeless. She and those others like her knew their duty and would do it. As long as the volunteers needed relief they would provide it. "Anne!"

"They have so little hope," she whispered. "And they are willing to die for us all."

No hope at all and, willing or not, they would die. The very structure of their suits would see to that. A man could exist for only so long cooped up in the artificial environment and, if nothing else, their air would be limited as would their water and food. But it was more than that as Aldcock had said when he passed on the news.

"Built in remotes, Mal! They offer to die and go ahead but still aren't trusted. They're sending out two to a unit and if one tries to change his mind they'll hit the button and blow his guts out. If that doesn't convince the survivor to play along they'll give it to him too."

Insurance against human fragility as Anne was a reward for being a hero.

That night Spragg cried in his sleep as he dreamt of Irene.

On the 7th day before impact they saw Thor at close hand for the first time. A probe had been sent out long before and was now close to the planetoid. In the control room Spragg sat together with Aldcock, Lauter and others watching the relayed images transmitted by the television unit incorporated in the mechanism.

"Jesus!" Aldcock was impressed. "Just look at that thing!"

Spragg was doing just that. Cameras were recording every moment and they would be played back and checked and rechecked for every scrap of obtainable information but, for now, he could sit and look and let his trained mind grasp the essentials of what the screen showed.

"It's strange," a woman whispered "Eerie and frighteningly alien."

A thing that had come from the furthest reaches of the universe. Which had been warmed by the heat of unknown suns and had passed through clouds of interstellar dust. An intruder thrusting towards them like a giant fist clenched to hammer a planet into extinction.

"Albedo is fantastically high," Spragg murmured. "As originally suspected. The surface seems to be smoother than is normal if the composition is similar to an ordinary asteroid. Temperature?" He frowned as the man monitoring the reception gave the answer. "So high?"

Space was an almost perfect vacuum with only drifting atoms of hydrogen and wide-spaced motes of dust found between the stars. An object moving at close to the speed of light could collect energy that would show itself in the form of heat by colliding with such debris but Thor was moving far too slowly for that. Then Spragg remembered the mysterious flare, which had caused, he thought, the dark spot on the otherwise bright surface. More evidence of a collision and the temperature level could be a sign of residual heat. Unless?

Aldcock voiced the thought. "Could the damn thing be antimatter?"

If so they were doomed. Antimatter, the atoms set in reverse order to their own, would simply merge with and negate anything they could throw against it. Merging energy would be released in vicious flares of energy which would cancel the missiles and leave space full of flying, broken atoms, but which would leave the bulk of the planetoid intact. An imbalance that would leave Earth open to impact by the remainder.

Spragg didn't want to think of what would happen then.

"No." Frazer shook his head as he studied the screen. "If that was antimatter we'd have known by now. Stray atoms would be scintillating and that area is full of tiny meteors. A single hit and the flare would be unmistakable."

"We had a flare," said Aldcock. "At the beginning, remember?"

"That could have been antimatter hitting Thor." Frazer was stubborn. "How about radiation emission?"

"It's there," said the technician. "But nothing too unusual."

"Magnetic field?"

"Zero—but we're getting a pull of some kind." He adjusted his controls. "I've sent a signal for the probe to back off."

Waiting they watched as the image grew larger. The surface seemed to hold a shimmer as if composed of trillions of crystals glowing with the reflected light of the sun. Spragg watched the movement of the dark spot, measuring the oscillation. It seemed not to have changed from when he'd checked it before.

"I need information," said Frazer. "What's that thing made of? How can I make calculations without knowing its density? It could be ice for all we know. Hey, that'd be one for the book! The Hammer of God a bloody lollipop!"

Lauter said, sharply, "That's enough! Concentrate on the job!"

Spragg said, trying to cool the tension, "What was that you were saying about a pull? An attraction of some kind?"

"Just that," said the technician. "The probe is reacting as if it's near a respectable planetary mass. Yet a thing that size can't have a high gravitational field. It doesn't make sense."

Not if Thor was composed of ordinary matter. Spragg leaned forward looking harder at the screen. "Could that crystal-like coating be a patina covering lead? If so would such a mass of the heavy metal account for the pull?"

Frazer shook his head when he asked.

"Damned if I know, Mal, but the computers will give the answer. What they won't tell us is how could such a mass of pure metal be out there in the first place." To the technician he said, "Is this probe only equipped to scan? Hasn't it any testing apparatus?"

"Some." The man was curt. "It was designed to check Mercury and adapted in a hurry. We've got most of what it can relay."

"Most? What's left?" Frazer bared his teeth at the reply. "Aren't you a cute little fellow? Here I am beating out my brains for an analysis and your little toy is equipped to obtain a spectrogram. So why not get it?"

"I will when I'm ready. Do I tell you your job? Right. Don't tell me mine." To Lauter he said, "We're set when you give the word, Colonel. Where do you want me to test?"

Frazer said, quickly, "The bulk is the more important factor. Aim anywhere but the dark patch."

"The coating could be thin and therefore of little value," said Lauter. The previous impact could have done some of our work for us."

"Or left an untypical residue. Damn it, Colonel, who's the expert here? Hit the goddamn coating!"

"The patch!"

"Make up your minds!" yelled the technician. "The probe's on its way out!"

Spragg watched as the man manipulated his controls, cursing the 3 minute signal-delay, the 6 minute total response time. On the screen the image veered, stars suddenly replacing the shimmering surface, the sudden glare of the naked sun. The probe, now rotating, was in the grip of invisible forces that negated all attempts to regain control from Earth.

"Damn!" Frazer stared at the screen, hands clenched, face contorted with rage. "Damn! Damn! Damn!"

A frustration Spragg shared. They had left it too late. The spectrogram should have been obtained ten minutes ago while they still held the probe under their command.

"Now!" Lauter shouted as the glimmering surface came again into view. "For Christ's sake, man, do something!"

Words weren't enough. The signal-delay made all attempts useless but the technician did his best. Grunting he lowered his hands.

"That's it," he said. "If we're lucky. If I've guessed right we might get something but I warn you now the odds are against it. All we can do it wait."

Wait as the signal flew at the speed of light towards the probe—3 long minutes, then to wait again as long for the answering transmission to return. Wait as somewhere outside the hut, high in the air, a giant roared its fury.

"What the hell—?" Frazer looked upwards. Like them all he had become accustomed to the sound for a regular lunch but this was different. "Christ! It sounds like a bomb!"

It was a bomb and Spragg flung himself down as he heard the thin, shrilling whine of falling debris. Somewhere high about the complex a launch had gone wrong. The vessel had exploded, venting all its fuel in a savage gush of flame and sound, which sent the torn fragments of its construction and load hurtling to all sides to rain down like a mass of jagged shrapnel.

An accident which had been inevitable from the beginning and Spragg felt his bowels turn to water as the thin, chilling sounds came nearer, aimed directly at him so that he cringed and tried to press himself harder against the floor, to press beyond it into the ground below, the shielding dirt.

To wait, quivering, until the world collapsed in sound and fury.

CHAPTER 16

"Mal?" The face was a blur but he could see the glint of golden hair. "Mal! Can you hear me? Mal!"

Fumes stung his nostrils and something stabbed at his arm and, suddenly, Spragg's vision cleared and he could see the woman at his side, the crisp uniform.

"Anne!"

"Of course. Who else did you expect would be here when you finally decided to wake up? How do you feel?"

"Lousy."

"A launch missed out," she said. "It was heading straight out to sea when it exploded. Bits flew everywhere and the hut you were in was hit by a part of the main engine. The roof caved in and they dug you out from under it." Pausing she added, "One of the tanks hit a hut in the enlisted man's sector. It still held fuel. The bulldozers are filling in the hole now."

"The load?"

"Fuel, supplies, water, tanked air. The nuke was safe-loaded. They're looking for the segments now."

"Anne—"

"You've nothing to worry about," she said comfortingly. "Some ribs broken, loss of blood, slight internal damage to lungs and liver, bruised pelvis, cracked bone in left leg, severe contusions to hips and stomach, multiple lacerations, concussion, shock and strained ligaments."

"That all?"

"We had to remove a kidney. Don't worry—the other one is fine. All you need to do is lie there and rest for a few weeks. We've used the latest techniques and you're healing fast."

He said, "The others?"

Frazer, like himself, was in hospital but with relatively minor injuries. Lauter had lost an eye. Sam Harvey was in intensive care with a ruptured spleen. Aldcock had been lucky and had collected only bruises. Frieda had died on her way to the hospital.

Spragg thought about her when Anne had left and darkness signalled the coming of night. He ached but drugs had killed most of his pain and those same drugs had made him a little light-headed. The mercy of modern medicine, he thought, the things given to those who had no further hope of life and so had no fear of addiction. The least the doctors could do for those who had ruined their bodies in an effort to save the lives of those who now tended them. Drugs which, perhaps, he shouldn't have been given but which Anne had supplied.

Frieda Osten—dead. Where had she gone? What had become of all that painfully acquired knowledge? Was life nothing but an endless joke in bad taste?

If the planets are inhabited then surely Earth must be their Hell!

Who had said that? Where had he read it? When?

The greyness closed in as he tried to remember, the cloud of painless detachment filled with bright images that enfolded him and carried him to a new bright world where Irene came to him and they were young again.

A week later Spragg refused his medication. "No."

"Why not?" Anne stood with the tray in her hand, the syringe, the swabs and pills.

"I want to get out of here. There's work to be done—"

"And others are doing it." She looked down at him shaking her head. "Your body needs rest and time to heal. Try walking now and you'll collapse. You could rip open the incision and haemorrhage. Damn it, Mal, get some sense!"

He glared at her. "How long must I stay here?"

"Five weeks, maybe six. Just get used to it, Mal, and stop acting like a spoiled child."

Frazer came to visit him during the third week. He limped and one cheek was puckered with an angry wound and a bandage made a turban on his head but otherwise he seemed normal.

Sitting he said, "You heard about Frieda?"

"Yes."

"A marvellous woman. Gone. The goddamned waste!" One hand clenched where it rested on his knees. "We were close, you know that? It wasn't just sex though she made that that wonderful. We thought alike and enjoyed the same things. She used to read me poetry and we played mathematical games. Hell, I was even learning German so as to be able to tell her I loved her in her own language. God, how I loved her!" Frazer blinked and looked away. After a moment he said, "I'm sorry, Mal. I guess you don't want to hear all that."

"It's all right, Harry. I understand." The man had needed to talk, to get it off his chest. Spragg heaved himself up in the bed. The bruises, lacerations and contusions had mostly healed as had the broken ribs and leg but the wound in his back continued to bother him and, at times, he spat blood. "How's it going? The work, I mean."

"The probe was a bust as you probably know. The records were hit by the wreckage so all we have is what we saw and can remember. They've sent out another probe—a souped-up missile adapted for the job, but it won't hit for a while yet." Frazer snorted his anger. "The fool! Trust the military to louse things up. Lauter should have got the spectrogram while he had the chance!"

He hadn't and it was no good crying over spilt milk. The new probe would do the job. Spragg said as much and Frazer nodded reluctant agreement.

"It's a matter of time," he said. "We need every minute we can get. Before I can determine a firing sequence I need to know what I'm shooting at. Ice, rock, nickel-iron, lead—it makes a difference."

But did it? Spragg thought about it after Frazer had left. The man was a specialist; a civil-engineer trained in the application of atomic power to cut channels, level hills, gouge tunnels through mountains. In such cases he would need to know the nature of the material he had to deal with. None of that applied to Thor. All that was needed was to kick the mass from its present path. Ice or iron—the basic difference lay only in the relative densities. It took less force to move a bladder filled with air than one filled with water.

That night, drugged, he dreamt of giants playing billiards using planets as balls.

* * * *

The new probe reached Thor at zero minus 35. Spragg, dressed, strapped in a web of bandages, weak but grimly determined gripped the arms of his wheelchair as Anne pushed him through the passages of the hospital and outside. She looked tired, red passion-bites showing on her neck, dark smudges circling her eyes. Spragg wondered if it was the drugs he'd been given or a sour jealousy coupled with his present inadequacy that made her seem less attractive than before.

He winced as the chair dropped over a kerb. "That hurt!"

"Sorry."

Like her face her voice revealed fatigue and he felt a sudden shame as he noted the thin lines meshing the corners of her eyes, the bruised appearance of her mouth. She was doing her best and who was he to blame her? Should a man be angry at the sun for shining on others than himself?

She swung the vehicle so as to avoid another minor crater. "Things aren't what they were."

An understatement—the installation looked as if it had been in a war. On all sides dumped and discarded containers lay in mounded confusion. The roads were scarred and pitted with the churn of wheels and tractors. Prefabricated huts stood huddled as if aware of the slums they appeared to be. Wind blown trash had drifted against every obstruction. The air stank with the smell of burning.

As with the equipment so the men. They moved in stained uniforms, red-eyed, bearded, drugged against fatigue as they fought their battle against time. A battle that produced too many casualties as Spragg well knew. He watched sombrely as an ambulance passed them heading towards the hospital, the crude extensions which ringed it. Another man with a broken limb, acid-seared lungs, chemical burns to face or eyes, fingers missing, internal organs ruptured or a mind gone under ceaseless strain.

"Anne, will—" He broke off as a siren wailed form far across the area and cringed as, in the distance, a launch spouted fire as it headed up into the air. Another load bound for space but would it make it? Would it veer, break from control, run wild? The fear died as the flame dwindled and he looked at his hands where they gripped the arms of his chair, the knuckles gleaming white beneath the skin.

"Mal?"

"Nothing." What was the point in asking her for a date? "I was going to ask if this trip will take long?"

"Five minutes. Relax."

Most were strangers but there were faces he knew; Lauter with a patch over his missing eye, Frazer, scarred but with his bandage set at a rakish angle, Aldcock who smiled and came forward to relieve Anne of the burden of the wheelchair.

"Nurse, you look marvellous! Did this crumb give you any trouble?"

Smiling she shook her head.

"Lucky for you, Mal. This girl's a friend of mine." Aldcock saw Spragg's expression. "Something wrong?"

"No." With an effort Spragg managed to control his jealousy. Aldcock had been up and capable while Spragg had been lying helpless in his bed. Well, to hell with it, he wasn't helpless now. "Help me up out of this."

"No, Mal!" Anne gripped his shoulder. "You stay in the chair or I'll take you back to the hospital." To Aldcock she said, "See he doesn't do anything stupid. I'll come back for him or send someone for him when he's ready to return."

"You aren't staying?"

"No. There's nothing I can do here and it's no time to slack." Bending over the chair she kissed Spragg on the cheek and whispered, "Be good, lover, and get well real soon. Remember, I'm waiting."

Aldcock said as she left, "That's a beautiful girl, Mal. You're a real, lucky bastard. You know that?"

"I know it." Spragg inched his chair towards the end of the room, the big screen hanging against the wall. "How long now to wait?"

Thor was as he remembered having seen it before; a huge, enigmatic lump of material, the surface glistening, marred only by the slowly oscillating patch of darker substance. The probe, he guessed, was at a greater distance, added amplification bringing the invader close. A guess verified by Lauter as he took his place beneath the screen.

"For those of you who've seen this before the probe is an adapted missile fitted with a projectile tube which can fire self-propelled thermite shells. For those who are with us for the first time this is Thor now at a distance of approximately 15,000,000 miles. In exactly 35 days it will hit the Earth unless we are able to deflect it. The purpose of this exercise is to determine, if possible, it's constituents. We shall do this by firing a thermite projectile at it and thus causing a portion of it to turn incandescent. The luminous vapour thus created will be recorded on a spectroscope. From the arrangement of the Fraunhofer Lines we shall be able to discover what kind of material forms the planetoid."

An explanation unnecessary to the majority of those present but Spragg guessed some of the strangers must be visiting politicians or others of high influence who needed to be put in the picture.

The image on the screen wavered and blurred. The signals coming over those millions of miles of emptiness, battered by the solar wind, affected by the impact of stray atoms, the magnetic field of the Earth itself, the mess of electronic 'noise' which clothed the planet. To get reception at all was in the nature of a miracle.

And then, as another technician had reported on the previous occasion, the man said, "We're getting a pull of some kind. Zero-magnetic field but we're getting a pull."

Frazer said, "Fire the projectiles! For Christ's sake, Colonel, don't let's louse up this chance too!"

A comment Lauter ignored as he snapped to the man at the board, "Fire one projectile!"

Spragg leaned forward in his chair his eyes intent on the screen. The command would take 80 seconds to reach the probe and it would take as long again before they could be certain it had been obeyed. A long time during which the image grew larger to suddenly reveal, to one side of the dark patch, a scintillating spot of brilliance.

"Got it!" Frazer shouted his relief. "Now try and hit the patch!"

A small target and one the projectile missed as, far to one side, another burst of radiant energy sprang into being. On companion screens rainbows flared to life; wide-banded spectrums marked with the dark Fraunhofer Lines. The spectroscopic images from each of the test-sites and, as far as Spragg could tell, identical.

"Hydrogen, iron, helium, sodium!" Aldcock read the lines as if he were reading a book. "Cobalt, lithium, Thorium? Yes, Thorium—nothing heavy as yet. Nickel and gold." He swore as the spectrums flickered. "What's happening?"

The probe was beyond control. Spragg heard the sharp interplay between Lauter and the technicians as he stared at the image on the screen. It grew larger, spread to dominate the area, passed beyond it, blurred now, fuzzy, details lost as it neared too closely to the scanners, then, abruptly, was gone.

"Damn!" Aldcock glared at the blank screens. "Well, it's no real loss. We'll have the recordings. What do you think, Harry?"

"A mix," said Frazer. "At least as far as I could see. Would you say it was normal, Earth-type composition?"

"Could be."

"What kind of an answer is that?" Frazer appealed to Spragg. "What is it, Mal?"

"I don't know and neither does Bud. The spectroscopic lines will have to be checked against known elements and even then we'll only know what is to be found on the surface. But it isn't made of ice or solid lead or iron or anything too alien. Basically it's a chunk of rock with an assortment of various elements in an unfamiliar ratio. If you want to know how it should be treated I'd suggest you handle it as you would basalt."

An answer and Frazer was apparently satisfied with it but other questions remained. Had they done more than test the surface patina? Was the mass homogeneous? And, above all, why had both probes been affected by a tremendous attraction?

* * * *

"A mascon?" Over the phone Ogden's voice echoed his bewilderment. "What the devil's that?"

"No one knows just what a mascon is," Spragg explained. "The name was coined for them way back when the Apollo landings set up seismometers on the surface of the Moon. Scientists were puzzled at the quakes that happened at frequent intervals and speculated they had to be caused by lumps of highly dense matter buried far beneath the surface. With me so far?"

"Yes."

"For a lump of matter to have a high gravitational attraction it must be incredibly dense. Both probes were pulled towards Thor when they shouldn't have been. There is no possibility of magnetic attraction. The planetoid isn't large enough to have exerted such a pull if it's merely a mass of solid rock laced with heavy elements so there has to be another explanation. I'm positive I've found it. Somewhere, buried below the surface, there has to be a mascon."

"Which, as you admit, no one knows anything about."

"I know it's there," snapped Spragg angrily. "Something has to be inside Thor for it to have exerted such an attraction. Call it a lump of neutronium if you want— God alone knows what a mascon is, but stop being a bloody fool and listen. You wanted information—well I'm giving it to you."

"Is it important?"

"Run out on the field," said Spragg dryly. "Take a kick at a football. What happens if someone's filled it with concrete during the night?" He listened. "Yes, now you've got it. If Thor contains a mascon, and I'm certain it does, then the planetoid is of a far higher density that we'd imagined. To knock it aside is going to take all the force we've got. So if we, or anyone, has been holding anything back get on their necks and make them cough up. You understand?" His voice rose a little. "I was at the UN, remember, and I can guess how those bastards intend to work. So get with it, man! Get with it!"

"This can be verified?"

"Yes. They know here already."

"Then leave it with me." Ogden added, in a softer tone, "Sorry to hear about you getting hurt. Better now?"

"I'll live. Have you any news of Irene? No?" Spragg felt himself slump. "Well, thanks for trying. If she should contact you—you know? Yes, of course, I'd forgotten. Do your best, eh? Thanks."

Hanging up he slumped against the side of the booth. No matter what happened now he'd done all in his power to do. Even to calling Ogden from an outside phone as he done before as they'd arranged before he'd come to Cape Canaveral. Cloak and dagger stuff, which he'd thought then and knew now to be utter nonsense.

He straightened, aware of watching eyes in the liquor store where he'd used the phone. The proprietor was suspicious. Spragg couldn't blame him. He must look like hell what with the drugs and hospitalisation not to mention the days of study during which he'd checked the records of both probes together with those from the space observatory. And the battle with red-tape in order to have certain tests and observations made hadn't helped either.

A horn blared from the street outside as he left the booth and headed towards the counter. "Give me Scotch," he ordered. Any brand." He found money and threw notes on the counter. "As much as the money will pay for. I'll see what my driver wants."

He was a big, beefy man with a red face and a shock of red hair beneath his stained uniform cap. He sat behind the wheel of the army truck on which Spragg had scrounged a lift.

He said, "Buster, I'm leaving. You coming or staying?"

"I'm waiting for a few bottles. I—" Spragg turned as the proprietor joined him at the door with his order.

"Good. Could you carry them to the truck for me, please?"

A mile down the road the driver sighed his satisfaction and handed the opened bottle back to Spragg. "Don't get me wrong, Prof. I'm not against you egg-heads. It's just that I got word there's trouble brewing at the gate. Some nuts wanting to give us a hard time. Leave it too long and I'd have had trouble getting back in time and I've a hot date with something special. You dig?"

"Sure." Spragg took a drink and handed back the bottle. "Keep it." The rest of his purchases he'd tucked about him.

"Uh, uh." The driver grunted as he slowed a little. "Look at the creeps!"

They were the usual crowd for whom demonstrations had become a way of life.

"You know what they want? They want us to stop work. They don't like what we're doing. The bloody fools!"

A man carried a placard adorned with a skull and the words DEFY NOT GOD! Another bore the appeal to REJOICE IN THE LORD! Spragg read THE END IS NIGH! On a placard thrust at his face. A girl with a mane of tangled hair and a face blotched with acne screamed, "Sinners! You work for Satan!"

The driver was fuming, affected by the alcohol he'd nipped during the journey, conscious of the passage of time and the prospect of missing his date. The truck lunged forward, horn blaring, lights flashing as it roared towards the crowd blocking its path. Spragg saw grim faces, eyes suddenly terrified, a mad scramble of those with the sense to recognise their danger. A woman, more dedicated than the rest, stood with arms outstretched. A willing martyr to the cause.

Spragg switched off the ignition as a man jerked the woman to one side. The engine backfired as he again twisted the key, the report echoing like synthetic gunfire. Ahead the crowd abruptly thinned. To one side of the road a gaunt, bearded character flung a bottle that starred the windscreen with a mesh of fracture-lines. The placard at his side read GOD IS LOVE!

CHAPTER 17

The bottles Spragg had bought were for his birthday, which he celebrated a few days later. The cake bore a single candle and rested on the chest of drawers of his old room. Looking at it Waldemar said, "One candle? Mal, my friend, I know you must be older than that."

"I've only had one birthday—all the others were anniversaries. Come in, Harry! You too, Bud! Carl, make some room."

Waldemar had arrived early and he dutifully moved up the bed. Spragg, as host, occupied the chair and waved at the bottles he'd set out on the floor beneath the window. Glasses and water rested next to the cake. Mixers were stacked next to a tub of ice on the floor.

Frazer said as he handed over a bottle. "Many happy returns, Mal. Hope you like gin."

Aldcock said, as he handed over his own contribution, "Why didn't you hold this shindig in the club?"

"Too many strangers."

"The hospital then?"

"Too many nurses and doctors telling me I mustn't drink." Spragg helped himself to whisky, soda and ice. "They must think I'm going to live forever."

He settled back, nursing the drink as others crowded into the room. Lauter had brought a friend, Major Judd, an expert in space medicine who favoured pungent cigars. A nurse and two WACs joined in and Spragg was appreciative when, complaining of about the heat, they removed their tunics.

Zach Cheyne thrust his head into the room and sniffed. "Who the hell is smoking old socks? They—sorry, Major, didn't see you. Hi, Mal, how goes it?"

"I'm fine."

"You look like death. Here, take a shot of Old Grandad, it'll warm you up." As Spragg obeyed Cheyne said, "I was saving that for a special occasion. I guess we're near it, uh?"

"Close, Zach, we've 22 days to go." Spragg studied the contents of his glass. "That's why I'm celebrating my birthday. I may not have time later on."

"None of us will have time. How about it, Colonel? When do we launch?"

Lauter hesitated then said, "We haven't finally decided yet."

"We've had problems," said the Major. "Things we didn't expect." He remembered the Colonel. "I'm sorry, sir, but—"

"Go right ahead." Lauter eased the patch covering his missing eye.

"Well, we've had trouble like I said. Accidents which shouldn't have happened and there's been some nasty incidents with the Angels. I guess you know about that?" He grunted as Cheyne nodded. "Of course. You'd be the first to get the information. A man can't crap up there without it registering on your dials."

"That's no longer quite true, Major. There's too many up there and we've too much to do monitoring the launches. We don't even monitor the Kamikaze."

"Them!" Judd swallowed his drink and held out his glass for more. Frazer provided it. "You ever wonder what makes a man want to throw away his life? Can you understand that?"

"Yes," said Spragg. "They call them martyrs."

"Those who aren't committing suicide but who are sacrificing their lives for a cause." Waldemar nodded. "I've always thought they had to be a little crazy."

"They are," said Judd. "They have to be to deny the survival instinct but the trouble is that instinct won't be denied. Once the euphoria of volunteering wears off it gains strength and begins to show itself in the form of diminished performance. The volunteer becomes prone to accidents and psychosomatic ills. He doesn't want to back out and he doesn't want to die, so anything which offers an honourable way out of the predicament is just fine."

Waldemar said, "I understand what you are saying, Major, but surely this was not wholly unexpected? Don't you have means at your disposal to correct the situation?"

"Of course, we have drugs and hypnotic conditioning and both have been used to maintain the state of euphoria. But to put it bluntly we can't keep the Kamikaze hanging around too long. We either use them or lose them." Judd emptied his glass. "Could I try some of that Old Granddad?"

"Sure." Spragg did the honours "How about the suits, Major?"

"You really want to know?" Judd glanced at the WACs. "Well, I guess they're broad-minded." They needed to be as he went into detail as to what life was really like cooped up in a personal coffin; the stink, the itches, sores, cramps, irritations and above all the claustrophobia to which none was immune. How long could a man remain sane once convinced he was buried alive? He ended, "So that's another problem. How long can we keep a man effective while in a suit?"

"The Angels—"

"Are only in suits for a short stretch at a time. How long do you figure the Kamikaze will have to wear them?"

Frazer said, "Burn at 1-G for 14 minutes and we will have matched Thor's velocity. To meet the deadline we should begin shooting this time tomorrow."

"Which means at least ten days in free fall while coasting to the rendezvous." Judd frowned through the smoke of his cigar. "I wouldn't like to guess how many of them would be functional at the end of that time."

"Would it matter?" The nurse had a pretty face but there was nothing wrong with her brain. "Once the missiles are close will they need further guidance?"

"Unfortunately yes." Lauter glanced meaningfully at Spragg. "That's one of the troubles we were talking about. Recent discoveries have aggravated the problem and we'll have to guide those missiles right up until impact."

"Couldn't we halve the journey time?" suggested Spragg. "Extend the burn or double the acceleration. The man should be able to stand 2-Gs."

"They probably can," agreed Lauter. "I'm not so sure about the units. A longer burn is probably the best solution. We can arrange for extra fuel to be carried in bowsers accompanying the units and so maintain the thrust. It'll have to be something like that—I can't mess with the basic design at this stage."

Spragg leaned back in the chair as the party dropped shop and concentrated on enjoyment. He felt sick and a little dizzy and his back hurt when he moved. His urine was an unhealthy colour and he wondered if his remaining kidney was functioning as it should.

Listening to the hum of conversation, the laughter from the man cuddling the WACs, the one with his arm high around the nurse, Spragg wondered what was going on in the real, political world. Waldemar could tell him and would if he insisted but it was easier to guess and, in any case, Carl was busy talking to Lauter. The big powers were now, Spragg guessed, showing their teeth. Either the small nations would cooperate to the full or, if the world survived, they would be crushed. And with the threats would come deals; all South America, Canada, Greenland and the Caribbean to the United States. Russia to spread west to the Atlantic, swallowing all Europe, the Balkans and Middle East. China to get Japan, India, Indonesia and Australia. Africa would be split and serve as the arena for future tripartite wars.

The hammer of God splitting the world in more ways than one.

"Mal?" Spragg jerked as Frazer touched his shoulder aware that he had fallen asleep. "You all right?"

"I'm fine." The sleep had done him good. Spragg looked around the room. Everyone had gone aside from Frazer. "What happened?"

"You just sat back and went quiet and we all thought you'd passed out. So we just got on with the party. Those who were lucky sneaked off with the girls and the rest of us talked shop for a while. I've stayed to make sure you're okay."

Frazer found two glasses and loaded them with Scotch, soda and ice.

As Spragg took one he asked: "Did they decide when to launch?"

"No, but it won't be tomorrow. Didn't you hear the discussion before you went to sleep? Lauter's waiting until they are ready upstairs." Frazer jerked his thumb skywards. "When they are he'll decide on the time and date."

"Worked out your schedules?"

"A long time ago. Pick a date and time and number of missiles and I'll tell you when to send then, how fast they should go and where they should be aimed." Finishing his drink Frazer turned towards the door. I'd better leave now. You sure you're OK?"

"Don't worry about me."

Frazer paused and looked back from the passage. "Were you really celebrating your birthday?"

"No," said Spragg. "My wedding anniversary."

* * * *

On zero minus 17 Earth launched its defence against Thor. It was too close and an unhappy compromise but the best which could be achieved. To increase the thrust would be to endanger the units, to launch too soon would be to risk the Kamikaze, to wait would be to let Thor come far too near.

Facts and figures, which every technician knew as did mathematician. As did Barry Dunne.

He waited in the revolving can that had been his home for the past 19 days. He was stripped and naked aside from shorts and his chocolate skin held a faint sheen of sweat. To one side lay his suit every piece checked and rechecked by both himself and the attendant who would help him into it. He didn't talk. He didn't want company. He just wanted to sit and lean against the metal wall and let his mind drift as the grab-rope leading to the airlock drifted in the zero gravity at the centre of the can. Like he would drift when, later, mounted on his assembly, he would be thrust into space to drift for 180 hours before destruction.

He was quite calm. Even when a man sitting to his left down the can began to croon a wailing chant he didn't look in his direction. The chant was as meaningless as the soft hiss of air from the tanks of his suit, the shuffle of feet over the metal of the can, the rustle of clothing, the coughs, snorts, gasps of his fellows. Noise that had no power to register on his mind at this time. He could think of nothing, feel nothing not directly related to his mission.

And the things he had seen and heard and experienced while in space had less impact than the childhood memories of tears and laughter.

"Ready Barry?" The attendant leaned forward a little. "Time to go, man. Up and in your shell."

Up and into the exoskeleton of metal and plastic and multi-layered fabric, the internal mesh and the braces and supports, the pipes fitted into the orifices of his body, the water nipple placed where his lips could find it as was the nipple dispensing the flavoured paste containing his food and drugs, and then the helmet and tanks and the air softly hissing and the mechanical voice coming from his helmet radio.

"All Kamikaze 34 through 78 report for assignment. Check in at the flashing green beacon."

An order repeated as Barry jumped and gripped the rope and led the way towards the airlock and through it and out into space. Out to where a green jewel winked with a soft pulsation and a grotesque construction of tanks and struts and flaring venturis and grimly menacing containers marked and starred with warning symbols waited with others to receive their human cargo.

"Askew and Clark—number 52. Elcar and Harris—number 53. Cook and Manning—number 34."

Men drifting like wingless birds, sparkling reaction pistols wafting them on their way to reach the units which they would ride, to settle, to seat themselves, to strap in to wait.

Dunne had drawn Fred Kika, an ethnic brother, as his companion. He barely remembered the man and took his place without attempting to communicate. A silence shared by them all now that the moment had come.

"U33—go!" A pause then, "U34—go!"

A stream of numbers at spaced intervals answered as engines flared to life and tongues of flame thrust the units out and away from Earth. Flame that ate the fuel even though reaching only a 1-G acceleration. A thrust that lasted less than 10 minutes.

Dunne felt the artificial gravity thrust him back against his support and held him as if he lay on his back looking up at the starry universe, the guide-screen before him displaying the dot that was his target-star. It was covered by another of a different colour and even as he watched it drifted to one site. A touch and it was back in place again only to drift to the other side. Another adjustment and the dots matched and held.

"Neat." The voice from his direct link to his companion was soft and precise. "You've got the touch, man. And the control too."

"I've got it."

And he wanted to keep it—while he did the guiding he was more than just a passenger or a safeguard in case of an emergency. Then he remembered why they were riding double, the reason they had been given.

"I'll maintain control for the first spell," he said. "After we refuel you can sleep if you want."

"Maybe. Any sign of the bowser?"

Dunne stared ahead seeing nothing but the blaze of stars that filled the heavens. Automatically he checked the guide-screen and felt satisfaction when he saw the coloured dot matched to the target-star. As he looked something dark occluded a glittering point.

"There!" Kika lifted an arm as he pointed. "See it? Over to the right and above."

It grew as they watched, becoming a grotesque creature of the void, tanks and struts and venturis the whole dotted with blazing lights, a cabin that housed the crew not on watch.

Dunne turned, seeing the other units that had left with him spread before and behind and to either side. An armada coasting now, identified by the winking beacons set high above where the pilots sat. As he watched a unit jetted fire to realign itself. Another, far to one side, was obviously in some kind of trouble.

Looking back towards the bowser he saw the flare of reaction pistols as suited men streamed from the structure and an open craft containing Angels head towards the straying unit. The ether was suddenly filled with a blur of voices.

"U38—for Christ's sake stay on course! U41—get ready to receive Angels. Mack! Harry! Get moving or we'll lose the bastard!"

Sections drifted away from the main bulk of the bowser; tanks handled by men, impelled by open craft. They reached the drifting units and steadied, matching velocities and direction, the men working with frantic haste as they touched.

"Steady! Watch what you're doing you fool! Hold firm, damn you! Move!"

Dunne felt his own unit shift a little as the Angels made contact. They ignored both him and Kika as they freed couplings, adjusted pipes, activated the pumps that filled the empty tanks. When the task was done a man thrust his helmet against Dunne's.

"Watch the bowser. When you see the top signal-light blink red-green-red blast ahead. Burn for seven minutes precisely. Got that? Seven minutes then out and coast. Use the rest of the fuel as and when necessary to hold position. Luck!"

Then he was gone and Dunne watched the guide-screen, the now parted dots.

"What did he say?" Kika was curious. He grunted when Dunne told him. "Top signal light, eh? You take it or shall I?"

"I'll take it. You keep watch in case some of the others come too close."

A risk and one to be guarded against—when he fired the tubes Dunne wanted a clear stretch ahead. He watched for the signal, adjusting the controls to match the dots again as he waited. He saw red, green, red again and felt the push of his back-support as he fired the engines. A push that lasted until the overall velocity had built up 6 miles a second.

And then there was nothing left to do but wait.

Wait and keep the dots matched and try to forget the hiss of air in the helmet, the pressure of the suit and the itches and burns and cramps to come. To forget the stunning vista of the universe and the emptiness all around and most of all not to remember that this was all he would ever know for the rest of his life.

* * * *

In his vision Thor began to dance and Spragg closed his eyes, seeing the movement against his closed lids, retinal flashes ringed with smaller points of fire, the flares of jetting rockets carrying men to their chosen sacrifice.

It had been something like the ritual dance of insects, he thought. The courtship flight of bees when the drones fertilise the queens then to fall and die. Or of fireflies painting elaborate pictures of light against the darkness of night as they wove minute flares of brief colour. The units had looked like that on the monitor screens as they had shifted in their elaborate saraband. It was hard to remember they had been fashioned in haste by the hands of men, each carrying a pair of heroes.

He looked again at the relay from the observatory. Thor was moving as predicted. But now tons of material were heading towards it and they would attract it with the same force as it would attract them.

But Thor, while big and heavy was not a planet and some slight deviation could be expected. But not as yet. If at all it would come later—more figures to add to the rest, more predictions and reports to be made.

It seemed at times as if the world was nothing but a mass of dancing figures with feet drumming on his brain.

"Mal?" Frazer had stepped into his room and was looking at the screens. "Well," he said, "it's done. The units are on their way. Now it's all up to the Kamikaze."

Frazer rubbed a hand over his stubbled chin. "We're doing it all wrong," he said. "We should have landed and drilled holes and set charges around the circumference and set them to blow all together so as to split the bastard in two. They would have passed over us; one section over each pole. If fragments had hit they'd have impacted ice."

Spragg said, patiently, "You're tired, Harry, or you wouldn't talk such crap. Drill holes—how many and how deep? A mile? Say they were a couple of miles apart you'd need something like 18,000 and as many atomic charges. And even then you'd have only ripped off the outer crust. What about the mascon?"

"If it's there."

"It's there." Spragg looked again at the relay. "I guess we'd find one or more in every planet or large mass of material. They could be responsible for its formation. Drawing atoms to itself over the eons or collecting them from the formation-clouds in the beginning. We know they are in the Moon and I'll bet they are in Earth too."

"Maybe." Frazer shook his head. "Holes," he mused. "Drilled with a laser. A mile deep and thousands of them. I guess I must be a little crazy. We couldn't have done that in a generation. Hell, we can't even do it here on Earth... I'm bushed," he admitted. "And you look as if you should be in bed."

The room was as he had left it two days before, the bed still holding the imprint of his body. A hidden bottle yielded six ounces of Scotch and he nursed the drink as he lay on the bed. He should, he knew, undress and get under the covers but the effort would be too much and it was better just to lie and rest and take warming sips and let the comfort of the spirit dull his nagging aches.

"To you Reverend," he murmured lifting his glass. "Wherever you are."

Destiny—who could defy it? Things happened because they must and none could know the reason. Yet Thor could provide the answer to everything. The doom promised by ancient Prophets and written in the sacred books. The punishment of God delivered by the hammer of His wrath. And against it they had only the fire of Satan. The fire and the blood of sacrifice.

* * * *

Looking at the glittering stars he let his mind wander among a plethora of bright images induced by the subtle drugs in his food, the hypnotic conditioning of his mind. One that stimulated euphoria, but a conditioning that was wearing thin.

Dunne sucked air and took a sip of water and looked at the guide-screen. The dots were far apart and he hit the controls to bring them back in line. The flare from the jets thrust fingers of flame into space and he felt the unit move beneath him.

"Cut or burn!" Kika's voice was thin, edged with harsh dissonance, the words a threnody of remembered pain. Dunne listened and felt himself grow tense with sympathetic rage. Kika was his ethnic brother. His anguish was that of them both.

"Fred! Fred Kika! What's the matter with you, man? Grab hold now. You're raving!"

"My head feels funny. I keep having the same dream. Fires and men with hoods and my grandpappy nailed to the log. Cut or burn!"

"It's just a dream, Fred. Look ahead now and tell me what you see. Anything in the way we're going?"

Lights from the beacons of other units as they slowly converged. Shapes that occluded the stars and presented baroque outlines. A suited figure that waved and Dunne felt the warmth of companionship.

Kika said, breathing deeply, "Barry, I don't want to die. I want to quit right now. To hell with the others. Let's turn this thing and head back home. I want out."

Out of the chafing suits and personal coffins. Out of the misery they had squatted in for days now. Too many days and too much strain even for the drugs and dedication to surmount. Back on Earth in the bunker a technician who had been monitoring the conversation waved at his superior.

"Trouble on U39. One of the pilots is acting up. Shall I—?" He gestured towards a red button.

"How far to strike?" The officer pursed his lips at the answer. "Give it as long as you can. Once they actually see Thor things could even out."

Madness replaced by dedication. The urge to survive smothered by the impulse to sacrifice.

Dunne said, "Take it easy now, Fred. We'll be remembered for all time. We're saving the world! All the kids in the kraals and those in the fields and all the brothers in the ghettos and those in school in Africa and all the other places we've heard about. Millions, billions of them. Give it time and we'll be the ones in power. But we have to give them that time."

Time and pride and all the things they could win by his sacrifice. By his and the others now riding closer as, ahead, a mote swelled into a thing of brightness, a disc, a ball.

"There it is!" Dunne pointed. "Thor!"

The Hammer of God bright with reflected glory and lying before them helpless to their attack. Their goal and target. Their tomb.

"No!" Kika twisted in his straps. "I don't want to die! Let's all get together and dump everything but the fuel and ride back and—"

The words died as he died. Ending as the destructive charge incorporated in his suit exploded as the distant technician pressed the red button. Dunne heard a dull thud and saw his companion sag as he fell silent. Now his would be the task and his the glory. His name remembered for all time as the saviour of the world.

But he must keep the dots in line. The dots in line...in line...in line...

Matching them as the unit swept on, now caught in the gravitational attraction of Thor. It and those with it, a stream of units loaded with nuclear destruction, merging, riding close, heading towards the glowing orb of their target. Faster...faster...faster...

Laughing as he dissolved in flame.

CHAPTER 18

The house was just as he remembered. The lawn was ragged with the scars of winter, dead grasses lying like thin bones over the new-born green, the green itself dotted with the bright points of early flowers. The curtains, he noticed, were drawn.

The gate squealed as Spragg pushed it open, closing with a clang as his shoes rasped over the gravel of the drive. He was almost at the house when he saw the car parked on the far side.

Dropping his bag Spragg headed towards it, hearing a rustle from the shrubbery shielding the rear of the house as he touched the bonnet. The engine was cold. He tested the doors and found them locked. The back of the vehicle was empty aside from two cans of petrol and another, sealed, of oil. Turning Spragg headed towards the rear of the house then froze as he saw the double-eye of a shotgun aimed directly at his face.

"Hold it!" The shape behind the gun was hidden by the shrubbery. "Who the hell are you?"

"I live here. Now just turn around and head back to the road and just keep walking or I'll blow your head off. Got it?"

"Live here? You bastard—I own this place!"

"You own it?" The voice changed. "Spragg? Is that you, Professor?"

"It is."

"Christ, man, you look awful!" Leaves rustled as Sam Eagan pushed his way through the shrubbery, gun lowered, eyes wide.

"I feel it." Spragg swayed, fighting giddiness. "Have you got a drink?"

He nursed it sitting in the chair facing the television in the living room, grateful for the fire Eagan had switched on, the pure malt doing more than the glowing bars to ease his chill. "What are you doing here, Sam?"

"I grew tired of city life and fancied a little rest and quiet. So I packed up a few things and came out here. I didn't know where else to go."

"And that?" Spragg looked at the shotgun.

"I borrowed it. I thought I'd find a rabbit or something."

"In the shrubbery late in the afternoon?"

"I'm a city-dweller. How the hell would I know the best time to hunt?" Eagan took a sip of his malt whisky. "You want me to leave?"

"No."

"Good." Eagan relaxed. "There are some little luxuries in the fridge and I've put the rest of this where it will come to no harm." He lifted his glass. "Your health!"

"Cheers!"

Spragg felt himself relax. He was glad Eagan was here, he took the chill from an empty house and he had always liked company when he drank.

Eagan said, "How was it, Mal? At the end, I mean."

"It wasn't nice."

"I heard a few things. In my job word gets around and not much stays secret. The pilots died, didn't they?"

"The Kamikaze. Yes, Sam, they all died."

Burning like moths in a flame as they went, laughing, singing, praying, and screaming to their destruction. Spragg remembered what he had seen and heard; the echoes of murder, the ravings, the pleas from those who had weakened, the courage of those who had remained dedicated but one way or another all had died.

Sparkles in his glass evoked flashes of memory. Frazer retching. Cheyne babbling like a child with tears streaming from his eyes. Aldcock standing, beating his head against a wall, blood smearing his face.

A technician who had killed with the pressure of his red button solemnly commending the souls of the departed to God.

And the flame that had burned his eyes. The feeling when he had staggered from the bunker to lean against a wall, trembling, sweat dewing his face. Needing a drink. Needing to sleep. Needing to forget.

"Bad," said Eagan. "But at least you managed to get back home. Land at Prestwick?"

"Yes. I managed to hire a car and driver to bring me here."

"You missed the big towns? You were smart. Things were getting nasty when I left Carlisle a couple of days ago. Riots, arson, looting." Eagan poured them both fresh drinks. "There's no reason for them to panic. They've been told over and over there's nothing to worry about. Listen."

He pressed the television remote. Spragg looked at a bland face mouthing bland nothings. It was followed by his own in a clip taken from an early interview.

"For Christ's sake turn that crap off!"

He rose as Eagan obeyed and headed for the kitchen, A vial held the tablets he had been given and he swallowed three waiting for the drugs to diminish his pain.

"Mal?" Eagan called from the other room. "You all right?"

"Yes." The tablets were working.

"Want something to eat?"

"Just a sandwich." He stepped to one side as Eagan entered the kitchen.

Spragg looked at his reflection in a mirror. His eyes were smudged with dark circles and he seemed to have lost most of his hair and the skin was meshed with lines.

"I don't wonder you didn't recognise me," he said.

"When I heard the gate I just—"

"Decided to go hunting?"

"That's right." Eagan's gaze was steady. He finished making the sandwiches. "Let's go and eat."

They ate and sat and talked and drank some more of the malt. Spragg caught himself as, dozing, he almost fell from the chair.

"I'd better get to bed. Which room are you in?"

"The spare in the front. Mal, I—" Eagan broke off as the gate squealed. Snatching up the shotgun he moved towards the rear door. "This could be nothing but I'd better make sure. Just sit down and relax."

Minutes passed and then Spragg heard the sound of the door opening and footsteps as someone entered the house.

"Sam? Is that you?"

He rose as there was no answer and stepped to the door leading form the room and then froze.

"Hello, Mal," said Irene. "Welcome home!"

She looked a goddess, a dream as she stood illuminated by the dying light, a vagrant beam of the setting sun aureoling her hair and misting her face so that it seemed to glow. An illusion as Spragg discovered when he blinked at the smart in his eyes and found them moist with tears. But there was nothing false about the sudden weakness that gripped him, turning his legs to water so that he had to grip the jamb to prevent himself from falling.

"Mal!" She was at his side, arms firm in their support.

"I'm fine." He forced himself to straighten. "I just didn't expect to see you. Eagan—the bastard!"

"He meant well," she defended. "I was here when he arrived and there seemed no harm in letting him stay. He liked you and I guess that was recommendation enough. But he couldn't know how I felt about you so he warned me you were here."

"Warned you? With a shotgun?"

"He insists on guarding the place. Maybe he wants to feel he's earning the right to stay." Her eyes widened as she searched his face. "Mal, you're ill!"

"I'm all right. I was in an accident and in hospital for a while, that's all. And you?"

"Fine. Mal, are you sure?"

"I'll live as long as you—I promise. Let's sit down and have a drink and talk—Eagan?"

"He's staying outside."

A delicacy Spragg hadn't known the man possessed but was glad he did when, later, he and Irene sat on the couch in close and warm proximity.

"I returned just after Christmas," she explained. "After I'd quit there seemed no point in remaining in the States and, well, I got homesick. Or perhaps I just wanted to make certain that your bitch didn't get my home."

"Myrna lied, you know that?"

"I found out. Women of that type make enemies and some of them can be cruel. Mal, after I left did you—"

"I threw her out and tried to find you but you weren't to be found. So I joined up with Waldemar and others at Cape Canaveral. You remember Carl?" As she nodded he continued, "He told me about Myrna, what she was doing and who with. Then, at the end, he helped to get me back home."

"You should have brought him with you."

"He didn't want to come. He's got ideas of his own and is staying in the States." He added, "Irene, I love you."

She made no comment but her hand touched his own.

"I don't mean just want you, it goes deeper than that. I—" He swallowed. "When I saw you it was like being shot. That's what made me stagger. It was the last thing I expected."

But the one thing he had secretly hoped for—what else had drawn him back? Hurt he had run like an animal to its lair. Hurt, she had done the same.

She said, "You'd better get up to bed. A bath and a good sleep is what you need."

"I've done enough sleeping."

"A bath, then. It will relax you and maybe you could take a nap afterwards." Her smile was tremulous. "Please Mal. I don't want you to fall ill now that we're together again."

"Are we together, Irene?"

"Yes, darling. And if that bitch tries to come between us—"

"I'll break her neck and bury her in the back garden." Spragg kissed her gently on the cheek. "Irene! We must never be parted again!"

Footsteps crunched on the gravel outside and a dark shadow passed over the curtains.

"Sam! He's coming back!"

"To hell with him! Irene—"

"No!" She pushed him from her. "Later, my darling. Now go and get your bath and try to nap a while whilst I get us all something to ear."

"We have eaten."

"Sandwiches?" She glanced at the debris. "I'm talking about real food. Now hurry, Mal, and don't forget to rest."

"Which room shall I use?"

"My room," she said. "Our room."

She had changed it around and cleaned it, removing all traces of Myrna.

Stripped he bathed and sent his hand to make little waves as he soaked in the comforting water. The pills he had taken had combined with the alcohol to give a slight fuzziness to his senses.

Water splashed as he rose from the bath, little rivulets running over his torso. Dried he padded into the bedroom and donned shirt and slacks from the bag Irene had carried upstairs. The bath had relaxed him but he was not yet ready to lie down. Instead he wandered about the chamber, looking, probing, opening the wardrobe and seeing expensive furs and gowns, racks of shoes, coats and hats. Closing the doors he looked in the dresser and found a plethora of cosmetics, perfumes, unguents all of the best quality. Drawers held filmy lingerie, One held a small sheaf of unpaid bills.

He crossed to the window and opened the curtains to look at the dome of the observatory looming against the darkening sky. She must have been coming from it when Eagan had intercepted her to warn her of his presence. Had she been visiting old friends? Susan and even Hammond? Reilly wouldn't have known her from the old days but must have heard of her from the others. And there would be others; technicians and laboratory workers who would have made her welcome if they were still there.

Perhaps he should ask but he felt no inclination to visit the place where he had spent so many years. The curtains closed as he turned away and sprawled on the bed. Some light still filtered through where they had badly joined and he watched the glow on the ceiling, remembering other times in this very room when passion had ruled—but those times had been the product of lust, not love and, surely he could be forgiven his weaknesses.

He slept, drifting, seeing again the flame, the men dying, hearing their voices long seconds after they had been turned into ash. Knowing the sick, helpless despair.

"Mal?" Irene called to him through the closed door. "Are you awake?"

"I am now. I'll be right down."

Slipping on his shoes and jacket and headed downstairs. Eagan sat at one side of the table, Irene facing him at the other, the place of honour at the head reserved for himself. As he sat Spragg looked at what had been prepared, nostrils twitching to enticing smells.

"A banquet," he said. "Irene, this is wonderful!"

All the foods they had once yearned to taste but hadn't been able to afford now set with costly glass and silver. It was a part of what he had discovered; the expensive clothes, rare perfumes, trinkets and luxuries, which Irene had bought without regard for cost. A self-indulgence as was the food and wine.

Reading his face she said, "Yes, Mal. Yes."

The observatory, of course, they would know and would have told her. But Eagan?

"The truth, Mal," he said. "For God's sake tell us the truth. What happened out there? What went wrong?"

For answer Spragg rose and went to the big window and parted the curtain with a rasp of runners. It was there as he'd known it would be, larger now, smeared like a blood-stained thumbprint in the sky over the dome of the observatory. A sign and a portent that even now men were pointing at as they screamed their warnings of doom to come. Shouting louder than the lying newscasts, which still insisted there was nothing to fear.

"Behold the Hammer of God," said Spragg. "Once it was just a ball of rock and minerals a few hundred miles in diameter but we took care of that. We weren't satisfied to be crushed to death we had to improve on the punishment of the Lord. Poetic justice—the Reverend Aird Gulvain must be laughing himself sick wherever he is. We tried to kick God's messenger in the rear and it blew off in our face."

"Mal?"

"We sent everything we had against it," he said not looking at her. "All the nuclear devices we could get into space and send on their way. The Fire of Satan with the Devils of Hell to guide them. And they did the job. They got there. They let loose with all that man-made destruction—and Thor hit back. Thorium," he explained. "Cobalt, strontium, lithium. Heavy metals. So we hit it and burned it and caught it alight and turned Thor into a plasma. Now we don't have a rock to worry about. We have a cloud of gas 10,000 miles wide and over 1,000,000 degrees centigrade." He ended, bleakly, "We've got two days."

* * * *

Spragg woke late on the morning of the second day and lay thinking of the festivities of the night before; a feast which put his homecoming meal to shame. Their last supper, the last time they would have the chance the sit and talk and eat and drink through the long hours before dawn. Then to bed and to make passionate love and to lie and talk some more but this time about the little intimate things that held lovers close.

Turning he looked at Irene. She lay like a child with her knees bent and her face snuggled into the pillow one hand lifted to rest below her chin. She was sweating, her skin dewed with moisture and he drew back the covers to reveal the rounded whiteness of her shoulders, the enticing lines of her back.

As he kissed them he heard the shout followed by the blast of the shotgun twice repeated.

"Mal?" Irene jerked awake. "What was that?"

"Lie still." Spragg slipped from the bed and dressed in shirt, pants and shoes. "I'll see what's going on."

Eagan met him as he ran from the house. The man was scowling, his face blotched and marked with scratches; injuries Spragg hadn't noticed before.

"What happened?"

"Kids from the village coming to see what they could find. I yelled and gave them both barrels. I wasn't aiming at them but they couldn't know that." Eagan touched his scratched face. "I got this from the shrubbery."

A possibility but Spragg wondered why the man had wanted to fight his way through bushes. Why he was out in the first place when he had seemed so drunk when going to bed.

"You'd better go inside and get washed and tell Irene what happened," said Spragg. "Give me the gun and I'll look around."

It was an unaccustomed burden but if Eagan had done what he shouldn't and men were after revenge they could mistake him for the other. A misjudgement, perhaps, Eagan could be as innocent as he claimed, but it did no harm to be sure and if some had the idea of raiding the house others could have the same object.

Following the road Spragg made the familiar journey to the observatory, turning away from the main entrance and skirting the village. A man in the distance lifted a hand to shade his eyes as he stared in his direction and a woman, cleaning windows, paused until he had passed otherwise he saw no one. Returning he circled the house and halted on a knoll to stare towards the road. Traffic was light, the normal rumble reduced to the faint whine of passing cars travelling at speed. The air held a hushed tension as if before a storm and swirling clouds covered the sky.

Irene was up when Spragg returned and watched as he settled the shotgun in a corner. She wore a thin robe, which stuck to her perspiring skin. Perfume enveloped her like a scented cloud and her hair shone like burnished gold.

"Coffee, Mal?"

"Tea. Where's Sam?"

"Upstairs. Did you notice he had blood on his shirt?"

"No. It probably came from those scratches."

"Or someone who put up a fight." Irene handed him a steaming cup. "Could he have gone out after we went to bed and attacked someone in the village? A woman or girl?"

"I walked through the village," Spragg sipped at his tea. "No one seemed excited and if those people he shot at had come after him for having committed rape they wouldn't have given up so easily." He added, "But if you think he's that way inclined you're crazy to dress like that."

The cup fell as she came into his arms and for a long moment the world was filled with scent and softness and the warm heat of demanding passion, which, somehow, changed to a fierce, protective tenderness.

After a while, Irene said, "Shall we go for a walk?"

"If you want."

"If Sam comes down keep him busy while I dress."

Eagan came down as Spragg was making another cup of tea. He nodded and sat in a chair facing the big window rolling himself a cigarette. He had washed and changed and looked what he was; an aging, dissipated man.

Without looking up he said, "When?"

"Tomorrow."

"But you said—"

"You don't have to jump into a fire to feel the heat. There's a miniature sun out there and it's hot! Once it reaches us—before it reaches us—hell, man, use your imagination!" Spragg watched as Eagan lit the cigarette and inhaled. "At least you won't have to worry about those things killing you."

"Nor anything else. I didn't, you know."

"What?"

"Rape a girl. I'll admit I had it in mind but when I got to the village I saw a man trying the same thing. She was screaming so I kicked him in the face and he got up and hit me so I hit him back. That's why I was outside with the gun. I guessed he'd come after me and he did." Eagan added, musingly, "I must have killed him. At least he fell down behind the shrubbery and didn't get up."

"It doesn't matter."

"I know. Drink?"

"No thanks. Irene and I are going out for a walk."

"To be alone? Maybe I should be the one to go out." Eagan blew more smoke. "No? Then I'll just sit here and have a few drinks and do some thinking. You're certain we're all going the same way?"

"Yes."

"Good." Eagan looked at his hands, at he knuckles white beneath the skin. "All of then," he breathed. "Every last, damned bastard!"

The inconsiderate, the uncaring, the unkind. Those who lied and stole and destroyed for the sake of destruction. The ones who loved to inflict pain. The thoughtless. The cruel. The indifferent. The bullies. The lovers of power. The ones who prated and practiced other than thy preached. The hypocrites. The manipulators. The haughty, the proud, the bestial.

"It helps," said Eagan. "By God, it helps." Liquid gurgled as he refilled his glass. "Join me?"

"Just a small one."

"You know, Mal, you live a life and at the end of it what've you got? Bad health, bad habits—and there isn't a soul who really gives a damn about what happens to you. And now it's over. Well, to hell with it." He began to chuckle. "Hell," he said. "what a joke if all along we've been on the wrong side and didn't know it. Bowing to the wrong God." He looked at the black tablet Spragg placed on the table beside him. "What's that?"

"An easy way out. It's what they gave to the Angels who'd been burned. It's quick—just bite and it's over." Spragg added, bleakly, "Don't play the hero, Sam. It isn't going to be pleasant."

Irene was waiting when he left the room. She was dressed in a loose skirt and blouse, her legs bare as, he guessed, was the rest of her beneath the clothing. Her hair was bound with a brilliant scarf and she carried a small basket.

"Picnic things." she explained.

They found a rolling meadow edged with trees and sat after long hours of walking to eat and drink and rest in the seclusion of shrubs sweating from the heat, which had turned spring into summer. The motorway now was quiet aside form the occasional whine of a speeding car, which made an accompaniment to the rustle and song of birds. Spragg plucked a blade of grass and studied it as if he had never seen grass before which, as he thought wryly, was near enough true as he studied the delicate tracery of fibres, the curl, the shape, the colour.

"This is so beautiful, Mal!" Irene sighed her appreciation as she lay at his side. "It seems such a shame it all has to go."

Burned, destroyed, seared to ash—had Eagan been right? Were they paying the penalty of failing to recognise who really ruled Earth? If the space programme had not been thwarted, if they had pressed on to take what was before them there would have been more machines, more trained men, better systems of control. They would have been able to hit Thor months ago, shattering it, spreading it through space in harmless fragments. Would God really have wanted to destroy his own? Could Satan have won had there been no interference?"

"Mal!" She whispered. "Mal!"

They made love in the shelter of the bushes her naked skin glowing like radiant pearls. A time of tenderness ruled by affection as he stored more memories and found a momentary forgetfulness. And afterwards they lay to look up at the branches ripe with budding leaves, delicate shades of green that veiled them from the sky.

And then to walk again, hand in hand, over the grass and along the paths, seeing no one and pleased to be alone.

It was late when they returned to the house and Spragg halted as he heard the voice then relaxed as he realised from where it came. Eagan had switched on the television and sat before it, immobile, one hand holding his glass. The voice was the usual stream of lying assurance promising all would be well and Spragg listened to it for a moment and then, with sudden rage, snatched up a bottle and sent it hurtling to smash the tube.

To Irene he said, "I've always wanted to do that. Now go and get your shower while I sort out some music. What would you like? Bach? Mozart? The Rolling Stones?"

"Just music. Something not too solemn. How's Sam?"

"He's drunk, I guess. You go along now while I take care of him."

Eagan was dead, his eyes open, his lips parted, a mote of black staining the lower lip. Spragg took the glass from his stiffening fingers and closed his eyes then, with an effort, heaved the man on his shoulders and carried him up the stairs to his bed. He sagged as he closed the door and leaned gasping against the wall, hearing the gush of the shower as Irene laved herself, seeing black motes and vivid flashes as he fought the pain searing his back. As the gush of water died he straightened and went back downstairs where he took a stiff drink and more pain-killing tablets. When Irene joined him dressed all in white like a virgin bride he was relaxed and smiling.

"You look beautiful," he said. "You are beautiful."

"You're biased. Where's Sam?"

"In bed. He's out cold." Spragg glanced at the music unit as the sound died. "Well, that's it. I guess the power's failed. What shall we do now? Drink? Talk?"

"Let's go outside."

Out into the garden there to lie side by side on the ragged grass now tinged with ugly, sombre hues. To hold hands and to feel the immensity of the universe and to know that, elsewhere, crazed humanity ran and screamed and aped the beast. But here they were alone.

"Mal, what will happen when it reaches us?"

"We burn. The air, the seas, the soil, everything. The trees will go, the grass, the ants and birds and worms and bacteria. The ground will fuse and turn into steam and the steam will be broken into atoms. When the plasma passes on the Earth will be nothing but a clinker."

And perhaps he would have caused it with his report on the mascon. If he had kept silent, would the nations have dug so deep into their no-hope chests and used everything against the invader? Would a few bombs the less have made any difference?

"Mal," she said. "Mal—I'm afraid!"

He rose so as to look down at her and recognised the terror held back so long. To burn. To feel the searing touch of fire on the skin, the fat running, the blood boiling, to twist and run and scream like a living animal locked in an oven—the punishment of Hell now to be felt by all.

But not by her. Never by her.

"Here!" He produced the black tablets. "Take one. Bite it. Quickly now you—" He sucked in his breath as her flailing hand hit his own and scattered the tablets far and wide in the ragged grass.

"Mal! Mal, for God's sake!"

He moved and found the other thing he'd obtained in the States and settled with it in his hand pointing at the back of her head. The short-barrelled revolver loaded in each of its six chambers. One shot was enough bringing instant, merciful death but he fired them all then, not wanting to see what he had done, turned to look at the sky.

The ghastly, glowing sky.

www.ingramcontent.com/pod-product-compliance
Lightning Source LLC
Chambersburg PA
CBHW022155260626
47155CB00018B/1935